Praise for

'*Mad Cows* should be renamed *Wet Your Knickers With Laughter* . . . read it, love it and be prepared to change your undies!' – *Company*

'Will comfort the millions already suffering from "Ab Fab" withdrawal' – *Daily Telegraph*

'Very funny – yet for all her tough sassiness, Lette writes movingly about the tenderness of a mother's love' – *Woman's Journal*

'Breaks through taboos with a wit so daring that you'll gasp at her bravado before you laugh out loud' – *Elle*

'Quick-witted fiction . . . ascending into the starry firmament of much-loved and bestselling comic novelists' – *New Woman*

'Queen of the wounding one-liner . . . she wisecracks like a cerebral Guy Fawkes party, raining glittery puns down on her delighted audience' – *The Scotsman*

'Fast, witty . . . ultimately an unconventional, strangely touching paean to motherhood' – *Q Magazine*

'Her take on motherhood, men and post-feminists . . . is a barrel of laughs' – *Sunday Telegraph*

'Wicked, warm and witty' – *London Magazine*

'Furious with puns and acrobatic sex . . . one of the few books about motherhood which makes you laugh' – *Marie Claire*

'Kathy Lette has brilliant, enviable one liners.
Like Mae West and Dorothy Parker she knows that wit is
the best revenge' – **Helena Kennedy QC**

'A female Lenny Bruce' – **Carmen Callil**

Kathy Lette

Kathy Lette first achieved *succès de scandale* as a teenager with the novel *Puberty Blues*, now a major motion picture. After several years as a newspaper columnist in Sydney and New York (collected in the book *Hit and Ms*) and as a television sitcom writer for Columbia Pictures in Los Angeles, her novels, *Girls' Night Out* (1988), *The Llama Parlour* (1991) and *Foetal Attraction* (1993), became international bestsellers. Kathy Lette's plays include *Grommits*, *Wet Dreams*, *Perfect Mismatch* and *I'm So Happy For You Really I Am*. Recently she has presented *Behind the Headlines* and *O1* on British television and *Devil's Advocate* for BBC Radio 4. She lives in London with her husband and two children.

Also by Kathy Lette

Girls' Night Out

The Llama Parlour

Foetal Attraction

KATHY LETTE

Mad Cows

PICADOR

To Georgie – with love, Calpol

and disposable nappies

First published 1996 by Picador

This edition published 1997 by Picador
an imprint of Macmillan Publishers Ltd
25 Eccleston Place, London SW1W 9NF
and Basingstoke

Associated companies throughout the world

ISBN 0 330 34746 2

3 5 7 9 8 6 4

A CIP catalogue record for this book is available from
the British Library.

Typeset by CentraCet Limited, Cambridge
Printed and bound in Great Britain by
Mackays of Chatham plc, Chatham, Kent

Contents

CONTENTS

Redwood Says Single Mums Should Have Babies Adopted

Tory MP John Redwood sparked fury last night by telling single mums: 'If you can't afford to feed your kids – give them up for adoption.' The Conservative leadership challenger said, 'Maybe the girl should consider letting a couple adopt her child to provide the home the baby needs.'

News of the World, 13 August 1995

PART ONE

After Pains

'Your new baby can go everywhere with you so long as you are composed and well-prepared. If you are well-organized and self-assured, outings with your baby can be a great joy, and the sooner that you start after bringing the baby home the better.'

Dr Miriam Stoppard's New Baby Care Book

1. Giving Suck

'*Mother Nature's a mingy, stingy, two-faced bitch,*' muttered Madeline, as she re-adjusted her jumbo-sized sanitary towel, hoicked up the baby papoose and hobbled painfully into Harrods in search of prunes to ease her post-natal constipation. '*We're talking Lady Macbeth with PMT and a Kalashnikov.*'

In the marbled foyer of this castellated and cupolaed folly, as magnetic to London tourists as Mecca is to Muslims, Maddy caught sight of herself in the mirror. An alien from the Planet Yuk stared back at her. Her misshapen body oozed from a floral jumpsuit which she didn't remember buying.

'Don't worry, dear,' the midwives had promised, 'after baba's born, your body will just *snap* back!'

Yeah, *right* – in time for the Ms Osteoporosis Spinal Curvature Contest.

It was one month since the birth and her tummy still dangled downwards – a flesh colostomy bag. And *hips*. She'd never had hips before. Two flabby sidecars rode pillion with her everywhere. What she needed were some control-top pantyhose; but for her *whole body*. Her distended breasts were so sore that it hurt to walk against the wind. 'Walk!' Now *there* was an optimistic word. 'List' was more appropriate. The nurses on Maddy's ward had instructed all the mums to empty only one breast per feed. The result? A lop-sided tilt and alternate bra-strap indentations only surgery could bloody well remove.

Madeline took a left through Cosmetics and continued her angled shuffle toward the food hall like a saddle-sore John Wayne in a B-grade movie. As if vaginal haemophilia wasn't enough, the 'wings' on her Kotex had slipped their cotton moorage and adhered to her pubic hairs. With every step she was giving herself a full bikini wax. Oh well. At least it distracted from the pain of the episiotomy scars. During the slicing of her perineum, the surgeon had uttered the worst word possible in the English language: 'Whoops.' She now had a goddamn blood clot the size of Roseanne Barr in her underpants.

Wincing and mincing, Maddy inwardly cursed all those beatific Madonna and child paintings. In not one of them is Mary crying in agony from cramps, cracked nipples, mastitis, constipation, haemorrhoids – or 'bottom grapes' as her friend Gillian so quaintly called them – hair loss, tooth decay, nor the sets of crippling contractions triggered by the baby's sucking. This was what Maddy meant about Mother Nature being scungy, grungy and totally bloody two-faced. Yep. God was laughing when he made women.

'Free skin analysis?' A manicured hand holding a tantalizing vial of transparent unguent stamped 'Tester' fluttered in Maddy's face. 'Take control of your life,' purred the svelte shop assistant, beaming euphorically.

Maddy rocked back on her heels. 'Hey. I've just had a baby. I can't even take control of my urine flow.'

The bionic beam dimmed. Good one, thought Maddy.

4

Readjusting her baby's hot little body in the pouch, she allowed herself a moment of complacent congratulation. Harrods, her big treat, was Maddy's first excursion since Jack's birth. After all those months of cerebral hibernation and hormonal collywobbles, her brain was at last coming back into orbit. She squared her shoulders. She commandeered the perfume tester. She aimed the nozzle at her neck and sprayed liberally . . . realizing too late it was hand-bloody-cream. Daubing at the beard of jism-like blobs frothing lobe to lobe, Maddy resumed her sleep-deprived Boris Karloff lurch toward the food hall. Boy, she thought. Am I a girl who knows how to have fun, or *what*?

The Hampton Court maze has nothing on Harrods. Bewildered, Maddy trudged past the Eiffel Towers of fruit – jellied, candied, brandied – the obelisques of rare biscuits and braided bread. She cast a greedy glance across the exotic fare before selecting her humble packet of prunes.

A boa constrictor of shoppers coiled back from the cash register. She joined the tail end and was just hoisting up the waistband of her maternity knickers (now *there* was a good look – undies in which you could hold a revival meeting) when she became aware of a dripping sensation on her foot. She glanced suspiciously towards the taxidermied geese and garrotted grouse which dangled from the ceramic ceiling. It was a full minute before she realized that the culprit was *her own tit*. A wet ring saturated her shirt fabric through which a small geyser of milk spurted forth. People were glancing at her, disconcerted. She was like some escapee from *The Exorcist*. Any minute now, her head would do a 360 degree turn in a blur of lime slime.

'Um . . . Haven't quite got the supply and demand thing going yet,' she explained lamely to the pin-striped men who cleared their throats and crabbed away from her to other queues.

Fan-fucking-tastic, whinged Maddy to a morose flock of tuxedoed penguins advertising the freezer section, I'm incontinent at one frigging end and constipated at the freaking other. Her leaking breast had now started to throb and she dimly remembered the midwives' advice that frozen peas made a soothing ice pack. Excavating a packet of Birdseye, she hastily bandaged them into her bra cup. Lemme tell you, it takes a lot of effort to achieve this much *savoir*-bloody-*faire*, she philosophized. Now, to find another goddamned till . . .

It was early closing and shoppers were manoeuvring towards counters with the grace of Iraqi tank commandoes. A sudden wave of people whirlpooled in Maddy's direction and she heard a woman's ragged cry: 'Stop! Thief! My purse!'

In the crush, Maddy stumbled. The jolt woke Jack, who whimpered in fright, then let out a lacerating howl. Maddy's milk haemorrhaged. This clutch-started more womb contractions. Her other boob began to weep, in sympathy. The need to give suck created a Saharan thirst. Sweat soaked her anxious armpits and beaded her face. She seemed to be having her own *weather*, for Christ's sake. Panic gripped her guts as she strove to regain her balance and the mêlée propelled her in the wrong direction. Protecting Jack's tiny head with one hand and lashing out with the other, Maddy beat a path towards the exit. She heaved out into the foyer, lowered herself on to the mottled marble steps, gritted her teeth and offered up her tender nipple to Jack's electric-pencil-sharpener grip.

'*Modom!*' The inverted scrubbing brushes of the doorman's epaulettes quivered with indignation. 'Harrods has strict dress standards.'

Maddy had become blasé about breastfeeding. She suddenly saw herself through his eyes: the milk stains, the grey maternity bra with the aesthetic appeal of an orthopaedic shoe. 'That's the worst thing about lactation,' she smiled, apologetically, 'the havoc it wreaks with your dress sense.'

The doorman looked her over with a flat, expressionless face. 'Strict dress codes are about remaining *dressed*. The nearest lavatories are on the first floor.'

'The nearest lavatories charge a pound a pee. Besides,' she said, 'would *you* eat in the toilets?'

The doorman ground his atavistic jaw. 'Store policy don't allow knockers.'

Young and bitter with a pimple plotting an appearance on the bridge of his nose, this was a guy who'd dived in the shallow end of the gene pool. 'Store policy allows you to sell the bloody nursing bras which makes public breast feeding more discreet, *don't* it, zit-features?'

Any hint of professionalism evaporated. 'Yeah, well, tough titty, Aussie. Time to go walk-about, yer mad cow.' In case his request had been too subtle for her, Grizzle-guts clinched her elbow and winched her skywards.

Inserting a finger between the baby's velvety lips, Maddy broke his seal on her pap. Jack's barely formed face twisted with fury. He let rip with a scream which sounded like a plane coming into Gatwick. His bowels opened with the suddenness of a bomb-bay. An ominous yellow stain appeared on his baby-gro and seeped on to Maddy's hand.

'Just let me change him,' Maddy pleaded, 'and then I'll be on my way, okay?'

The doorman obviously late for his Charm Class, shoved her towards the doors.

Maddy, clutching the baby with one hand, fumbled her blancmange of a mammary back into its elasticated hammock. Hey, just call me, Suave, Urban Sophisticate she thought. It's a *gift*. Wheeling around, she delivered her parting shot; a frisbeed, sodden nursing pad. It found incongruous sanctuary on the gold-braided ottoman atop the doorman's shoulder before flopping between his mastodon feet.

Out on the street, the low, leaden sky was soggy with rain. A Jag with a grinning platinum number-plate splattered them with grimy spray. Maddy, shielding Jack from toxic farts of taxi exhaust, darted through the drizzle into the claustrophobic warmth of the tube station. She fed her ticket into the mouth of the chrome carousel, perfectly positioned to reopen a woman's episiotomy stitches. She was just contemplating the less painful option of pole-vaulting over the barrier, when her arm was wrenched up behind her back. She spun round, knee raised in Mugger Mode, but the artificially 'casual' clothes – the too-new trainers, the ironed jeans, the tan leather jacket that had never been in the weather . . . Uh oh. Maddy only knew of one species which dressed in sheep's clothing.

*

The store detective shanghaied her back into Harrods. The office into which he eventually steered her was already inhabited by a po-faced pen-pusher and a black lady of advanced years whose smile, upon Maddy's entry, revealed a glittering diamond embedded in her left front tooth.

'*Lord* have *mercy*,' she hooted. 'It not enough to pick up a poor, old lady whose doin' no harm to nobody. Now youse pickin' on a helpless woman and pickne. Shame! Shame on you.' She was large, bottom heavy and of awe-inspiring rotundity. If she were a map of Britain then her handbag was Ireland, full, so the store detective alleged, of other people's possessions. The old lady extended her salmon-pink palm in a high-five. 'Mamma Joy,' she crooned.

The store detective meanwhile was rifling through Maddy's belongings. She had forgotten all about the prunes until he produced them with an officious flourish.

'Oh, Christ. Look, I meant to pay for them . . .'

Jack bleated. Once again Maddy unfastened the left cat-flap in her bra. He latched on fretfully. 'I need one of those . . . what do you call them? Alert Bracelets, which reads "Brain-Dead Breast-feeder. Handle with Care".'

Maddy was many things; subtle as a falling piano, as culturally refined as, say, a turd in a cocktail – but she was also as warm and natural and *genuine* as a bather's bum turned sun-wards on Bondi Beach. Surely they could see that? She was just about to do the Naive Aussie Tourist Thing, when the doorman's distinctive aftershave invaded the office. But it was the chip on his shoulder the size of a caravan park which gave him away.

'Is this the woman?' asked the store detective.

'Yes, Guv.' He was holding, between fastidious forefinger and thumb, the pale, pulpy poppadum of breast pad.

'Oh, gimme a break. I *would* have paid except Ack Attack here pushed me out on to the goddamn street.'

'I neva touched 'er.'

'Yeah, right. And Elton John has his own hair.' Maddy had got more sarcastic since the birth; since she'd given up on blokes. If love was a drug, Madeline Wolfe had been the all-night chemist. But not any more. As far as men were concerned, she'd closed up shop. She liked her new, tough persona. Like her cropped haircut, it suited her somehow.

'Do you want to ring the baby's father?' the Harrods official, touched by Jack's dreamy gurgle, pushed a phone across the plexiglass desk.

Maddy laughed so strenuously that she choked. It had been a month since she'd seen Alex. The last words he'd ever said to her in the maternity ward were, 'Let's keep in touch.' She opened her mouth to answer the Harrods Inquisitor, but her lips distorted and her strong chin trembled with the effort not to sook. It wasn't that she still loved Alex. It was just, well, when you've been addicted, there were bound to be withdrawal symptoms. Although she was definitely getting better. Lately, *whole seconds* had elapsed where she hadn't thought of him.

'Don't think waterworks'll get you out of it,' the doorman snarled. 'Only the guilty ever blub.'

'Don't be rid-ic – ?' Maddy fought to gain control of her vowels ' – ulous. It's the baby, that's all. I cry at the Andrex puppy ad. I cry in the movies . . . and *that's* just in the *trailers*.'

'Obviously,' Mamma Joy announced, superciliously, 'de poor gal's postnatal.'

'I'm not de – de – ' Maddy sobbed ' – pressed.' She tried to look contemptuous – pretty hard with mascara blobs skid-marking your chops and milk yoghurting your clobber.

'Gal, you is sadder than a solar-powered vibrator on a rainy day.'

Jack began to wriggle and whinge. Maddy held him at arm's length, frightened by her own ineptitude. She loved him more than life itself – but if only he'd come with operating instructions.

'Them would laugh you outa da courtroom, boys,' the old lady chortled at the wavering official and the professionally nondescript detective. 'Iinn. Not to mention de newspapers . . .' Scotland quaked and collapsed into Wales during her seismic seizure of laughter.

'Stop fartin' about and call the fuckin' Plod,' the doorman urged. This guy had a personality guaranteed to give a shrink wet-dreams.

'Go on. *Do.* De Babylon gunna *love* dis call. Especially now when they're tryin' to lower dere black crime figures.'

As the store detective and the Harrods official conferred, Mamma Joy's big bright mouth leaned towards Maddy, diamond strobing. 'When it's rainin' shit,' she whispered hoarsely, 'get a brolly.' Scooping Jack into her bulky arms, she excavated a space on the desk top and changed his nappy. She then laid him across her knees and rubbed his back in a soothing, circular motion. Maddy, marvelling at the large woman's ease, touched her son's delicate, immaculate head with awe. Like the beginning of any love affair, Maddy was nervous and idealistic. She loved irrationally, without the inoculation of familiarity and experience. A month into motherhood and he still felt like some precious accessory . . . in this case, to the *crime.*

'S'pect you get to Buckingham Palace for dis, boys!' In the

place of pearl chokers, rolls of rich fat encircled Mamma Joy's neck. They joggled now as she chuckled. 'A poor new mudder and a menopausal woman . . . hee, *HEE*, hee, hee . . .' The baby's milky burps punctuated her remarks as she handed Jack back to his mother, who held him like a breakable object.

Defeated, momentarily, by the disarming mixture of sobbing and sarcasm, the Harrods official wrote 'No further action' on Mamma Joy's form.

'Menopausal! Must be the longest menopause in medical history,' he yowled. 'You must be in the fuckin' *Menopause Guinness Book of Fuckin' Records.*'

Mamma Joy added a two-fingered salute to her operatic range of gesture.

'You are banned, however, from the store,' the Harrods official added, in a final face-saving flurry. 'Both of you.'

That might have been the end of it, if the store detective who was repacking Maddy's possessions had not come across the money pouch. It was nestled – a brown, furry marsupial – in the seat of the baby papoose. As he extracted it from its warm little burrow, Mamma Joy pushed to her feet.

'Lord have mercy! It's a fit-up.' Her huge body was not just vibrating with rage, it was avalanching flesh. The men drew back. The ferocity of her movements dislodged a sack secured beneath her skirt. Before she could scrabble it back into position, the cotton bag slipped to the floor, spilling its cargo of contraband across the carpet. Mamma Joy exploded into a furious, take-no-prisoners patois.

The doorman gloated. He tweaked his underwear and realigned his epaulettes. 'I think it's time, gentlemen, to get in the Old Bill.'

The baby's contented little pink face snuffled and truffled at its mother's breast, unaware that life had just handed them a one-way ticket: Destination – deep doo-doo.

For Maddy, it was a case of 'fasten your sanitary belt . . . we're in for a bumpy ride'.

2. Mr Wobbly Hides His Helmet

'So, Officer . . .' the clapped-out desk sergeant looked up from his notes and addressed the young constable who had brought Maddy in for questioning. 'What led you to the belief that the defendant might be an illegal alien?'

'She doesn't pronunciate her words properly.'

Maddy snorted with laughter. Jack smiled, probably with wind, but Maddy liked to think he saw the joke.

'Do you realize,' the sergeant monotoned, 'that the discovery of stolen merchandise found on your person is the causation of your appearance here at the police station?'

'I always dress this way.' Maddy resolutely refused to take this situation seriously.

'Do you realize that failure to input into the present interface may give impetus to a detention scenario? What do you think about that?'

'I think you should arrest that sentence and have it sent down for life.'

The sergeant rubbed a toilworn brow. 'Let's start again, shall we? Name?'

Maddy stared into her cold styrofoam cup of coffee. The Chelsea police station had the tiled ambience of a urinal.

'Occupation?'

'Mother.'

'Working mother?'

Now there was a redundant phrase. '*No*. As in Theresa . . . Look, can I go home now?'

'Home address?'

Right now, Siberia was looking like a more attractive residential abode.

'Sorry, I can't say.'

It wasn't that she particularly wanted to mountaineer up this poor man's nostrils, but Maddy couldn't possibly reveal the location of Gillian's flat. Gillian Cassells had been in more banks than Ned Kelly and, like him, proven faster on the draw than the deposit. Her Versace tastes somewhat hindered by the Lloyd's débâcle – a strange phenomenon, Maddy thought, to go broke saving money – it was credit-card fraud for which she was actually wanted, but Maddy felt confident her best friend had notched up a few other misdemeanours *en route*.

Maddy's mute performance soon entitled her to an interview room. She sat at the desk, concentrating on a cigarette butt embedded in a half-eaten kebab on the carpet at her feet. Each knock on the door heralded the appearance of bigger and bigger policemen. It reminded her of those Russian dolls you stack inside each other. The biggest of all sat opposite her, a dirigible of cigarette smoke hovering over his head. Clad in a dark suit of the sort you wear when somebody's died, with sweat patches in the armpits of his shirt, and a polyester tie, he didn't have to open his mouth for Maddy to see him for what he was – a wolf, in wolf's clothing.

He levelled at her an icy, opaque gaze. 'Do you know who I am?'

Maddy wiped away the little bit of spit which had projectiled into her eye. 'Um . . . President of the Saliva Bank?'

'Regional Crime Squad. Detective Sergeant Slynne. In charge of Operation Big Dipper. Investigating foreign gangs, these days usually Algerian or Nigerian, but historically Aussie. Work seasonally. Tourists. Hard to catch. Post the proceeds home. Same day. Kaput. No evidence.' During his mechanical explanation, the dirigible drifted out of orbit to be immediately replaced by another. 'If deported, you simply scamper off home for a holiday at the taxpayer's expense, then return using false docs. Do you have a passport?' His manner was Teutonic. 'Is the name in the wallet an alias?' All that was missing were the jackboots. 'What's the name of your gang leader? How many dips are you doing a day? Four? Six? What are you making from wallets? Two thousand, three thousand pounds per shift?'

Maddy looked at the slowly turning wheels of the tape deck. There seemed to be enough recording equipment in the room for a Beatles reunion album. She couldn't quite believe this was happening to her. Maddy had always seen herself as lucky. Apart from men problems (now *there* was a tautology) the lowest blows life had ever dealt her were soggy *croûtons* in a salad; lack of toilet paper in a public loo; the arrival of her period on a night of passion. This was a woman who walked under ladders.

'Its very Faginesque of you to use a baby.' Jack, tightly swaddled, was sleeping soundly in Maddy's arms. 'Is it yours or some poor Albanian brat you pay to bus in from the East End for the day?'

The allegation shattered Maddy's composure. 'Of course he's mine!'

The Spittle Projectionist's yellow, dingo eyes looked right through her. 'Single mother, eh? Thought "ovulation" was a warm milk drink before beddy-byes, did you?'

The other policemen in the room Del-toned his smug chuckle with a chorus of ha-ha's. Maddy eyed Officer Slynne narrowly. He was the type of guy that if your plane crashed in the Andes and you had plenty of rations and a rescue helicopter had been spotted, you'd *still* eat him.

The Russian Doll policemen stacked themselves to the side to permit their superior access around the desk. With no warning he pounced, wresting Jack from Maddy's grasp. The baby woke with a start, took one look at Officer Slynne and exploded into a paroxysm of rage.

Maddy tugged the baby back; her arms, fleshy parentheses around his precious body. His sobs immediately subsided. 'Excellent judge of character, children, don't you think?' she remarked sweetly.

One of the Russian dolls tittered. Slynne's face, gorged red with fury, silenced him instantly. 'Interview suspended at the time of five thirty-five p.m.' Punching 'off' buttons on the telltale tape, he harpooned her with a hateful stare.

'Get Social Services to take that bloody brat!' he commanded. 'What kind of mother are you? Found out too late for an abortion, is that it? Too out of it no doubt . . . On the game, I bet. Your pimp keeps you sexually active, does he?'

'No,' she replied with droll hostility, 'I just lie there.'

Detective Sergeant Slynne crushed his coffee cup. Styrofoam splinters dandruffed to the floor. Maddy had a vague idea that things were not going well.

'I don't suppose you're remotely entertaining the idea of bail. You won't give us a name. You have no address. You were found with some hookey gear and we haven't checked your immigration status.'

If he *spat* on her once more, she'd confess to the Birmingham bombings.

'Look,' she sighed, acquiescing, 'I was in Harrods. All I remember is someone shouting and a crush of people. The thief must have shoved the money pouch into the baby papoose. My only crime was to forget to pay for a packet of bloody prunes. I'm really tired. If this is some kind of joke, like, what's the punchline?'

'The "punchline" is that you're about to be put on remand at Holloway Prison. If you'd just cut the bollocks, come across and give us some names, we could do a deal.'

Maddy nearly laughed out loud. The only bars she'd ever been behind were to pull schooners. The most dishonest things she'd ever done were to break a wholemeal recipe chain letter; not to leave a note under the windscreen wiper of a car she'd bumped; serving up M & S gourmet as her own. She was pathologically honest, well, except for the time she'd used the paraplegic cubicle to have sex with Alex. But they'd needed the elbow room. Maddy was the type to feel guilty if she wore a back-to-front baseball cap emblazoned with the name of an American city she hadn't visited. Even when playing Monopoly, she never picked up the 'Go to jail' card.

Things had gone far enough.

'My name is Madeline Wolfe, okay?'

'How do we know that's not a load of old pony.'

'For Christ's sake . . . okay, okay. There is someone you can call to confirm my identity. The baby's father . . .' Gosh, was she looking forward to *that* call. It was second on her list of fun things to do – after a clitorodectomy. Until now Alex had been about as useful as a . . . well, as a father in a delivery room. She didn't want to be the first to get in touch, but shit a brick. At least he could get her the hell out of here. Humiliation, she lectured herself, is character building. But she had enough character already. Too *much*, according to Alex's well-connected friends amongst London's chattering classes.

'Ah . . .' Slynne gave an impatient snarl. 'So there *is* a man in this equation?'

Maddy pondered. 'Yes, I think he can be scientifically classified as a vertebrate.'

'Am I to take it you are not on good terms with the father of your child?' It was the Sarcasm Olympics and both Maddy and Slynne were going for Gold.

'I'd like to tweeze out every single one of his pubic hairs and then transplant them back with a blunt needle . . . but otherwise we get on *fine*,' she said, cutely.

'Oh, let me guess.' Officer Slynne leaned back, balancing on the legs of his chair, and regarded her with listless mockery. 'It was *"rape"* . . .'

When he'd first entered the room, Maddy had mistaken the close-set eyes and hang-dog expression as taciturnity. She now knew that he'd just been studying his prey. She shook her head.

'If he's such a pillock,' he pried, derisively, 'then why'd ya shag him?'

'I dunno . . . *somebody* had to do it.' Maddy didn't think

19

the police would appreciate a description of her attraction to Alex's highbrows. He was the first man she'd ever met who could listen to 'Nessun Dorma' and not think of the World Cup. Not only did he know all the Mozart K numbers and hold six degrees in biology, but he actually *read* the books short-listed each year for the Booker Prize. To Maddy, who'd left school at fifteen, this was pretty impressive stuff. The only examination *she'd* ever passed was her smear test.

Yes, it had been love at first sight. But then she'd taken a second look. It was as if she'd been wearing a sign on her heart which read 'In case of Emergency, Break'. The emergency being that no sooner had she ricocheted half-way across the world to be with him than she found out that he was married with twins and, as soon as she'd broken up with him, that she was pregnant.

An entire squadron of John Player cigarette air-ships were dispatched ceiling-wards before the detective spoke again. 'Well?'

'The fact that he has a sequoia-sized penis helped . . .' Maddy teased, dangerously. 'Amazing. A sequoia tree takes two hundred years to attain the same girth it took him 2.6 seconds to achieve at the merest glimpse of a fish-net stocking.'

Slynne's face contorted into a gargoyle grimace. 'Cut the bollocks. I want his name and his fucking number. If you don't co-operate I'll have you on remand faster than you can say "legal aid".'

*

Maddy breastfed while she waited. The frozen peas she'd stuffed down her bra had cooked from the heat. She took out the packet, tore it open with her teeth and ate them with a plastic coffee spoon. The policewoman guarding her dutifully added a packet of peas to Maddy's charge sheet.

At the thought of Alex's imminent arrival, a wave of relief washed over her – the sort of relief you feel when you think you're up the duff and it turns out to be a twenty-four-hour flu bug. The truth was, Maddy had said 'No' to love . . . but it hadn't listened. In the past month, she'd shown more self-restraint than Pavarotti's panty girdle . . . while all the time secretly hoping to see more of him . . . and even perhaps his perfectly symmetrical tool. Alex's trouble was that he suffered from F.O.C. (Fear of Commitment). When it came to committing to anyone, he was as cautious as a naked bloke climbing a barbed-wire fence. But Maddy had since discovered a sure-fire cure for F.O.C. – the tiny token of their affection nestled beside her. Her spirits rose irrationally.

The Detective Sergeant returned shortly afterwards wearing an ersatz smile. 'The renowned Alexander Drake, British naturalist, host of own BBC nature series, denies any knowledge of you or your bastard.'

It was a simple sentence, said perfunctorily, and it immediately changed everything. Reality slapped Maddy in the face like a car-salesman's cologne. The selfish mongrel! But – she reasoned – calling Alex selfish was like calling a dwarf short. Somehow she'd overlooked her ex-lover's ego. We're not just talking *BIG*, she fumed to herself. We're talking Visible From Outer Space. She bet it was sodding well there on the satellite photos, along with the Great Wall of China and the Barrier-bloody-Reef.

She filed her hurt away under 'Revenge' – cross-referenced in 'You'll Keep, You Bastard.'

'That's the other thing I forgot to tell you,' Maddy said, camouflaging her shock. 'He's also a founding member of Assholes Anonymous.'

In that nanosecond, Maddy plumbed the depths of the crapola. 'I want a lawyer,' she announced, with all the confidence of a beehive hair-do in the rain.

Ostentatiously reaching for the list of duty solicitors, the Detective Sergeant suggested a firm. Maddy was escorted to the 'rape suite'. It was just like a normal cell, only painted pink to enable the vermin to stand out more. A woman lay on a bunk, weeping.

'We're letting you wait in here 'cause of baba,' the policewoman announced, as though doing Maddy a great favour.

'Oh! A dream come true!' Maddy was having trouble disguising her trepidation. After the water-logged woman was led away, the three of them lay on the bed – Jack, Maddy . . . and Maddy's stomach. She looked at her baby, his arms and legs flexed like a dead beetle. Unperturbed by light or noise, his eyelids moved in his sleep, as though experiencing the happiest Technicolor dreams.

Maddy tried to sleep but couldn't. She counted flocks of woolly sheep, shorn sheep, lamb cutlets . . . She tried counting other boring and inane creatures – Liberal Democrats, New Men, Gary Barlow without Take That, the Martini man in the wet shirt in that cinema advert, the ex-love of her life, televisual spunk rat Alexander Drake . . . and awaited her saviour – legal eagle R. M. Peregrine.

*

The abdomen entered the room first. It looked like the third trimester of pregnancy – not a good look on a man. The face which followed would qualify for National Disaster relief. Above the fruit-fly larvae complexion was a clump of dyed-brown hair resembling a yak which had been dead a decade or two. Maddy, visibly repulsed, drew back from the sauerkraut body odour. Rupert Montgomery Peregrine grasped her hand before she could stop him.

'Ms . . .' he consulted his file, faltering.

'Wolfe.'

'Peregrine. Expert in criminal law. Which is actually an oxymoron, when you analyse it. As is "even odds", "minor miracle" and "bad sex" . . . So, what can we do for you?'

Maddy wiped her damp hand on her dress. 'A few laps in a swimming pool of disinfectant would be nice. A jacuzzi dip in penicillin . . .'

'Grotty, I know.' He misunderstood her. 'But better than the cells.'

Her heart sank. It was obvious by the cheap stained suit that Peregrine was the sort of lawyer whose office is located by the neon sign outside it. He was all stubble and Old Spice.

'Just get us out of this hell-hole.'

'Ah . . . that all depends on the Magistrate . . .'

'I've got a one-month-old baby, for Christ's sake.'

'The only thing which moves a London stipendiary, my dear, are his bowels.'

'But I'm innocent.' Even her own ears cringed at the cliché. Her day was rapidly turning into a bad country-and-western ballad.

'Of course you are, dear.' Peregrine, ignoring the chair, lowered his bulky frame on to the bunk. The bed springs moaned in protest. 'All incarceratees are innocent. The reasons they are innocent range from' – he counted them off on his pudgy fingers – 'One, incompetent lawyer. Two, incompetent judge. Three, incompetent jury. Four, incompetent lawyer, judge *and* jury. Five, an over-dressed defendant. Six, an *under*-dressed defendant. Seven, too cold in the court room. Eight, too hot. Nine, racist jury, anti-*black*. Ten, racist jury, anti-*white* . . .'

Peregrine, Maddy adjudicated, was the sort of guy who should come stamped with a warning – 'May Cause Drowsiness.'

'The fact of the matter is that the Bill have got their nuts in a knot over LA-style "girlz'n'hood" gangs. That all-woman attack on Liz Hurley really excited them. Statistically the number of young women in jail is steadily increasing. This has convinced the Plod that they have an inner-city crime phenomenon on their hands.'

Maddy slumped. If she'd been operating a machine, she'd have been on the brink of an industrial accident.

'Which is why the judiciary want to make an example of uppity girls like you . . .'

What jolted her from her coma was the sight of the aubergine-coloured slug poking its head out of her solicitor's trousers. It lay in his palm. He stroked it absentmindedly as he spoke, as though it were a family pet. This could *not* be happening. If her life of late was a used car, nobody would bloody well buy it.

Now that he had her attention, Peregrine got to his

unsavoury point. 'No magistrate will grant you bail unless you have surety. Now, I can find a respectable person who'll swear he's known you all his life, guaranteeing ten thousand pounds. In exchange for this service, a woman would obviously want to show her gratitude . . .'

He had a coldsore in the crease of his lip. Maddy stared at it in stupefaction. Hey – it was a better view than anything else on offer. Maybe she was dreaming . . .? (If so, then where was Brad Pitt and why was she still clothed?) Or having some kind of out-of-body experience? Yeah, *right*. Answers on a self-addressed plasma beam.

Her solicitor crossed to the door and made sure it was locked. Turning, his eyes travelled the six foot length of Maddy's muscular body with slow appreciation before snaring at 36D level. 'Now, isn't it time we got to know each other better?'

'Oh, I've got a pretty good idea who *you* are. *You're* the kind of guy Ricki Lake builds an entire show around.'

Peregrine chortled, enjoying her obstinacy. 'So, shall we play Mr Wobbly Hides His Helmet?'

'What do you use for contraception?' Maddy stalled. 'Your personality?'

Peregrine's tone darkened. 'You don't seem to be taking your situation very seriously. Forget *Porridge*. Not all inmates have their own TV sitcom. Some of them are psychotic lesbian axe murderesses.' He slouched back on the bed, resurrecting his manhood from the folds of his underpants.

'Okay. Enough kidding around,' Maddy rebuked. 'Now show me your *real* penis.' Two strides and she was at the door, ready to shout through the grille for help. 'I mean, what kind of an idiot do you think I am?'

'The kind of idiot who allows the Regional Crime Squad to select her solicitor for her,' he gloated. 'Oh, forgive me. That observation was intended to be parenthetic. And don't even think about trying to report this. A single mother, suspected fraudster and illegal foreigner? You have about as much muscle as, well, Christopher Reeve.'

Maddy was sick with disbelief as the Kafka-esque turn to her day. These kind of things didn't happen to people like her. She listened to *Desert Island Discs*. She cleansed with Clarins. Moisturizing before toner was a *major* misdemeanour. She worried about whether her twenty-four hour deodorant would run out after twenty-three hours. She looked up words she didn't know in the dictionary. Recycling was a daily ritual. As was gum massage . . . Maddy glanced across at her tiny baby. His hands fluttered in his sleep, as though conducting an invisible orchestra . . . with no idea that the score had suddenly switched to Berlioz's 'March to the Gallows'.

'Well, Ms Wolfe, what's it to be?'

3. The Hood, The **Mother Hood**

As the police car drove through the dark arched gates of Holloway Prison, the sense of certainty that Maddy had taken for granted all her life was obliterated for ever. The magistrate had not granted bail, which was why she and Jack were being herded, with the other incarceratees (Maddy had seen their shrunken abstracted look before – on sheep) into what was laughingly called the 'reception area'. Her nose, mouth and ears were inspected by a jailer with a black, Beatle-wig haircut, blue eye-shadow, beige support knee-highs and a chest which started at the neck and ended at her navel.

'Get yer gear off and give us a twirl.'

'Hey,' Maddy said, with strained joviality, as she stepped out of her underpants, 'aren't you even going to buy me dinner first?' She rotated obediently, a knot of anxiety mangling her innnards. 'What's the Mother and Baby Unit like? I mean, it's not as bad as the *real* gaol . . . is it?' She was about to learn that Her Majesty's prisons are home to the world's record number of Mensa-rejection slip holders. They're called prison officers.

'Put it this way,' the Mensa flunkee chortled, 'last night the inmates played soccer with a wet nappy . . . *still attached to the baby.*' Maddy slipped her finger into Jack's half-clenched fist.

He gripped it, hard. Oh, thank you, Alex. How *would* she thank him? A huge amplifier outside his bedroom window playing a Wings album at top volume would be nice.

Maddy was hosed down in a tepid shower and her possessions bagged and tagged. Jack was also strip-searched. 'Heroin. In the nappy. Major drug route.'

Make that a Linda McCartney back-up vocal *on an isolated track.*

She was then assessed by a doctor to see whether or not she was suicidal. (In these circumstances it would surely save time to see who *wasn't.* By now Maddy's mood was so black you could view an eclipse of the sun through it.) She was ordered to exchange her own dirty clothes for a stylish little piece of prison haberdashery: charity-donated crinoline slacks and a psychedelic tank-top three sizes too big – a fashion statement which could only be described as Albanian.

Swathed in this fluorescent tarpaulin, she billowed behind her captor whose hush-puppies echoed squelchily as she marched the length of 'B' wing. Jack slept throughout the journey, occasionally jumping in his dreams, as though zapped by invisible electric currents.

'Wonder what yews are havin' thrown into your cage for dinner then?' pondered Maddy's jaunty companion as they approached the Mother and Baby Unit.

All that seemed to be on offer was an aperitif of drugs from the medication trolley. It was 'cocktail hour'. The equivalent to social drinking in prison is a quick gargle with washing-up liquid, a clandestine sniff of bleach lifted from the laundry or a pill-chill. Women, cradling irritable babies, buzzed around the nurse, downing plastic cups of iridescent tranquillizers. Dinner itself consisted of a bread roll, still frozen in the middle, and a bowl of stew which looked to Maddy like the sort of liquid in which frogs would spawn. Pastel animal mobiles rotated half-heartedly beneath the strip-lighting. She took her place at one of a cluster of plastic tables next to a young brunette, cradling a baby about Jack's age.

'What beautiful red hair!' Maddy broke the quizzical silence. 'Does her dad have red hair?'

'Dunno. He neva took off his balaclava.' The other mothers hooted with derision.

'Oh!' Maddy retreated. She suddenly had that haemophiliac-in-a-room-full-of-switch-blades feeling. Jack stirred, looking for tucker.

'I neva wanted anuvver kid,' chirped a teenager opposite, banging on the bottom of an HP sauce bottle. 'Tammy's farver promised he'd only put it in a little way. What's yer sprog's name?'

'Jack.'

'A *male*,' the young woman lamented, cheerily. 'Still, I don't think we should hold that against him.'

It didn't take long to suss that most of the women in Holloway's Mother and Baby Unit had been involved with blokes who made Claus Von Bulow look like the perfect husband . . . They were even worse than her heart's resident ratbag: supersonic sleazebucket, Alexander Drake.

'Got any putt, gear, blow?' whispered another mum. 'Any of yer visitors gunna keep yer sweet?

At the appearance of a patrolling male prison officer, all ten mums were suddenly gazing at their babies the way people look at aquariums, tuned into Baby Channel. The screw rapped his knuckles on the table top in front of Maddy. 'Don't breastfeed at the table. It's unhygienic.'

A rat the size of a football sauntered casually over the bread basket. 'Sorry.' Maddy gestured towards her fellow mothers, confident of their support. 'I thought this was a B.Y.O. establishment.'

'You're only breastfeedin' to turn on the male screws,' accused Tammy's mum, emerging from her trance to wrap herself around a stale slice of bread and to cadge a fag.

'*Nobody* breastfeeds,' snarled the brunette. She stood over Maddy with the thrust-out pelvis of a store mannequin. 'Ruins yer titties.'

The officer smiled disparagingly, then flicked Maddy's tray to the floor. The clank and rattle set all the babies crying simultaneously. 'Oh, what a shame.'

The nasal twang of the tannoy announced the collection of the dinner trays.

'Hey,' complained Maddy. 'Lactating mothers aren't sup-posed to skip a meal. We've got to eat *some*thing . . . even if it's only five or six courses per bloody second . . .'

Maddy was issued with a brown paper bag containing toothpaste, comb and a cake of soap thoughtfully mono-grammed with the Queen's initials, then escorted to the door of her new home – a cell so small she could hardly turn round without having sex with herself. There was a cot for the baby and a narrow iron bed for her. The slatted perspex windows – Maddy had to climb on the bed and crick her neck sideways to look through it – offered a charming view of the prison wall, bristling with a crew-cut of barbed wire. Interior decor con-sisted of a bucket, scrubbing brush, grey scuffed linoleum and thin, white-washed walls. The Mother and Baby Unit gave mums the perfect opportunity to share some quiet moments together ... listening to each other plotting the penile dismemberment of their respective 24 carat cads.

In an effort to avoid a Jules-Verne trawl through the depths of despair, Maddy decided to cling to her routine. It was bathtime. She was undressing Jack with philatelic care, painstakingly folding his clothes, when the door detonated open.

'And whose little population explosion are you?' The voice emerged from a glowing face which played host to the kind of button-features pastry chefs tend to pipe on to kiddies' cakes. It oozed goochie-goos before its owner planted a polka-dotted posterior on the narrow bed. The nose tissue permanently wedged into one fist and the armour-plated shoulder pads signalled to Maddy two tiresome words – social worker.

Maddy's single-mum status in hospital had brought her into close contact with this species. There were two breeds. The big dangly earring-wearing, Doc Martened, it's-all-a-capitalist-plot ones, or the Advanced Scarf Drapers. The woman whose namepass read 'Edwina Phelps' was draped in a scarf *and* a pussy bow, alerting Maddy to the fact that she was Crafty; the sort who collect poignant porcelains, mail-ordered from magazine adverts. Her spare time would be spent drying flowers and spraying tiny pinecones silver for the home-made potpourri she handed around the office at Christmas. The sun would never set on an empty slow-cooker in Edwina Phelps's house. Her petrol gauge would invariably read 'F'. The date of her next period would be circled on her desk calendar; a rain bonnet in a plastic travel pack at the ready in the drawer. She was what the English call Head Girl material. The type who carries an emergency tube of Canesten in her bag for the thrush she never got but read about in womens' magazines. The type who would go to the Chippendale male strip show and look at the *audience*.

'My friends call me Dwina. And as your psychologist we *will* be friends, Madeline.' She looked at Maddy the way an alcoholic looks at an unopened bottle of Smirnoff. 'You mustn't feel alone. *All* my girls in the Mother and Baby Unit are scarred, emotionally.'

'I really don't need any psychological plastic surgery, okay? What I *need* is a court hearing.'

'All of us long to connect with our inner child.'

Maddy winced. 'Um . . . it's called pregnancy. And I'm in touch with him already.' Indicating the wriggling worm of her son, Maddy made an artless fumble at the press studs of his baby gro.

Dwina waggled her forefinger. 'Beneath your bravado, Madeline, there's a little girl inside who's hurting.'

'Does she get a child allowance?'

'You're only being glib because you're in denial.'

'Of course I'm in bloody denial.' Peeling off Jack's nappy, Maddy's fingers stuck to the adhesive tapes. 'I'm in *jail*.' She flapped her hand back and forth through the air, trying to shed its soggy consignment. 'I'm denied fresh fruit, late nights, good coffee, nice clothes, sleep-ins, newspapers, *crème brûlée* and hot jungle sex with the horndog Himbo of my choice . . .'

Edwina cocked her head to one side and smiled patronizingly. 'I'm not as straight as I appear. I've undergone Transactional Analysis.' She uttered these words as though they were a magic talisman. 'I believe you must Own Your Anger.

How else can one understand transference and rejection? I'm currently part of a rebirthing workshop.'

'As long as I can rebirth myself as a millionairess love goddess with no stretch marks.'

'Primal therapy is not beyond my grasp,' she confided, unperturbed.

'Oh, great. Just the ticket.' Maddy, balancing Jack's naked body in the crook of her arm, filled the sink with warm water. '*Cheer yourself up whilst in prison by reliving your unhappy childhood* ... Um ... I don't think so. Besides, I had an unfashionably *happy* childhood. Sandy beaches, blue skies, nothing more dangerous than a bad prawn for miles around in any direction ...'

Dwina seized on this with glee. 'Hidden Memory Syndrome, dear. We therapists find that the more a patient denies being abused as a child the more assiduous the search for evidence should be!'

Maddy was only half listening. 'Ah-uh ...' As the sink's water-level peaked, she twiddled at the taps with one hand. Testing the temperature with her elbow sent a tidal wave over her feet. Adding a squirt of prison-issue baby oil, she slowly submerged Jack. He promptly spurted out of her hands and went under. 'Shit!'

'Just look at the facts, Madeline. Lack of career success, low self-esteem' – the 'L'-plated analyst itemized Maddy's shortcomings on her disinfected fingers – 'a jail sentence, single motherhood ... Is *this* the product of a happy childhood?'

Each time Maddy grabbed hold of Jack's slimy body, he'd squirm free of her trembling grasp. She was dunking him up and down like a teabag. Shoving Maddy aside, Dwina, with dextrous panache, extracted Jack and swaddled him snugly in a towel. Maddy, overcome with her own inadequacy, felt a sob rising in her throat.

'I know how you feel, Madeline, I really do. You're not a criminal, dear. You were driven to crime for *his* sake.' With nimble-fingered deftness, Dwina sluiced water on to Jack's delicate head, towelled his hair-fluff and placed him on the bed in a shower of powder. 'A victim of circumstances. But what I want you to take on board, is that you can *change* those circumstances. There are many, *many* loving couples out there who would give this sweet little baby a fulfilled and *normal* life.' A cold tentacle of dread suddenly coiled around Maddy's abdomen. 'Such a gesture on your part would make any judge sympathetic. You could start over, unfettered. I think you feel these things, but don't dare express them.'

Maddy dive-bombed her baby and clenched him to her. 'You know nothing about me!'

'I'm training as a psychotherapist. It's my business to know.'

'Who are you training under? Doctor *Seuss*? I am not giving up my baby.'

'The point is, Madeline, if you're going to get a sentence over eighteen months—'

'Eighteen months!'

'Oh yes. These days, the quality of mercy is severely strained. I've never known a government with such an enthusiasm for punishment!' A chain dangled from her waist, holding a large key and a whistle. She tucked them into a leather girl guide-type pouch on her hip. 'It's cruel keeping the baby with you now, only to have to give him up further down the track to a foster parent. Imagine it. He'll come out into the world terrified of traffic noise, of dogs barking! Why not place him with a happy, loving family now? I can arrange it . . . Or would you rather he be taken into care?' Dwina extracted a compact from her pouch and examined her reflection. 'As far as Detective Sergeant Slynne is concerned, you have no fixed address, no money, no paternal or familial support. It will be easy for him to paint you as an unfit mother.'

Her words twisted in Maddy's guts.

Frowning into the mirror, Dwina tweezed an impudent hair which had dared to sprout on her chin. 'You've seen the women in the Mother and Baby Unit? Only kids themselves. Now *their* kids will be in care, perpetuating the cycle.'

It was true. Maddy had been able to tell the women who'd been brought up in children's home. They ate quickly, hunched over their plates, having learned to protect their food from an early age. Maddy felt rain seeping into her veins. 'Would you please go now?'

Edwina Phelps snapped shut her compact, offended. 'Why?' she asked, sarcastically. 'Busy?'

Maddy refused to let this headshrinker get the better of her. 'Well, there's my Please Note Change of Address cards . . .'

*

After Dwina's departure, Maddy fed and burped Jack before tucking him into the paint-chipped crib by her own cramped cot. Beside him, she placed the only toy she'd been able to scavenge – a legless, plastic Pocahontas. Someone had put out their cigarette in the leg socket, which had melted grotesquely.

Jack coiled his little arm up to the doll's face. Great, he'd be a pervert when he grew up. An amputee-philiac. *She had to get him out of here.*

The eerie silence was punctuated by coughing, by copulating pigeons, by a morse-code tapping on pipes, bronchial plumbing, shrieks, rattles, slamming doors, the sound of muffled sobbing. From all over the prison, women called out to each other through the windows, a desolate chorus of 'I'm gonna punch your poxy head in' and 'I fuckin' love you's.

A screw flashed a torch through the hatch in her cell door, the beam briefly illuminating the dismal graffiti on her wall: 'Here today and here tomorrow.' There was only one person who could save her.

Maddy knew she was on the edge of an emotional precipice. What she didn't know was that she was about to take a giant leap forward . . .

4. Baby, It's Cold Inside

'I suppose it wouldn't be entirely sympathetic to ask if you've been up to anything new lately?'

'Ask me that, Gillian, and I'll be in here for manslaughter.'

Maddy had used up her entire ration of phonecards to track down her best friend. Her first dialling destination was the real-estate offices of Belgravia. Gillian had confided that the way to find a rich husband was to pretend you were house hunting in a posh neighbourhood. A house on the market often indicated a divorce settlement, and men were so easy to catch on the rebound. Maddy's next attempt was the Concorde guest lounge at Heathrow. Gillian's trick was to book herself a seat, loiter seductively in the lounge, setting up dates with every powerful man present and then refunding her ticket at the last minute.

Maddy struck luck at Sotheby's. Gillian maintained that a *collector* of expensive antiques often turned out to *be* one. All a girl needed to do was pepper her conversation with 'Jacobean' this and 'Georgian' that and . . . she'd soon be sending him 'baroque', furnishing her for life.

'You called me away from the most div*ine* man.'

'Yes,' Maddy ribbed, 'I'm sure you have just *so* much in common.'

'We most definitely do.' She paused. 'He has a Caribbean island, and I want one . . . So, how's the food?'

'Okay . . . if you like rat's sperm.'

Gillian, looking noticeably louche in the grim surroundings, leant back in her chair to allow the males in the visiting room a generous view of her sheerly stockinged legs. Her designer-suited entrance and finishing-school deportment had created quite a sensation amongst the prisoners' raggle-taggle collection of unshaven boyfriends. Looking under-dressed without their ski masks they slumped over full ashtrays, eyeing Gillian with the hungry look of half-starved greyhounds.

'Have you ever seen so many shell suits?' Gillian enquired, agreeably caustic. 'Think I'll pick one up, put him to my ear and listen for the Atlantic,' she snorted with self-satisfaction.

Observing Gillian in the poisonous green light of the remand-wing visiting room made Maddy ponder afresh how they had ever become friends. She reminded herself that despite appearances, Gillian's siliconed décollétage was *not* the only deep thing about her.

She seized her friend's hand. 'Listen!' Maddy sputtered, with earnest desperation. 'They're going to try to take Jack! You've got to hide him!'

Gillian's response was not exactly what Maddy had antici-pated. She laughed until her mascara ran, inking two big racoon rings beneath each eye. Semi-composed, she blotted at her face with a lace handkerchief and replied, 'Dah-ling, did they take your brain out at the same time as your baby?'

'I come up for bail again in a week's time. Then I can clear up this godawful mess . . .'

'The thing is, dah-ling, I only know how to look after *dogs*. The child will be cocking its leg on trees within *days*.'

Maddy was leaning so hard against the table between them that her ribs were bruising. 'Gill, I'm shitting razor blades.'

'You're serious!' Gillian's tone was one of doleful dismay. 'Dah-ling, I don't know how to operate a baby.'

'Fun tips for beginners,' whispered Maddy, facetiously. 'Kissing, cuddling, tickling, toe-nibbling, tummy-raspberry-blowing . . . That's about all he requires.'

'So did my chihuahua . . . and *he* ended up down the waste-disposal unit.'

'Feeding times are about every four hours . . .'

'Just like at the zoo . . .' replied Gillian, displaying the compassion for which she was internationally renowned.

'The two most popular brands come in Boy and Girl and—'

'Be sensible. How on earth do you propose I get him out of here? In my *hand*bag?'

Gillian was thirty-six but didn't look a day over forty. Her make-up requirements had recently reached the special-effects stage. She needed a handbag the size of an aircraft hangar to accommodate her chemist shop of lotions and potions. 'Precisely.' Maddy tipped the carry cot in Gillian's direction. 'He's a completely portable lap-size model. He'll go to sleep after his feed and then we'll transfer him.'

Gillian tried to push back her chair. 'I went to Roedean.' It was bolted to the floor. 'I wear Issey Miyake.' She struggled to standing. 'I am *not* the type to be seen drinking from a Postman Pat flask.'

'He sleeps between one and six hours between meals. He'll cry between one and four hours in every twenty-four so don't panic and—'

'Has it crossed what's left of your mind,' Gillian interrupted sternly, 'that this is a *prison*? Where they have a tendency to *search visitors*?'

'Gillian, generally people in jail want things smuggled *in*.'

To illustrate her point, a woman near the windows was unceremoniously dragged away from her boyfriend. Dope, cling-filmed and kept in his mouth, had been transferred during a tongue-kiss, to be lodged half-way down her throat and sicked up later, with shampoo.

'Now sit down for Christ's sake!' Maddy tugged Gillian back into the chair from which she had just escaped.

'It's im*pos*sible,' Gillian announced to the wilting carnations she'd brought with her.

'Gill, we're talking about a little baby. A little baby in *prison*. The tooth fairy will have to commit a crime to leave the twenty pence under his pillow. His knowledge of primary colours will stop at grey . . .'

'Speaking of which . . .' Gillian glanced furtively around, then spoke funereally. 'I found my first grey pubic hair this morning.'

'He'll be teething on steel bars. He won't be learning to read from *Spot Goes to the Circus* but graffiti along the lines of "Die Police Scum" . . .'

'Of course I plucked it out. But, let's face it, *there's more where that came from!*'

'I want him to be able to count, sure, but not in lieu of knowing people's names. Will number two-three-six please pass me my bottle . . .'

'The point is, I'm past the marrying age. Which means it's time to confront the job market, which is impossible to do with an infant in tow.'

'Hah! The only job you've ever had was on your nose.'

Gillian's hand leapt protectively to her pert proboscis. 'This is my *real* nose!'

'Gill, if you don't look after him they're going to take him into' – Maddy could hardly say the word – '*care*.'

'Care?' Gillian calmed the material across her thighs. She uttered a heavy, half-relenting sigh. 'A *week*. No longer.'

Relief flooded Maddy's body. Jack, who'd been waving his pygmaean arms, got more agitated. Maddy picked him up. He attached himself to her nipple with sea-anenome suction. His teeny hand stroked Maddy's breast; feathery, soft little movements which soothed her beyond belief. A drowsiness seeped over her. The throb of the central heating, the drone of voices, she was soon slipping under the meringue of Gillian's words; all sugar and air. A kick in the shins promptly roused her.

'On the whole,' Gillian's curt voice karate-chopped, 'I prefer not to wake a friend who falls asleep while I'm talking to her but it's Ciao time . . .'

'Sorry.' Maddy yawned. 'For some reason Jack is the only living creature in prison who thinks they don't wake us up early enough. Three a.m. and Hey! It's Party Time!'

'Oh, tickety-boo,' said Gillian, with not altogether fraudulent alarm. 'You kept *that* information quiet.' Leaning forward, she inspected her new accessory with an irritable disdain. 'Ugh! What on earth is that *hole* in the top of its head? My God! He's not going to *spout*?'

Maddy was going to explain about the anterior fontanelle,

but her voice was muzzled by emotion. Although the bells were signalling the end of visiting time, she wanted to top him up with milk, camel-like, to last the whole week. They were sitting in a shadowy corner. Gillian positioned her back to the rest of the room. She extracted her massive make-up kit and pushed it across the table. Maddy tucked it into her carry cot. She then took a last look at Jack – her eyes, lens shutters, photographing him in her head.

'Hurry up,' hissed Gillian.

Maddy traced his delicate eyebrows, the colour of caramel toffee. She kissed his ivory eyelids; the lashes so long you could positively hike through them. She buried her nose in his crest of blonde hair and inhaled. To a mother, that baby smell was as moreish as opium. Steeling herself, she broke Jack's liplock and handed the precious, swaddled parcel to Gillian. 'Try to pretend not to be impressed at receiving *the* Most Beautiful Baby Ever Born On This Planet, okay?' she said bravely. He looked so vulnerable, she had to bite her fingers to stop herself from snatching him back. She bit them till they bled.

'Dah-ling,' said Gillian, in a rare spasm of concern, 'look on the bright side. A women's prison – at least the toilet seat will never be up.'

'Take good care of him,' Maddy implored, as they got to their feet.

The handles of Gillian's voluminous valise closed over their unusual cargo. 'Next time you see him, he'll heel when called.'

*

Staff shortages meant that Maddy got back to her cell undetected. She lay on the narrow bed. A mournful clock tolled the hours since Jack's departure. The humidi crib atmosphere of the prison pressed in on her. She had kept back one small item of his clothing. It was all she had to remind her of her cherished angel. Aching body and soul, she buried her face in his minuscule cotton cardigan, breathed in his soft, sweet smell and wept, helpless as a newborn.

5. The Standing Offer

The sky lightened to a bitter, jaundiced yellow, to find Maddy bent over the tiny sink in her cell, applying hot flannels to her breasts. Until now, Maddy thought that only performance artists 'expressed' themselves. But no. Not just streams, but *Niles* of milk gurgled down the plughole. Every noise triggered her milk flow – distant car horns, clock radios, kettles, other babies crying. She could have opened a goddamned dairy in there.

This was how the prison officer found her, baby AWOL, missing, presumed dead. Slynne was called; the harmonic wheeze of the cell-door hinge heralding his arrival.

'Apparently you've' – he cleared his throat with mock theatricality – '*lost* your baby.'

'Have I?' Maddy hammed. 'Oh, well, he's probably with my car keys, then.'

'Have you killed it?' His alert, rodent eyes scurried over her face scavenging for a confessional crumb.

'There's nothing in the cell, sir,' vouched the prison officer.

'Dismembered it? Cannibalized it, perhaps?'

Maddy, feigning nonchalance, studied her interrogator. Brutal and brusque, he was also vain. That hungry hyena smile suggested an intimate knowledge of periodontal work prac-

44

tices. And there was something too solid about the hairline. A closer inspection revealed a Grecian 2000 stain behind his right ear.

Slynne banged his fist on the wall. 'What kind of mother are you?' His grip on her arm was that of a jack-hammer operator. 'You're not even worried about your own baby!'

'Oh, I *was* worried,' Maddy contended, wrenching free, 'but then I thought, hey, why torture myself when you can do it for me?'

'Infanticide is a very serious crime.'

Maddy felt her stomach fall through to the floor. This copper was a magnifying glass who would not go away.

'What rot!' The voice was Dwina's. She stood panting in the doorway. Having completed stages one and two of Basic Scarf Draping, she had now graduated to the reverse neckerchief foulard model. She shed her coat and fell on to the kettle. 'It's a recognized psychological post-birth trauma. I've run a workshop on this just recently. This woman is a Recovering Hormonal Addict.'

Prison, Maddy was discovering, was full of recovering people. Recovering from smack, barbiturates, solvents, bad marriages. Inmates boasted membership of Nymphomaniacs Anonymous, Cake-aholics Anonymous, Men Anonymous, *Anonymous* Anonymous.

Dwina placed a possessive arm on the back of Maddy's chair. 'If you'd attended my workshop, Detective Sergeant, you wouldn't be so ignorant of female endorphins.' She gave Maddy's head a condescending pat, as though she were a child. Maddy flinched. Edwina Phelps was a candidate for '*Nice*-aholics Anonymous'.

'No baby' – Slynne bounced on the balls of his feet – 'no Mother and Baby Unit. Let's see how her "endorphins" go down with the nonces.'

Edwina Phelps's hand halted in mid-air, post-pat. 'The Nonces?!'

'Paedophiles and perverts,' stipulated a voice located somewhere behind a cigarette. 'Most loathed people in prison. Segregated so the other inmates don't waste them.'

Dwina angrily workshopped a cup of coffee, rattling a spoon into a chipped enamel cup. 'Over my dead body.'

Maddy thought that maybe she wouldn't enrol Dwina in Nice-aholics *just* yet.

'Oh, well,' retorted Slynne. 'Everything has its price.'

'No corpse, no crime. The baby is missing.' Dwina replaced the spoon in a sugar bowl, encrusted with brown granulated balls. 'Not dead.'

'Yes,' said Slynne, craftily. 'You're right. Much better that I send her into prison proper . . . where she'll be beaten up as a "beast".'

'How can that happen when no one but the people in this room know about the missing child?'

'You know how word travels in prison.' The Detective winked in the prison officer's direction. She reciprocated with a cruel, collaborative grin. 'Especially when a woman has killed her baby . . .'

Dwina, savouring her Ph.D.'ed smarts over the clueless detective, unclipped one earring and rubbed the lobe. (Maddy presumed she'd attended a workshop for that also – Earring Management in Telephonic Situations: A Psychodynamic

Approach.) 'I don't believe she's hurt her baby. She's hidden him with someone. Didn't you have a visitor yesterday?'

Detective Slynne opened his mouth to speak, but Dwina got in first, forcing him into a goldfish impersonation.

'Madeline, all that talk of adoption, it all felt so cold, didn't it? So clinical . . .' She squatted down in front of Maddy. 'But what I didn't explain is that there is another way.'

Slynne, ferociously drawing on his cancer stick, rocked from his toes to his heels and back again.

'What once took just one man, one woman, one bed and Ravel's "Bolero" has become, for many couples, a bureaucratic nightmare. There are ten million childless women in the "civilized" world. And yet the number of babies offered for adoption is falling. Can you imagine the pain of couples longing for a stake in the next generation?' She retrieved a tissue from her sleeve and delicately blew her nose. 'It's heart-breaking.'

The Detective Sergeant, sighing tetchily, lit a new cigarette from the embers of the old. To him, pyschology was nothing more than a guess with a goddamn degree.

'The beauty of a *private* adoption is that *you* can *choose* the adoptive mother. I see the chance here of saving four lives. The hopeful couple's, Jack's and above all, *yours*, Madeline. I'm offering you a chance to *start again*. Just tell us where your baby is?'

All eyes were on Maddy, whose eyes were on her shirt in anticipation of the kettle's cry.

'Otherwise every bleedin' broom handle you see will have your name on it.'

'Detective!' Dwina fumed. 'Centre yourself! You're pro*ject*-ing!' She impounded the police-officer's cigarette and extinguished it. 'A cigarette,' she lectured, 'has a fire on one end and a *fool* on the other.'

'You don't understand,' Slynne whinged. 'Ms Smartass here likes a bit of a joke. Liked making an ass out of me in front of my coppers down the nick. How do *you* like it when the joke's at *your* expense?'

Maddy's mouth was in gear before she knew she was driving. 'Have you heard the one about the inmate who cut off the Detective's testicles and wore them as ear ornaments? Dwina could have a workshop. Earring Management – the *psychotic* approach.'

The kettle shrieked. Maddy, mopping at her shirt front, could have kicked herself. What was wrong with her? She'd have to run her own workship, entitled 'How To Lose Friends and Alienate Everyone'.

A convulsive start rattled Slynne's frame, from hair tint to toe-nails. Edwina Phelps, defeated, shook her head in despair. Slynne elbowed her aside and began his sarcastic mantra. 'You do not have to say anything unless you wish to do so, but what you say may be given in evidence . . . do you want your lawyer?'

*

Few things in this life are more reassuring than being in the hands of a legal-aid lawyer – one is sitting on a jumbo jet that's about to make unscheduled contact with the Himalayas. This was the thought in Maddy's mind as she waited for legal-budgie Rupert Peregrine in the dank, dimly lit legal-visit room, soured by decades of over-wrought armpits.

'Look,' she announced urgently as he lumbered into the room, 'they can't do anything to me. Not without a body.'

'It's touching, your naivety.' Peregrine put down his brief-case and struggled out of his jacket. 'Two inmates have already made statements saying that they saw you kill the baby.'

'What!' The heat of injustice flushed her face. 'But that's crap. Why would they say that?'

Peregrine lowered his great weight on to the swizzle chair opposite, which gave the customary moan of protest she'd come to except from any piece of furniture unfortunate enough to be in contact with her para-legal's posterior.

'Prison, Ms Wolfe, is full of roach-like reprobates desperate to ingratiate themselves with the Powers That Be.' Scuttling his chair backwards, he checked the doorlock. This guy had the single-mindedness of a cruise missile. 'I could help quash these reports, lose relevant files on the computer' – he rolled the chair closer to his quarry – 'if I had the right incentive. My offer still . . . how shall I put this' – a trail of slaver hit the table between them – '*stands.*'

Maddy looked over her Law Society-Approved knight in pin-striped armour. Yesterday's coldsore was now slick with ointment. 'If I'm feeling masochistic, Mr Peregrine, I go shopping for a new swimming costume. That's about as self-loathing as I get.'

'But when the microchips are down?'

Maddy contemplated a subtle little hint to let him know she wasn't in the mood – like smashing the ceramic ashtray over his head. 'The answer is still no.' She pointed to his glistening herpes. 'Besides which, your enthusiasm is kind of catching, you know?'

'Your court appearance is on Thursday.' The gunshot click of the catches on his opening briefcase made her jump in her chair. 'Until now, the case against you was fairly flimsy. An illegal immigrant, yes, but white, so we politely call you an over-stayer. Only circumstantial evidence – the stolen wallet – to link you to credit-card fraud and a defence both plausible and tear-jerking. But now, infanticide? The judge will not even consider bail without someone of substance to stand surety. Madam' – he hooked pudgy thumbs through straining belt loops – 'my joy pendulum awaits you.'

Maddy's heart sank into her socks. 'You know, this conversation is strangely familiar.'

'*Strangely familiar.*' Her solicitor winced, retreating into his professional demeanour. 'Oxymorons are to me abhorrent. Please remember that, Ms Wolfe.'

Maddy could feel a headache gnawing at her temple. 'Rupert?'

'Yes?' Leering hopefully, he rolled up his shirt sleeves, exposing milkbottle-white forearms, formidably shagpiled.

'Fuck you and the synthetic suit you rode in on.'

Peregrine laughed disproportionately, slapping his massive thighs. Undeterred, he covered Maddy's hand with his own. 'Now' – his adams apple yo-yo-ed up and down with excitement – 'I've always found cunnilingus to be a good opening courting gambit.'

Maddy snatched back her hand. 'Why are you like this?' But she knew why. For all his declarations of love, Alex was little more than the same – a heat-seeking penis which did not report to Mission Control. 'Wouldn't you occasionally like to have sex with someone who didn't press charges later?'

'Sexually exploiting my clients has the advantage of requiring no more than fifteen minutes of my day, leaving me more time to lavish on the love of my life – a Burmese kitten called Butter Truffles.'

'In case you've forgotten, I've just had a baby. There's an out of order sign on my underpants, okay?'

He rolled down his sleeves and snapped shut the gaping black jaws of his cavernous briefcase. There was a terrifying finality about it which gave Maddy a panicky feeling in her belly.

'Anyway, I'll be out in a week.'

Peregrine stood up abruptly. 'Don't make any plans.'

'A week I can handle,' she stated, bravely. 'I mean, there's a library, a gym, educational facilities.'

'With Advanced Rug Munching on the curriculum.' Peregrine wrestled his way back into his jacket. 'When I say don't make any plans, Ms Wolfe, I do *not* mean putting your Women's Reading Group on hold. I mean write your will and kiss your loved ones goodbye.' Peregrine gallumphed to the door. 'Rug munching . . . a rather resonant euphemism, don't you think?'

Maddy read the graffiti carved into the back of the door which her solicitor had just slammed – 'Kill All Bitches'. Madeline Wolfe had a terrible feeling that the writing on the wall was about to include her name.

6. There's A Baby In My Bath Water!

'Let's get one thing straight. *I don't like babies.*' Gillian's gigantic face swelled into Jack's myopic vision. 'I'd rather have a pedigree Weimaraner. At least you can sell them. You wouldn't even *be* here if it weren't for those five years at Our Lady of Maximum Humiliation and Hypocrisy Convent. A Catholic upbringing, my dear, is a life's excursion on a guilt trip. Comprehendé?'

The baby's hands jerked past his face. He didn't seem to realize that they were attached to his body. Alternatively amused and intrigued, he watched his own fingers fly by as though they were performers at the Moscow State Circus . . . Oh well, Gillian reflected, he wasn't the first male she'd met who could be entertained by bits of his own anatomy.

*

'I'd like some baby clothes,' said Gillian, gruffly, to the Mothercare assistant.

'Yes, Madam. What sort?' The shop girl was so enthusiastic Gillian thought her face might fall off.

'*I* don't know,' she snapped. '*Clothes* for a *baby*. Oh, and nappies.'

'What size?'

'How the hell do *I* know?' She wrenched open the handles of her handbag and pointed contemptuously at Jack ensconced within. '*This* size.'

Gillian was too irritated to appreciate the incongruity of the situation; she, in her false eyelashes which looked, when she blinked, like tarantulas mating, and a four-and-a-half-week old baby, held at arm's length like a contaminated package. Watching the startled sales assistant assembling the basic-maintenance kit, Gillian idly pondered that she actually knew more about babies than she'd realized. Essentially they were just like designer cars; the fuel tank needed constant topping up and it was impossible to get any replacement parts.

'Well, rug-rat,' she said, going through her wallet with painstaking care, 'the silver spoon one was born with has somewhat tarnished. We've got just enough money to keep us until your mother gets back, unless I feel the urge to buy anything. Like *food*, for example.' Gillian thought of the money she'd squandered when she'd been solvent; if only she'd known its worth.

There wasn't much in life that the worldly Ms Cassells hadn't sampled. She'd hot-air-ballooned with Richard Branson. She'd Glyndebourned with more Royals than you could shake a corgi at. She'd joined the Mile High Club on Concorde (no crew, someone new and not in the loo). She'd lain on private yachts, in Parisian hotel suites and under the knives of Hollywood plastic surgeons.

But work was an unknown phenomenon.

'It's not just the grey pube,' Gillian confided to her handbag, as she sashayed up Regent Street. 'The other night, during a romantic encounter, I remarked to my partner that he was skilled enough to do it professionally and, dah-ling, do you know what he said?' She didn't wait for Jack's reply. 'He said that he *was*. And that the payment would be fifty quid. It was then I noticed the V.F.M. tattooed on his penis. Value For Money.'

She paused to examine a bikini she was far too old for in the windows of Liberty's. 'You see, Jack – one thought one would be on to one's third or fourth hubby by now, getting richer by decrees, dah-ling.' It was an exquisite bikini. Perhaps with a little cosmetic enhancement? Gillian sighed, pulled in her stomach muscles and marched onwards. The only plastic surgery Gillian Cassells was now likely to experience involved banks cutting up her credit cards.

At Oxford Circus tube station, she bought a newspaper. Tight-lipped with embarrassment, she flicked to the employment section.

'From queen bee to drone, dah-ling,' she despaired to her hidden kiddie contraband. 'It just ain't natural.'

*

As inexperienced as she was, Gillian suspected that arriving one hour late for her job interview was perhaps not the best way to impress a prospective employer. It was not her fault. Despite inflating condom balloons to amuse him, Jack had howled the whole night. Once he *did* go to sleep, he became a capricious clock radio, going off unpredictably and tuned into long-wave static. But when she *needed* a wake-up call, he'd slept right through. Hence her flustered arrival on the threshold of 'Ronald La Roux Fine Art'. An ice-cream van inched along the pavement, the syrupy music dripping out on to the street.

'Listen,' Gillian pleaded desperately to her small, whimpering ward, 'they're playing your song!'

Gillian was in the middle of her pitch on depersonalized perceptions of abstract dichotomies when the ice-cream cone propped in the pram lost its soppy sanctuary and slid in slow motion on to the work of a primitive (not so Naive, to judge by the number of zeros on her price tag) Fauvistic Impressionist.

'Kid loves art,' Gillian gushed on the brink of her own Premenstrual-Tension Nervous Breakdown Blue Period. 'His first words were Mama and Dada,' she added pathetically, then left before Roland La Roux was tempted to break Jack down to his most basic geometric form.

*

Her foray into exotic kitchenware fared no better. Despite Gillian's limited culinary credentials – as far as she was concerned capers were things you got up to, preferably with recently divorced shipping magnates – she was busily bluffing her way into the earthenware traditional Peasant cooking-implements department of Selfridges, when the sales assistant she had paid to mind Jack, appeared, grimacing.

'I think,' the nineteen-year-old (nose pinched between acrylic nails) informed the job applicant, 'he needs changing.'

'Yes,' hissed Gillian, resentfully. 'Preferably for the heir to an oil fortune.'

Not the way to conduct a job interview, she silently fumed, lying Jack on the office carpet to swab and daub.

'Well, that's a first,' she began lamely, resuming her seat and glancing at the bewildered personnel manager across the desk. 'The only male I've ever succeeded in changing. Oh, I got close with Milo Roxburghe,' she floundered, name-dropping frantically, 'the Hair Extension King? An ex-fiancé of mine, do you know him? That man wore white *shoes* when I first met him.'

Gillian couldn't believe how often babies defecated. 'You're *male*,' she lamented to her homo sapien soupçon, as they were ejected from the store. 'You're supposed to disappear into the lavatory with a copy of *Sporting Life* for hours on end. Don't you know *any*thing?'

*

Worse than the endless poo were the air-to-surface mucus missiles. Gillian had to resort to going to the corner store in her taffeta ballgown, because the rest of her wardrobe was covered in baby slime. By Wednesday morning she'd taken to wearing only fawn and cream. Not her colours, but it cut down on washing.

Gillian felt that years of attending the Paris fashion shows had equipped her for the job of Fashion Editor on *Harpers Bizarre*. All you needed to do was describe everything as *fab*ulous, am*az*ing, or 'tastic. This just meant that you hadn't seen anything like it in the last five microseconds. As babies were this year's ultimate accessory – all the Fashionista from Madonna to Michael Hutchence were sporting them – Gillian felt that finally Jack would be an asset.

'Oh, look!' The female fashion journalists – who used their heads solely as a place to prop their Sony Walkmans – emerged from behind their six-foot flower arrangements, and, ignoring Gillian, rushed to gush over Maddy's offspring. 'Isn't he *gorgeous*?'

Gillian stared down at Jack. He lay squiggling on the carpet like something larval. She couldn't see it. 'I suppose someone said that to Saddam Hussein's mother,' she japed. Oblivious to the magazine editor's censorious glance, she prattled on. 'Can you imagine the indignity of being a baby and having to wear those hideous all-in-one baby-gros? Now *there's* a fashion victim!'

The editor, in arctic tones, replied that she didn't know what Gillian was talking about. Standing up to show Gillian the door, she revealed her lamé jump suit – with press-studded crutch for easy access.

'Oops.'

Jack gurgled happily all the way down in the lift. 'Oh, grow a neck,' she scolded him. 'And *then* we'll talk.'

*

It was the same story all week; whether posing as a Prue Leith graduate (she'd landed the job to deliver hampers of salmonella and egg sandwiches to posh boardroom lunches) or an opera buff (when the Covent Garden PR director asked her how she would define her understanding of various plots, she'd flirtatiously ad-libbed, 'Just follow the bouncing dagger!') every opportunity was sabotaged by Maddy's little crumb-cruncher. 'Talk about gumming the hand which feeds you!'

*

'Indulge me,' Gillian pleaded with Jack on Friday morning. 'I'm a severely economically inactive, neurotic, middle-aged celibate with suicidal tendencies. *Please be quiet.*' She plugged a dummy into the baby's mouth and watched, astounded, as he plummeted, pell-mell, into unconsciousness. This time Gillian checked him in with her coat at Blake's Hotel, cocooned in the depths of her carpetbag.

Half an hour into the interview, not only did she have the job of Exotic Plumage Importer, but the boss, Simon, an elegantly dressed stud-muffin in his mid-forties with bedroom eyes and a bionic bank balance, had asked her to lunch. It was then the coat-check girl arrived with the writhing handbag.

'Shit!' said Gillian, eloquently. Responding to her voice, the handbag emitted a high-pitched wail which seemed to be imitating a backed-up insinkerator.

'I'm sorry,' Simon retreated. 'You didn't mention a child.'

'It's not *my* baby,' Gillian jabbered. 'His mother's off stamping due dates for the prison library.' Her employer's eyes bugged out. 'Not that I make a habit of fraternizing with felons, but . . .'

'This job, Miss Cassells, requires long hours and late nights.'

'I need to fit him with a silencer, that's all.' Gillian groped urgently through her bag, excavating the contents – a half-chewed rusk, a rattle, a musical frog, one soiled diaper and a tube of iridescent pink nappy-rash cream – on to Simon's desk. 'He needs the Betty Ford clinic for dummy addicts,' Gillian said, above the howling. 'A dummy de-tox unit. Do it cold turkey, no-neck,' she snapped at the child, *sotto voce*.

Her employer winced with alarm.

'I mean, one must be cruel to be kind, correct?' Gillian gave a fake laugh in an effort to salvage the situation. 'After all, boys will be boys. Mind you, so will a lot of octogenarian business men I know.' The look on Simon's face alerted Gillian to the fact that this may not have been the most tactful comment.

'Though obviously, not *you*.' It was the sleep deprivation, that's what it was. She'd been taking lobotomy pills.

*

Later that day, Gillian invested in a play pen and incarcerated the baby without trial. Like mother, like son, she thought dismally. 'Call Amnesty International. See if I care.' She would add a sign – 'DANGER. Put Fingers Inside Bars At Own Risk.' She dropped a bottle into the baby's mouth. 'Drink it,' she demanded, delivering her version of the starving millions in Africa spiel. 'You know, *there are children in Knightsbridge with eating disorders!*' It was only then that it struck her that she was actually conversing with an infant.

Pouring a large gin and tonic, she tried to talk herself off the psychological windowledge where Maddy had pushed her. Failing, she put her hennaed head in her hands and sucked morosely on the plastic pacifier.

7. The Clit-lick Hilton

Maddy's eyes had not adjusted to the dimly lit corridor of the remand wing. She had a distinct sensation that she was being watched. Not particularly perceptive of her, as the surrounding gloomy shapes were breathing adenoidally. The hairs pricked up on her arms. She backed instinctively towards the wall. She thought of those air fresheners people have on toilet cisterns and the backs of car seats which exude alpine and eucalyptus aromas. In prison, there's an invisible scent-tree too, only it impregnates the atmosphere with paranoia and fear of imminent death.

'H-h-hello?' Like a bat, Maddy sent off conversational sonar bleeps to gauge the positions of the oglers.

A thin, wiry shape with the dress sense of Liberace stepped out of the shadows and prodded Maddy in the throat with a scalpel nail. 'What choo lookin' at?'

Shaved into this woman's dyed purple hair were the words 'Made in London'. Maddy wondered if the charges against her were 'Assault with intent to kill a hair colourist'. Her adversary's footwear, the sort which could crush light aircraft, propelled her to the daunting height of six foot two. She launched into a 'you slag this' and 'you slag that' diatribe, punctuated by an oyster of phlegm which hit Maddy full in the face before beginning it's slow, gruesome descent down her chin. She told herself that she wasn't frightened. She told herself that she'd been in scarier situations – lip electrolysis, labour without an epidural, dinner with the London literati . . . But then *why were her teeth fillings dissolving*?

More lurking inmates came into focus, sporting that over-experimented-on lab-rat look.

'Who's it, Sputnik?' demanded a specimen with dirty blonde hair, red satin shorts, a ruby nose ornament and a facial expression a little too canine for comfort.

'It's that kid killer, wotsits,' Maddy's assailant declaimed, in the staccato of the seriously tense and totally deranged. Maddy noted the small pupils and the choppy, twitchy movements of a woman sweating out a drug high. The nickname was disconcertingly clear. Sputnik was in her own orbit.

'Ja know what I'm gunna do to ya, beastie?' She gave Maddy a look which meant pain.

'Gee, I don't know . . .' Maddy took a wild guess. 'Braid my labia?'

'Punch your fuckin' head in, nonce.' Tough? This was a woman who did her own bikini waxes.

'I didn't hurt my baby, okay?' she faltered.

'Why thuh fuck should we believe ya?' With one swift punch to the stomach, she concertinaed Maddy to the cold, cement floor. Sputnik stood over her; a brittle body encased in jeans so tight you could trace the outline of the sultana she'd had for breakfast. Maddy's eyes frantically sought out the prison officers at the far end of the association room. They roamed, big, bored cats, completely blasé about Maddy's life and death drama.

'I have two words for you,' Maddy panted. '*Social Services.*'

This stonkered them. To women who've been handed the stiff cheese from fate's *fromage* trolley, these were the most terrifying words in their limited lexicon. The miserable herd stopped jostling and glanced indecisively at Sputnik who answered their silent query by pitching her high-heeled Doc Marten down hard into Maddy's side.

'They were going to . . . take him away . . . into care.' Reasoning with Sputnik, Maddy surmised, was a little like pissing into a hurricane. 'I smuggled him out.' She braced herself as the psychotic Rockette prepared for some more fancy footwork.

'Lord have mercy! Can't you smuggle me out too?'

The old lady was so submerged in her own flesh that although each step was bringing her closer, she seemed to be moving in ten directions simultaneously. Beneath the diamond-encrusted tooth enamel, a familiar flight of chins led to a balcony of bosom above the gargantuan stomach. The thought of Mamma Joy being smuggled out in anything less than a greyhound bus sent titters through the edgy scrum.

'Or, preferably me man, *in* . . . without his wife knowin' dat is.' She bundled Maddy up off the floor and into a bear hug. 'Where dere comes no beau, de cobwebs grow.' This was a woman who made Zorba the Greek look introverted. 'I know dis lady. She love her ba-by. Wot you chargin' her wid, eh? Aidin' and abettin' the escape of a minor? Hee *hee* hee hee hee.'

Sputnik's phlegmy growl indicated her displeasure. 'You ain't tryin' to fuck me around are yer, yer fat cow.'

'You are just as high in my opinion as ever, gal.' Mamma

Joy turned, depositing a breathy aside into Maddy's earhole, 'On crack, dat is . . .'

Maddy in tow, she parted the anti-climactic throng with breast-stroke movements and waddled, as though wearing tights two sizes too small – towards the few library books shelved in the corner of the association room. As they pretended to flick through the fascinating range of donated reading material – *Taxidermy for Fun And Profit, Bulgarian Nautical Commands For Beginners, The Ghost in the Invisible Bikini – a Novel* – Maddy whispered gravely, 'What brought *you* here?'

'Mini bus, what cha think?' Mamma Joy chortled hoarsely.

'I didn't think people got sent to prison just for . . . I mean, shop-lifting?'

Mamma Joy narrowed her eyes. 'You tink I did a murder? I was tinkin' about it . . .' She erupted into that stagey cackle. 'No. Me neva done no murder. I'm guilty though – of *gettin' caught*. Tings can get a little awkward when a fella put he hand into him pocket, to find yours already dere.'

Maddy watched Mamma Joy's mouth – bright red, even without lipstick – with the fascination of despair. 'How long before you up infronta de Judge?'

'I dunno . . . about a week.'

'Dat no time at all. I know *marriages* lonelier dan dis.' Mamma Joy patted Maddy in a magisterial way. 'Time passes.' Yeah, thought Maddy, avoiding Sputnik's rapacious gaze, like kidney stones. The three-thirty dinner bell brought a cadence to her conversation. 'And stay away from Sputnik. She *was* goin' to anger therapy classes . . . till she head-butted de psychology woman. Hee, *hee*, hee hee . . .'

But staying away from Sputnik was not as easy as it sounded. The woman was fixated. At meal times she'd position herself a fork-prong's distance from Maddy, skewering her with a look of mild hunger. It was clear from the way Sputnik attacked her sausage – stabbing it with the plastic knife, twisting, yanking it out, then stabbing it again and again – that GBH was a vocation.

Sputnik also seemed to specialize in full bladder synchronization. Every time Maddy ventured into one of the two bathrooms on the L-shaped wing, there she would be in her peripheral vision, sniffing primordially. Maddy would have avoided the showers altogether, except hot water was the only relief for her lumpy-as-boarding-school-porridge breasts. The milk Niagaraed on to her feet. There was so much hair clogging the drain that Maddy was tempted to get down and shampoo it. It was the only plug hole she'd ever seen which needed a cut and blow-dry. But bending over in the near vicinity of Sputnik would be a major misdemeanour. 'Bend Over; I'll Drive' was the woman's motto. Maddy watched her with what could only be described as mounting apprehension.

*

As Sputnik's only reading material contained dialogue in balloons, education classes seemed the best way of avoiding her. To alleviate the bum-numbing tedium, various do-gooders made regular, condescending appearances through the prison gates. About once a week some pulped biographer, antediluvian backbencher or remaindered author of *How to Make Loo-Roll-Holders Out of Hubby's Shirt Cardboard* and *101 Uses for Old Egg Cartons* would offer inmates their pearls of wisdom – make that fake pearls, make that *paste*. 'Nicksniffers,' Mamma Joy called them. The announcement of an acting workshop, however, was met with universal enthusiasm. The remand wing's drama qualifications were that they were bored shitless and would do *any*thing not to be banged up twenty-three hours a day. The trick was to get a walk-on part, no dialogue. This was going to be a play with a *lot* of walk-on parts, no dialogue.

*

In the gaol gymnasium, Petronella de Winter glanced nervously towards the door, where two bored kennel-keepers were bent over a copy of *Hello!* magazine. She took a deep breath and introduced herself as an Actress. Judging by the combination of cleavage and IQ, Maddy felt sure she'd got her start in films entitled *Moist Choir Girl* and *Make Your Own Benwah Balls.*

'There is always a chance of like, dying on stage, especially when it's being, you know, shared with a couple of murderers,' she quipped.

Maddy's cellmate, Chanel, so-called because she was daughter number-five, lifted one bottom cheek off the chair and let rip with one of her famously resonant farts.

'All right' – the blond actress pointed a painted finger into the audience – 'which one of you naughty girls stole my car radio?'

The hostile silence finally persuaded this presentative of the Sheer Blouse, Blank Brain Battalion to abandon her appalling, ready-made patter. She then got all Sincere, confiding that she was donating her time because she didn't see the assembled inmates as social outcasts but as victims of circumstance . . .

she also just happened to have along with her a BBC documentary crew intent on filming her humanitarian gesture for an *Everyman* programme on selflessness.

Petronella's breathy request that they all sing 'Kum By Yah' as a little 'ice-breaker' (you'd need an arctic frigate to break *this* ice) lost any remaining potential audience.

Mamma Joy closed her eyes. 'Me goin' to say me prayers, now. Anyone want anyting?'

'Mel Gibson,' a woman called from the back row.

'Yeah, he's perfect.' Chanel's hot-pink Lycraed buttocks pivoted past Maddy. She stretched out on the lino, revealing flanks so dimpled they looked as though they'd been hit in a hailstorm. 'If I ever stop hatin' men, he's the one I'm gunna stop hatin' first.'

Maddy scoffed. She'd once thought Alex was perfect, until she'd discovered he had the emotions of a Klingon. The guy probably went home at night and peeled his face off. 'There's no such thing as the perfect man.'

'Unless you find me a fella wiv a twelve-inch tongue who can breathe through his ears,' barked Mamma Joy.

'Men,' Maddy continued bitterly, thinking of her ex, 'are the reason God invented cake.'

'Sure. You say that *now*,' Chanel groaned between sit-ups, 'but as soon as you get out? You'll be after that sperm liqueur faster than you can say *swallow*. Truth is, I've been on remand so long, whenever I see a man, *any* man, I just leave a snail-trail a mile long,' she lamented, scissoring her hailstorm thighs. 'The chicks in this nick are so horny, you can *ski* on all that love-juice. You can sit on your fanny and slide.'

The whole row erupted into hoarse cackles. With a twitch of embarrassment, Maddy readjusted her creeping underpants.

'Watch it, girl!' Chanel mocked. 'More than three adjustments in a row qualifies as a wank, ya know.'

Blushing, Maddy submerged her hands into her pockets. It was then she found the chocolate. 'Ah, the sort of happiness money can't buy,' she said to Mamma Joy, facetiously. 'Freedom may be fun, but does it have this ecstasy?' Half-masting the white flag of surrender she'd been running up to fate, Maddy main-lined that Malteser.

'Atta girl!' Mamma Joy enthused. 'Anudder day up de Judge's arse, eh?'

It seemed to Maddy that the reality of prison was not a rampaging throng of Patty Hearsts and Ulrike Meinhofs, but a flotsam and jetsam of sad little junkies, fine defaulters, the homeless, the jobless, people who couldn't afford to pay for a television licence or who'd fiddled the electricity meter ... people who belonged in prison the way a Mormon belongs in the Addams Family. Except for Sputnik, of course. Maddy was convinced that this was a woman who'd missed her calling, say as Medical Researcher at Auschtwitz.

'What's all the farkin' noise in 'ere. It's a farkin' loony bin innit?' Wearing a knicker-skimming mini-skirt – what Gillian called a pussy-pelmet – and white stilettoes, Sputnik swaggered through the gymnasium doors and across to Maddy's row. 'Some old slag's stolen me Maltesers.'

Inmates in the near vicinity lost the will to talk. Hell, they lost the will to *live*.

'Which one of you fat cows is the poxy wossit what's nicked

'em? Come on then – breave out – so as I can find the slag.'
Sputnik shoved her nose into Chanel's face. She exhaled in
mute supplication. Maddy's throat dried. She was next in line.

Mamma Joy sat up straight. 'It was me, gal. All right?'

'Wassat?'

'I have a size twenty body to maintain here.'

'I 'eard, right, that you, right, have got such a fat arse, right,
that they 'ad to drop you in to the nick with a crane.' Stacey
killed herself laughing at this bit of, no doubt, vintage crim
humour. 'But it weren't you.' Sputnik's pupils contracted,
dulled, then bore into Maddy.

Back on stage, Petronella, struggling to be heard above the
din of metal chair legs scraping over cement floors and women
jabbering in Gujerati, was gushing about the fact that her
famous director had just been nominated for a Bafta Award for
Best Documentary of the Year. She made a feeble aside into
the mike about all his programmes being 'cell outs', before, in
desperation, diving into the desultory audience and seizing
Sputnik's arm for a soprano rendition of Bob Dylan's 'I Shall
Be Released'.

Maddy felt an appreciative silence was the best policy to
adopt at this point. On the pretext of a pee, she made for the
door at a trot, stumbling over the tripod being set up by a
lighting cameraman. That is why she heard him before she saw
him; jerking at the sound of his melodious voice like a fish on
the end of a line. When Maddy did finally focus on Alex, it was
to register the fact that her little baby boy looked just like him.
Her eyes were too hot, too sore to cry.

Alex stood open-mouthed, mid-Bafta-nominated-direction,
as petrified as a Pompeii dog.

'Thank God you're here!' Maddy peered around for the ventriloquist who was uttering these words in *her* voice. This was *not* what she wanted to say. What she *wanted* to say was go juggle with chainsaws, dingo-dick. Much to her astonishment, she then flung herself at him, clung to his neck, gazed up into his handsome face and broke into a smile which wasn't reciprocated. She tweaked his freeze-framed cheek. 'Um, it is customary when you're feeling pleased, to like, notify your face.'

For God's sake, Maddy thought. Was that *me* flirting? It can't be me. It's someone else. Someone who doesn't have a purple vagina and cracked nipples; someone who hasn't dreamt every night since the birth of stringing this man up by *his* nipples.

Steeling herself, she stood back and appraised Jack's dumbstruck father. He looked tanned, taut, edible – it had to be said – in his black Levis and white, buttoned-down Oxford-cotton shirt. A shirt so crisp she could imagine him skiing down it at Klosters (the holiday resort he usually took his wife to, mid-winter). 'You're growing a beard?' She tucked her fingers into her palms, so that she wouldn't be tempted to touch him.

'What?' Alex tugged Hasidically at his jaw. 'Oh, yes . . .'

'Why? As a substitute for your masculinity?' That was better. That nailed the bastard. If only she could also now stop fantasizing about him dining alfresco on her nether regions.

'Maddy, look, about the police station . . .' He ran his hands through his luxuriant hair as though tossing a wilted salad. 'I'm so sorry . . . I had no idea they were going to in*carce*rate you. My God. It's just . . . I was about to announce my intention of going into politics. The publicity would have been . . . How can I expect people to vote for me to help save the environment, when I can't even clean up my own act?'

It was Maddy's turn to imitate Harpo Marx. '*You're going into politics?*' she queried, finally relocating her voice.

'Liberal Democrats.'

Maddy ruptured into an unoiled motor, gear-cruncher of a laugh. Alex was the sort of Liberal who had copies of the *Big Issue* home-delivered. So democratic, he'd voted not to tell her about his wife, until Maddy found Felicity's short and curlies on the underside of his socks. She guffawed so hard she had to sit down.

'Okay, I lie, I cheat on my wife, I drink, I won't identify ex-girlfriends when they call from cop shops in the middle of the night, but name one *really important* short-coming?' Alex unleashed a lopsided smile of irresistible roguery.

'But Liberal Democrat? Hey, I get it. It's like when you called yourself a "new man". It's just a *phrase* you're passing through.' They always talked like this; verbal ping-pong, with mouths as bats.

Alex cocked one hip in casual arrogance, then lowered his muscular frame on to the bench next to her. 'It's a smaller organization. Easier to get things done, get changes implemented.'

'Oh, I get it. "Smaller organization", meaning that it'll be easier to get a Peerage.' During the year they were together, Maddy had learned to read between Alex's lies. She turned her palm towards him, traffic-cop style, putting the brakes on his protestations. 'I don't care, okay, as long as you treat me like a voter.'

'What's *that* supposed to mean for Christ's sake?'

'Be nice to me for once. Look . . .' She sighed. Maddy had expected detestation when she saw him again. But all she could think about was Alex, emerging from the shower in the mornings, his tanned torso swaying above the knotted towel; tangoing buck-naked on the dining-room table singing Cole Porter songs; the time they'd licked the fresh caviar of Caspian sturgeons from each other's navels. 'I don't know what came between us.'

'Um – you had a baby against my wishes and then rejected me.'

'Rejected you?' Maddy reeled around violently to face him. 'Oh, I'm so sorry. It's just that I obviously needed an etiquette guide entitled *What To Do When Your Fiancé is Still Married.*'

'You never asked if I was married with children,' he said curtly.

'Go tell it to the Male Excuse Hall of Fame, okay?'

Alex impaled Maddy on his topaz gaze. 'My conscience is clear.'

'Well, buddy, you've obviously got amnesia. It doesn't take a mathematical genius to work out that it takes two to make a bloody baby.'

'Don't try and guilt trip me, Maddy,' he whispered, suddenly alert that the lighting man might overhear a suck and tell story worth selling to the *News of the Screws.* 'You made the decision to have the child – despite my objection. You've always been your own person.'

'Only because I was nobody's else's,' she said sadly. It had rocked her to her core, seeing him again.

'I tested positive to allergies to nappies, Lego, and broken sleep. Remember? You *knew* that.'

A shudder ripped through her. Marooned in Holloway Prison, this conversation was about as relevant as arguing over who would sit at the Captain's table on the *Titanic*. 'Look . . .' She coiled her fingers around his warm, brown forearm. 'It doesn't matter. What *matters* is that you're here and can clear up this whole god-damned mess.'

'Of course . . .' Alex replied neutrally.

She strengthened her grip. 'You will help me, right?'

'Yes, yes . . .' he said in the trouser-adjusting voice men use when they're being all Male and evasive. 'Though, of course, it must he handled delicately . . .'

Delicacy was the last thing on the mind which was vaguely attached to the toothpick legs, pale and goosepimpled, which pushed between the two ex-lovers at that precise moment. Maddy had just opened her mouth to reply to Alex, when a tongue not unlike a slab of condemned salami shoved its way down her throat.

'J'know what I need, Malteser-breath?' Sputnik asked in a voice both aloof and viscous.

'Some double-strength Fem-fresh?' Maddy ventured, gagging.

'Body heat.' Sputnik jerked her bony pelvis into Maddy's frame, pinioning her back against the wall.

'Really? You could get equally warm by wetting your finger and sticking it into an electrical outlet,' Maddy suggested.

'Do what?'

Maddy rolled her eyes. 'Oh well, at least the screws know that you're not taking any mind-expanding drugs.' Not just

Alex, but the whole prison seemed to hold its breath. Sputnik tightened her pneumatic embrace on Alex's former girlfriend.

Now if Maddy hadn't been walking around with two Ayers Rocks strapped to her chest; two huge, hard, insanely sensitive Ayers Rocks which were agony to the touch, she wouldn't have done what she did next – at least not without protective head gear and a good surgeon on tap. Letting out a low roar, she landed a punch to the side of her tormentor's head. Sputnik retaliated, forcing Maddy into a lop-sided waltz. They hydraulicked about, scratching, tearing at each other's hair, sinking teeth into any bit of accessible flesh.

From broad-side, Chanel appeared, seizing Sputnik's head and buffeting it against the bench. Stacey let out a blood-curdling whoop and pug-slugged Chanel in the snoz. It split spectacularly open. Blood geysered over them all. Chanel ju-jitsued Stacey who cannoned on to the floor. And then it was on. Caught in the eye of a tornado of Lycraed limbs, tattooed arms and shaven legs, Maddy lost sight of Alex.

Fights were inevitable in a women's prison. There was only a window of about one day a month in which they weren't all either suffering PMT, the menopause, ovulation cramps or post-natal depression. Even the prison cat was a female. It was like 'Welcome to Hormone World! Step right up! Ride the Emotional Rollercoaster of Your Choice!'

Maddy was dimly aware of the harrowing pulse of the 'aggro bell'. Through the human squall, she could see Mamma Joy flailing about in an ineffective semaphore. If she'd been ground staff, she'd have landed a whole fleet of jumbo jets by the time the herd of overweight officers lumbered along the jail's concrete intestines. They ran heavily as if trying to steam-roller the linoleum back into place, flattening a distraught Petronella and the directorless film crew against the wall.

'Okay, girls, let's talk it through,' demanded the officer in charge.

Sputnik and Maddy, in a gesture which made Pamela Anderson look articulate, were in a hair-lock, wincing with pain, both refusing to let go. A gnomic male screw pinned Sputnik's arms up into the restraint position.

Maddy was similarly half-Nelsoned. In her hand was a wodge of Sputnik's purple hair. She could taste blood trickling down the back of her throat. Through eyes which were rapidly swelling shut, she noted that Alex was nowhere to be seen.

'Who started it?' the officer in charge persisted.

Maddy shrugged. 'I don't know her name.'

'Can you describe her?'

'That's what I was doing when she walloped me, nong-brain!'

The officer nodded to his off-siders and Maddy was woman-handled to the surgery on C wing.

*

A doctor Maddy suspected had gained his degree from the Botswana Woodwork and Handicrafts Department was making a half-hearted daub with a disinfected swab at Maddy's more serious abrasions with what looked like a recycled corn pad – when Dwina goose-stepped into view.

'Where's Alex?' Maddy asked desperately. 'Did you talk to him?'

'Well,' Dwina hhumphed. 'This is certainly a unique method of obtaining bail.'

'He's here! My baby's father! He can straighten everything out.'

Dwina, wearing her Hostess with the Mostest expression, patted Maddy's hand. 'You're suffering from post-natal depression, dear.'

Maddy thrashed to sitting position and swung her long legs to the floor. 'You've got to find him!'

Dwina and the doctor forced her back on to the examination table, tethering her down with leather ties. 'You're neurotic and highly stressed.'

'Gee, you're right . . . Maybe I'm not getting out enough.'

'I don't think you realize just how seriously this little incident could set you back.' Dwina stroked the creased material in her lap as though soothing a fractious cat. 'Officer Slynne is going to object to bail, on the grounds that you may well be charged with infanticide.'

Where was Alex? Maddy thought frantically. She refused to believe his Vamoosing Gene had kicked in. Not again. 'Now he can add a count of grievous bodily harm. The Governor tends to lock troublemakers like you in the strip cells.' *But if not, then where the hell was he? Was the father of her child really so determined to make a footnote of himself as the Biggest Bastard Act in Recorded History?*

'The Segregation Unit is the grimmest, dirtiest, coldest corner of the prison. Are you listening to me?' *Maddy realized with a jolt that he hadn't even asked her about Jack. She made a mental reservation at Anguish Café. Never kick a woman unless she's down. Was that his credo?*

'You must centre yourself, Maddy. Stop projecting. I mean, what on earth do you think you are doing?'

'Um . . .? Rounding out my prison tan?'

Dwina waited until the doctor had left the room before taking Maddy's face in her hands. 'You can trust me, Madeline. I am your friend.' She untied the leather restraints. 'Your *only* friend. I'm offering you an intimate human interaction . . . yet all you do is put up barriers.'

'Hey, six in a cell getting into their pyjamas simultaneously makes intimate human interaction sort of unavoidable, you know?'

'Where is your baby?'

When Maddy didn't answer, Dwina made a disappointed adjustment to her mouth. The voice now emerging from it had taken on a tone of weary admonition. 'So you smuggled him out. So what? Even if you do ever get out of jail, which after today's little demonstration I doubt, you'll just be one more single mother.' *Maddy had to face facts. Her Prince had come, seen . . . and pissed off as fast as his chauffeured car would carry him.* 'Children of single mothers have their noses pressed into life's rectal canal. They consistently obtain lower educational qualifications than their IQs imply. They get the worst jobs. Is that what you want?' Dwina folded her arms and glared at Maddy, who was staring despondently at the shelf of self-help books – *Constructive Depression: How To Make the Best of Feeling Down.* 'Obviously you like theatre – I saw you signed up for playgroup. Well, all the world's a stage, Maddy. And *you* can write the script. Think of your child. Think of *Jack.'*

Maddy swallowed hard. As if she had done anything else. She was constantly savaged by daydreams. Was Gillian giving Jack toys which were chew-proof? Was she checking whether plastic wheels could be pulled off? Maybe he'd swallowed one already? Did she know what to do if he was choking? Maddy tugged agitatedly at the paper napkin she was wearing, incongruously called a gown – she'd written shopping lists on paper longer than this.

'Is it a financial incentive you want?' Dwina continued with controlled urgency. 'Demand for adoption has never been higher. Babies are a commodity. A rare commodity. Loopholes in the law mean that richer couples can gazump those going through legal channels . . . *are you with me*?'

The sullen doctor sidled back into the surgery with Sputnik in tow, a mauve ellipse beneath her right eye. He tossed Maddy her clothes, indicating the conclusion of the consultation. The worst thing about being sick in prison was having no place to stay home from.

As Sputnik painfully mounted the examination table Maddy had just vacated, she slyly regurgitated a small swodge of paper from beneath her tongue and secreted the crumpled note into Maddy's palm. On the pretext of tying her laces, Maddy unscrunched the note. 'You rottn cow. Do wot I want or yor ded meet. Lawndry. Fursday. 5 p.m.' The dots above the i's were plump little circles and every second word was highlighted with an inky aura of penstrokes.

Oh great, Maddy thought, gingerly shrugging on her cardigan; my baby's busy bonding with a woman whose main concern is the number of shopping years left until the turn of the century; my boobs are on the point of a nuclear meltdown; my social worker is after my inner and *outer* child; I'm still in love with the sort of Male Feminist who thinks the 'glass ceiling' is a club for coprophiliacs; chances of bail are Jody

Kidd slim and I'm about to be raped by a woman who has the words 'Hoover My Love Rug' tattooed on her lower abdomen.

Her only hope was acceptance into some sort of Witness Protection Scheme, with immediate relocation somewhere safe – say, deep space with Captain Kirk and Scottie at cruise speed. All she'd done was to go to Harrods for a packet of prunes and *now* look at her. If only she could rewind events and start again. Take Two. If all the world's a stage, Maddy thought to herself morosely, then where the hell was her dressing room?

8. Taking The Bitter With
The Suite

One toddler had the plastic submarine from a cereal box wedged up his nose. Another was making a pudendum out of playdough. Two were noshing ecstatically on the styrofoam packing which had housed the brand-new Hamley's Fireman Sam engine they were resolutely ignoring. All the wooden rattles and posting boxes bought by over-anxious stage-parents at vast expense lay idly cast aside. The best toys you could give an infant, Gillian realized looking around, was a half-masticated earthworm or a Black and Decker power drill (complete with small sibling).

The pre-speech bababa dadda babble at the Rosy Futures Child Modelling Agency was deafening. Baby pit-stops popped up everywhere across the mottled shagpile, as thirty or so mothers laid out their change-mats and descended with 'wet-ones' to wipe up Dijon-mustard-coloured 'poopies'.

Babies, lying on their backs, frantically bicycle-kicked, as though competing in the Tour de France. Those not pedalling to Paris lay on their tummies, tiny heads raised like periscopes to peer beadily around at their pint-sized rivals.

'One of life's mysteries, drape-ape,' Gillian philosophized to her bonsai charge, 'is that less is more. The smaller the bikini, the more expensive. The less food, cuisine minceur for example, the more expensive. No food at all proves to be the most exorbitant of the lot. I'm talking Health Farm, rusk-breath. Which is also why a weenie little ankle-biter like you gets up to eight hundred pounds plus residuals for a TV commercial requiring you to display slightly more cognitive development than an inebriated stockbroker on a Friday night.'

Jack answered her with a loud and resonant raspberry from his rear end. 'Do you *mind*?' Gillian protested, mopping up a dead-sea of drool from his chin. 'We'll have no heckling from the stalls. In the money department, however, less is well, less. So from now on I'm redefining our relationship. Forget that Mum-Mum rubbish. Em-ploy-*er*.' Gillian pointed to herself. 'Em-ploy-*ee*.' She gestured to Jack. 'Yes, I think you'll make a wonderful member of my staff. At least you won't always be flirting by the drinking fountain or clogging up my phonebills with personal calls.'

Rosy – the lace and leopard-skin trussed, nauseatingly young (she made Gillian feel positively Paleolithic) agency manageress – was culling the A-babies for photographic sessions and screen tests in the studio. The B-babies were being sent unceremoni-ously home. Mothers clenched the heads of squealing tots between their denimed knees, to coat microscopic eyelashes in mascara. Teeny-weeny cheeks were surreptitiously rouged; itsy-bitsy mouths were secretly tinted darker shades. To say that the atmosphere was competitive would be like saying piranhas are caring and sharing. Edgy and tense, mascara-wands poised, lipsticks uncased, the mums sneaked sideways glances at the miniature contenders; curling a sceptical lip at any infant they felt wasn't quite up to par.

All around them, babies were bribed with chocolate to go into their 'child-in-a-manger' routines. Jack, on the other hand, was busy eating his snot. Only a few days to go, tops, Gillian thought elatedly. Then she could hand It over to Its mother.

'Next?'

'Stop making that "I-don't-want-to-go-anywhere-with-any-body-at-any-time" face,' Gillian threatened, snaffling Jack up. 'You'll thank me when your mug is on that toilet roll.'

'Name?'

'Jack Wolfe.'

'Age?'

'Five weeks.'

Rosy's rough, careless hands prodded Jack's body with practised indifference. She did everything but mount him on a microscope slide.

'Hmmm,' she said, dismissively. 'Milk spots.'

'What?'

'Look. Little pinhead spots around the bridge of his nose.'

'*Acne*? You're saying he's got acne? At *his* age? Oh, *fab*ulous. What's next? Miming Jimi Hendrix guitar solos and setting fire to his farts?'

Rosy was scratching at the baby's scalp with a stiletto nail. 'Cradle cap.'

'What the hell's that?'

'Dry flaky skin. You should oil it, you know.'

'Dandruff? You're rejecting a child with *his* looks and personality because he's slightly dermatologically challenged?'

Rosy was checking her watch and casting a professionally calculating eye along the waiting row of potential ad fodder. 'Also oral thrush, sucking blisters and sticky eye.'

'If you knew this child's gene stock . . .' Gillian propped Maddy's baby up on a desk already over-burdened with photographic paraphernalia. 'This is the stuff of which high-octane Tycoon types are made! Dah-ling, we're talking Gene-Pool. *Designer* gene pool . . . Gene Pool Gaultier . . .' Jack chose that moment to give himself a euphoric whack on his forehead with a rattle.

'Indeed?' said Rosy, archly.

Gillian found herself executing a Mr Bean repertoire of facial grimaces to entertain Maddy's baby. 'Smile!' she urged, through clenched teeth. Jack responded with a blank stare. 'Smile, you little bastard!' she snapped. His tiny face concaved in misery. 'Oh, good God. Don't cry . . . Your eyes will go puffy.' Unable to locate the dummy, Gillian shoved the knuckle of her index finger into the baby's wailing mouth. 'I know it's not the real thing, nose-miner . . . Look on it as methadone,' she ordered him, furiously.

Holding her contempt in check, Rosy tapped her well-shod foot irritably. Gillian could feel a case of 'don't call us; we *won't* call you' coming on. Smiling ingratiatingly, she continued in an uncharacteristically unctuous and pianissimo tone. 'Normally, I am not prone to grovelling. It so ladders one's stockings. But . . . the problem is,' she whispered, 'I am deeply insolvent. *Cement* is more solvent than I . . .'

'If he were *black*,' Rosy adjudicated with a shrug 'or even taupe . . . I could get him *heaps* of work then. Or handicapped in some way. *Beautifully* handicapped, of course. You know. The Benetton thing . . . But blue-eyed, blonde-haired babies? Puh-lease. I get three hundred of *those* every week.'

Too late for a quick application for Instant Tan or a leg amputation, Gillian inhaled slowly. 'The point is, one is a month behind in one's rent and about to be evicted.'

'Well . . .' Rosy scrutinized Jack for the last time. 'He *could* work,' she hypothesized, 'if he had a bit more colour.' So saying, she pinched Jack's cheek, hard. His face crumpled at the short sharp shock of pain.

Gillian caught Rosy's hand in mid air and counted the fingers aloud, '1, 2, 3, 4 . . .'

'What are you doing?'

'Just checking you've evolved. You see, we don't treat children like that in this century.' Then, in a spurt of what observers took to be maternal rage, she slapped Rosy's face.

Pressing Jack to her wonderbra, Gillian pushed past the picture postcard, rose-lipped Botticelli babies and the floral flotilla of their mothers' frocks, out on to Hackney Road. She'd reached the Old Street roundabout before she realized, with a jolt of horror, that she was humming a little song for him. She stopped abruptly, eyes darting in a self-conscious search for witnesses.

Jack's newly rouged face lit up. 'Don't try to wheedle yourself into my affections,' Gillian said, pausing to study her tube map. 'I know you only do that when I'm around 'cause of *food*,' she told him brusquely, plugging a bottle of milk into his maw. 'You're like a film crew when the catering van appears.'

Still, she secretly liked the intense way he studied her. No matter how curt she was with him, he looked at her as though he was going to write her biography. Even in the mornings, when she had alcohol-sodden breath and bags under the eyes, there it was – that look of utter adoration. She liked that in a male.

*

Back at their dismal little basement flat in Clapham, Gillian packed Jack's baby essentials, called a mini-cab on an account she didn't intend to pay and directed it to the Savoy.

Waiting at the reception desk, she thought about her plight. No address, no friends, no funds, no training, no job, no prospects, a wailing curtain-climber for company and another grey pubic hair. She scrunched up the audition card for Rosy Futures. The trouble with the future was that it just wasn't what it used to be.

'A suite with a river view,' she pronounced in an upperclass accent sharp enough to draw blood if you were shaving your armpits with it. She'd rung ahead – hotels are suspicious of what they call walk-in's. 'Redecorating' was her explanation for such spontaneity; a house full of hirsute workers with builders' bum. Luckily it was raining when she arrived. She used this as an excuse to get out of handing over a credit card for an imprint; her purse, she lied, was in her suitcase which had already disappeared upstairs with the porter.

'I'll change the baby and have a hot bath first.' She also

knew to inform rather than to ask permission; to palm around a lot of tenners; and to be constantly extravagant. 'And a bottle of Krug immediately.'

It might be lonely at the top, Gillian pondered in the sumptuous art-nouveau elevator, but by God – the shopping was better.

9. Anything You Say Will Be Distorted Beyond Belief And Used Against You

Maddy could have been getting ready for a débutante ball, there was such excitement over the preparations for her court appearance. Mamma Joy and Chanel had been hauling her in and out of a Barbie-doll selection of their clothes since 6 a.m. Descending on Maddy's chassis, like a pit-stop crew in a Grand Prix, they shaved and waxed and tweezed and creamed. When the cells were opened at six-thirty, Mamma Joy had collected Stella, the 'Hair Hostess' of Block 3B. It wasn't that she had any training, but scissors were her speciality; she'd once kebabed her boyfriend on a pair of garden shears.

The women talked as they worked, instructing Maddy on court procedure. It was all about body language. Now when it comes to body language, the English are not particularly fluent. In Maddy's experience a sign of sexual euphoria in an Englishman was abandonment of his socks in bed. Suspending her disbelief, she allowed her friends to teach her how to sit virginally: knees together; hands cupped in her lap; with demure, downcast, Princess Di eyes. All things considered, the girls thought it better not to do the 'silly-me-I-forgot-to-wear-knickers' leg cross to the judge. Well, not unless things got *really* desperate.

'Ouch!' Having hacked away at Maddy's red fringe, Stella was now applying a smear of hot wax to her client's top lip. She yanked hard, taking half Maddy's face with her. 'Bloody hell!'

'Sorry, love,' said Stella with cavalier cheer. 'Bit out of practice. Been in hospital.'

'Stella had a big run-in with an inmate,' Mamma Joy, buttery with body lotions, elaborated mischievously. 'She give her turd-degree burns from an underarm wax.'

Maddy recoiled.

'It's all right,' Stella assured her, hot spatula in hand, 'I've read the friggin' manual now.'

'Lordee!' Mamma Joy was bent over Maddy's earlobe with a floral ornament. 'Can't find de hole.'

'Bet you haven't said *that* for a while,' Chanel cackled, unwinding the cottonwool from between Maddy's painted toe nails.

'At least not since childbirth!' Mamma Joy's raspy laughter expired in the air. Apart from the ever-present weaving pulse of reggae, it was so silent all of a sudden, that Maddy could hear her eyebrow being tweezed. Swivelling, she saw that it was Sputnik, wearing a 'We're Here, We're Queer, We're Going Shopping' T-shirt, with the ubiquitous Stacey hot on her high heels.

After casting the usual aspersions on the toilet training, parentage and genital hygiene of every inhabitant in the cell, Sputnik shoved her face menacingly into Maddy's. 'Laundry. Fursday. Na neva fronted. And I want yer.'

'Why?' Maddy stalled, uncoiling her hair from its coronet of plastic rollers. 'Are you out of Maltesers?'

Sputnik's lips gaped open to reveal a grand piano of teeth. 'You and me's gettin' moved into a two-person cell. It's all sorted with the Guv'ner. The less, the bleedin' merrier, eh?'

Maddy watched the chemise-lifter execute her caricatured saunter out of frame and back to her cell for the 8 a.m. lock-up. Maybe I'm dead, thought Maddy hopefully, and this is Limbo.

'That lezzo stuff . . . it's like real chic now, you know.' Chanel whooped as Mamma Joy's tiny silver eye-hook finally found passage through Maddy's fleshy lobe. 'Cindy thingyme-bob and what's-her-name Foster.'

Stella sighed and indicated the huge hole she'd accidentally weeded in the middle of Maddy's eyebrow. 'You're just gunna have to be brave and Do It, girl.'

'Oh, *what*? A case of stiff upper hip?' Maddy angrily pencilled in the missing brow acreage. 'I don't think so.'

'Listen.' Chanel was taking aim at Maddy's other ear. 'You know the craft workshop? Well, the last person who turned down Sputnik "fell" into the lathe and made a coffee table of herself.'

Mamma Joy uncapped a deodorant. 'Takin' on dat woman is like life,' she philosophized. '*You don't get out of it alive.*'

Maddy banished their grave and preoccupied expressions with an indifferent laugh. 'What are you people taking . . . *drowning lessons*? Tomorrow I'll be back with my baby!' The overwhelming relief at the thought of being able to feed again set Maddy's breasts into cappuccino mode. She surveyed herself in the mirror. For all their good intentions, with her half an eyebrow and swollen lip, all she needed was a tattoo to complete the barcoding which read 'CRIMINAL'.

When the screws came for Maddy, her cellmates kissed her goodbye. All the way back to 'reception', she was serenaded with traditional Holloway songs: 'If you sprinkle, when you tinkle, be a sweetie, wipe the seatie.' 'Have a bonk for me, or then again have three . . .'

Things were looking up. Not only was Maddy about to be released but something spectacularly joyful had already happened. After Jack's birth, it had been easier to reunite the Serbs and the Croats than the teeth of her fly. That morning Chanel had lent her size 10 Levis. And, for the first time since the birth, Maddy had *actually zipped up a pair of jeans.*

*

In the cells beneath the magistrate's court, Maddy's optimism dissolved like aspirin in aqua. The bare walls, the hard bench, the stench of urine; it was wintery with despair. All along the corridor, prisoners were calling out for a loo or a light, begging to be allowed to open their bowels, see loved ones, talk to after-shaved solicitors, or get a nice hot cuppa. In the hallway, it was chaos. Maddy could hear all the other solicitors and social workers bellowing to their clients through the cat flaps. 'So you were abused as a child? Who *wasn't?*' 'Bottom line is – the girl, she suffered no physical harm, right, apart from being raped.'

The spy hole in Maddy's door flipped open. Dwina's face, shrouded in a cloud of Body Shop secretions, appeared in the grim porthole.

'This is your last chance, Madeline. Your solicitor—'

'Peregrine? Oh don't tell me,' she replied sarcastically, 'I bet he's fired with enthusiasm.'

'But you *can't* fire him. Not under the new legal-aid rules. That means unless you tell me the whereabouts of your baby, he'll blow your bail application and it's back to Holloway.'

The slight tremor in her voice caught Maddy off guard. She made a casual inspection of her new lacquered nails – when really all she wanted was to put them in her mouth and gnaw them *up to the elbow*.

'One struggles not to get too involved – to keep one's distance. But there are always the cases which stay with you. Like *yours*, dear.' Maddy had a crick in her neck from bending to converse through the hatch. Behind Dwina, the building's dark entrails wound out of sight. 'I shouldn't have pushed you on the adoption. You need time to think about what's best for baby. I can see now what a good mother you are.'

Grief gushed into Maddy's throat. Dwina had hit an emotional artery. Maddy torniqueted her feelings, tight.

'The first three months is the critical bonding period between mother and child. The skin contact, the closeness . . .' Maddy detected a subdued sob in the psychologist's voice. 'Imperative in avoiding psychiatric disorders in later life.' Maddy had never felt so tired. She had the resilience of a Claes Oldenburg sculpture. 'Madeline, let me get your baby back for you.' Dwina's words were like anaesthetic. 'The address, Madeline. I need the address.'

The door opened. The key-jangling jailer called her name in a ten-pack-a-day voice. 'You're on now, darl'.' Maddy stood, automatically. Dwina's hand was warm and soothing on her arm as she passed.

90

'I've done my best, Madeline.' Dwina's voice sounded bruised. 'If you don't give me that address, I'm throwing in my psychoanalysis books, and off to the Cotswolds to open a little craft shop.'

Maddy gulped for air. Her breasts hardened and milk seeped through her nursing pads. Thoughts of Jack left her euchred, washed up and totally wasted.

'16a Ludgate Street, Clapham.'

The look on Edwina Phelps's face was not unlike the look of a born-again Christian making a convert.

*

Maddy concentrated on the expanding slit of light as she climbed the stairs into the well of the court. She was hours, maybe minutes from freedom. She had found the silver lining inside her dark cloud.

*

'Bail refused,' the magistrate intoned, with less deliberation than he'd give to a sandwich order.

'What's he saying?' Anxiety coated Maddy's tongue. Forgetting her body-language instructions, she gripped the dock's metal railings, knuckles tight and white, tendons taut.

Peregrine cleared his throat. 'There's a regression, time wise, on your bail application.'

'A *what*?' She felt glazed and unfocused.

'We'll have to appeal to the Crown Court . . .' he whispered. 'The infanticide thing. They want psychiatric reports . . .'

Maddy couldn't breathe. The courtroom billowed, the walls spun, her temples pounded, although the rest of her appeared still to be functioning because her mouth was moving and words were coming out.

'But I've told you about the baby. I told *her*.' Maddy jabbed desperately in Dwina's direction. Dwina was handing Slynne a packet of Nicotinell, which he was receiving with a sheepish grin. A ragged flicker of doubt zig-zagged across her brow. 'Dwina! Tell them.'

A few people glanced at Dwina who gave a light 'what can you do?' laugh at the absurdity of the suggestion – the way Salome would have laughed, post-head. A cold blade of realization knifed into Maddy. Edwina Phelps had been friendly in the way an intestinal parasite is friendly. This woman was a top order predator. Dwina, She-Bitch of the S.S.; the sort who'd like to become the Führer's play-thing. Edwina Phelps had wanted her to sign Jack over for adoption. Now she wouldn't even *need* adoption papers, because everyone believed Jack was dead. All Dwina had to do was seize him from Gillian's flat in Clapham.

'She just wants to keep me in jail so she can steal my baby!' Maddy blurted.

'Not even the O.J. jury would believe *that*,' quipped Dwina to Slynne.

'Don't tell me,' Detective Sergeant Slynne mocked for Maddy's benefit. 'It's a miscarriage of justice.'

'Arresting me in the first place was the miscarriage of justice. *This* is the curette!'

'Silence! Call the next case.' The usher drowned out her pleas. Only Slynne's voice was distinctive – 'If you can't do the time, don't do the crime.' And then finally, the stentorian tones of the magistrate – 'Take the prisoner down.'

In a state of advanced disbelief, Maddy was bundled into the prison van and seated next to Joyce, a thin, prim woman in a grey cardigan and seed pearls whose husbands made a habit of leaping between her carving knife and her chopping board. (Joyce didn't call it murder. She preferred to look on it as a Kidney Transplant Scheme.)

'So,' Joyce asked, extending a packet of Polo mints, as Maddy clambered past, 'you didn't get a result, dear?' She made it sound like an exam.

Maddy glimpsed the faces of the other failed applicants, slumped in mute desolation. 'My baby! She's trying to get my baby!'

As Maddy pressed her knees to her chest and rocked back and forth on the seat, Joyce tried to console her by reeling off a list of Edwina Phelps' crimes against humanity: the young girl in Holloway who'd tried to commit suicide after Dwina had her daughter taken into care; the forced adoptions – 'Babies just seem to disappear into her bureaucratic briefcase.'

Maddy had underestimated Dwina's powers of persuasion. This was the sort of woman who could kill her husband and make you sympathize with her for being a widow.

'I'll tell the press!' Maddy shouted frantically as the prison officer slammed the steel door in her face.

'There's a mass of restrictions on public access to family cases. Judges issue injunctions against the media which stop them publishing anything.' Joyce had to raise her voice to be heard above the shopping-mall muzak tinkling over the van intercom. 'It's all secret hearings, my dear. *Ex parte.*'

The intercom dee wah diddy dum diddy dee-ed all the way back to Holloway. Shit a brick, Alex! Maddy panicked. Thank you for landing me in this crapulous shemozzle. As far as the owner of the BBC's Best Buns was concerned, Maddy was starting to have fantasies involving cattle prods and private parts.

When the van stopped, Maddy listened to the engine ticking as it cooled. To put the icing on another fun-packed day, one of the screws informed her through the steel grille that she was now going to be charged with contempt of court. Well, thought Maddy. They got *that* right. Contempt was exactly the right word.

There were no slices left in the justice pie. They'd shown it to her, she could see everybody's fingers in it – then they'd put her on a diet. No pie for you, baby. Well, diets were for breaking. Still, the thought of what she had to do turned her stomach.

10. Pre-coital Depression

Penises, like snowflakes, are each of them different. And Maddy liked them all. She liked them in different shapes and sizes. The lean, slinky, kinky ones. The thick, succulent types. The low-slung, gunslinger sort. The stubby button mushrooms. The round-heads. The hooded eyes. The meat and two veg, packed-lunch variety. She liked them long and strong and ready for action. She liked them all coy on a cold winter's morning. All this male angst over size. It's *attitude* women are interested in. Women like a penis which says, 'G'day! God, am I glad to see *you*.'

This is what Maddy reminded herself, as she contemplated having sex with her solicitor on the interview room table of Her Majesty's Prison for Women, Holloway. She'd thought over every alternative. She could super-glue breadcrumbs to her arms and legs and let the pigeons fly her over the wall. She could sew all her cellmates' femidoms and cervical caps into a wet suit and flush herself. Or she could sink the sausage with Rupert Peregrine.

Maddy sat down hard on the straight-backed chair and massaged her cramped toes. She would have to fake it, of course. Faking it didn't come that naturally to her. She had always thought there was little point in encouraging a male partner in practices which were not going to get her anywhere. By anywhere she meant the usual desired female destination of over the moon, off the edge of the planet or into another orbit entirely. But, she admitted to herself, all women faked it a little *tiny* bit. Not in a grand, theatrical *When Harry Met Sally* kind of way. But, face it, when women wank, do they call out, 'Oh God! Don't Stop! Oh! Oh! *OH*! Give it to me big boy!' It was all theatrics, she persuaded herself, to *some* degree.

Maddy felt less convinced when Peregrine entered the room, all eighteen stone of him, secured the door and plonked a packet of condoms on the table between them. *Pre*-coital depression set in.

'Did you see him?' She couldn't keep the jangled anxiety out of her voice. 'Did you see Jack?'

'After our harried communication in the court cells in which you begged me to go to an address in Clapham to verify the existence of your son, I perambulated to the designated rendezvous as promptly as decorum would allow – '

'Yes! Yes!' Peregrine's concupiscent expectations had made him even more verbose than usual.

' – to encounter a most agitated Edwina Phelps.'

'That low-life! That two-faced Hitler on heat—'

'The basement flat of Number 16a Ludgate Street, Clapham is now inhabited by a . . . what would the correct collective noun be? A "litter" of Pakistani children. Ms Phelps was alone and as lost as I.'

'But 'cause you bumped into each other, she'll have to file an official report, won't she?'

'Yees . . . But it also makes your confession of the baby's

whereabouts look false. The baby is *not* thereabouts. Nor is the alleged accomplice, Ms Gillian Cassells.'

'Just get me into the Crown Court. I'll spill my guts to the judge. Gill's lived in that basement for at least six months! And I want my case for bail heard urgently. This week. Plus' – and here Maddy heaved a resigned sigh – 'that substantial surety. I'll pay your price.'

Peregrine lolloped behind her chair with the natural grace of a steam-roller. 'Done.'

'Done over, you mean.' His clammy hand was on the base of her skull, massaging muscles macraméd with tension. 'How do I know I can trust you?'

'Because I'm a professional,' he mumbled. His lips were on the nape of her neck. It felt like a couple of slugs having a cardiac arrest. 'A member of the Law Society.'

'What about AIDS?' Maddy blurted, desperately. 'Hey! Why don't I just strip off and you have a quick squizz. I mean, you don't want to put me in your *mouth*; you never know *where* I've been . . .'

'Why do you think I chose you? You're none of the H words – Haitian, haemophiliac, heroin-addicted or a promiscuous male homosexual.' His hot flaccid tongue was in her ear, swirling in a laundromat effect.

'Rules.' In a burst of abhorrence, she slapped him away. 'Don't touch my ear. Okay? I've got an infection. Nor my breasts, for that matter. They're sore. Or anything below the navel. I've just had a baby, for Christ's sake. My vagina's closed down due to renovation.'

In reply, Maddy glanced up to see his big fleshy mouth

descending upon hers. Peregrine had ointmented his cold-sore into remission, but not the pustules she could glimpse, at this close range, beneath his black polo.

In an attempt to dodge his mouth, she hauled his jumper up over his head. Peregrine stood there, straight-jacketed for a moment, arms up in surrender, head wedged in the neck hole. Maddy was tempted to shout for the screws, but she thought of Jack. The truth was, she couldn't *stop* thinking of Jack. When she'd given him to Gillian, she should have asked the doctor for a Nicorettes for baby-addiction – a progeny-patch, which released small doses of baby into her system; less and less each day until she got over him, so that she wouldn't have to be doing this.

Peregrine executed a clumsy accidental mambo as he wrenched his head free. It emerged from its cashmere burrow wearing a lascivious grimace. Maddy watched in horrified fascination as he started to unzip his fly. She could see the dark stripe of hair descending from his navel – a strand of licorice, glued to his dank abdomen. He placed her quivering hand on to the grey flesh of his gargantuan stomach.

She would simply think about something else. Her overdue book at the prison library. Her new moisturizer . . . the war in Chechnya.

Peregrine pulled her roughly against him as he yanked down his trousers. His skimpy underpants were wittily patterned with little red devils carrying pitchforks. The bulge inside strained skywards. It looked more like the sort of thing you climb into to await countdown, 10, 9, 8, 7 . . . 'Touch me,' he ordered, cold spittle staining her cheek.

With repulsed reluctance, she ran her hands over the bumpy

topography of his skin. Her fingers felt clumsy, as though wearing oven mitts. Peregrine removed her numb paw from his back and placed it between his legs. 'You're special, Madeline,' he panted. 'You're not like the rest. I really do like you, you know . . .'

'It's just the novelty of being with a female you don't have to inflate.'

'Take off your top.'

With leaden fingers she fumbled at her iridescent tank top, peeling it down to waist level. 'So when do I get to meet your Oldies?' she said, with bitter sarcasm.

'Take off your bra.'

Biting back her nausea, Maddy acquiesced. Peregrine knelt before her in ogling wonder. Her breasts launched out at him, two rising Zeppelins. He sighed reverentially. Reaching out a tremulous hand, he touched her right nipple.

Maddy felt the hot, dragging gush of the 'let-down' a split second before she saw the white arc of milk spurt forth and squirt her solicitor in the eye. Her left breast started lactating in sympathy. She was like some Michelangelo fountain in a Roman square, geysering milk.

Peregrine capsized backwards, sodden and repelled. Spluttering, he mopped his face and hair with his hands. Everywhere he turned, to get out of the line of fire, Maddy swivelled in the same direction. A repressed laugh unrolled down her face. What started as a slow dribble of mirth swelled into a cascade. Laughter shimmered off her.

'I told you' – she could hardly get the words out – 'I told you – not to touch my—'

'Shut up!'

'You'll smell like yoghurt for weeks.'

Her solicitor's penis deflated faster than a pump-up plastic lilo at the end of a beach-side holiday. As he scrabbled for his clothes, Maddy plunged into another vortex of laughter. 'I see that the age of *shrivel*ry is not dead!' She cackled. She roared. She realized that she hadn't laughed like this, completely abandoned, for the longest time. It felt better than champagne. It felt better than valium.

'Go on! Laugh!' His face had gone apoplectic-maroon. 'You'll have plenty of time to laugh whilst contemplating your long sentence.'

'Oh, well. As long as they don't put a preposition at the end of it,' she countered contemptuously.

Peregrine was reinstated in his vest, shirt and polo neck sweater; his arms hung down, ape-like, to pull up his underpants and trousers. His detumesced appendage resembled a par-boiled party frankfurter blu-tacked to his groin.

'So, tell me, Mr Peregrine,' Maddy asked, as he made for the door, 'does this count as a date?'

11. The Deposit

....

If there was one thing Gillian had learned from life it was that when the cat's away ... she's more than likely been squished flat under a car tyre. (That, and not to change a tampon whilst wearing a diamond ring over 20 carats.)

It had been two and a half weeks, and still no word from Maddy.

For someone with the maternal instincts of a Guppy fish (Gillian had encountered this aquatic type prone to dining out on its young in one of Alex's nature documentaries) two and a half weeks with a baby had been quite an alien experience. ('It's a lifeform, Jim, but not as we know it.') But not as alien as the out-of-money-experiences Gillian was having at the Savoy. The bill they'd run up now resembled the national debt of a small South American country. Gillian's best tip about being rich was to treat money with contempt. This enabled her to ignore the polite 'we neglected to obtain your method of payment – perhaps at your convenience, you could drop by the desk?' requests for at least a week. Then she'd palmed them off with paper – it would take five days for Barclays to put a bounce in her cheques. She had exactly twelve and a half hours to think of something.

'This may be news to you, Prince Poop,' she postulated,

trowelling yoghurt from her breakfast tray on to a teaspoon, 'but you can't actually absorb food *through your skin*. It has to actually go *into your mouth*.' In reply, Jack irritably smeared the lumpy white putty through what passed for his hair. 'Dullsville, dah-ling. Good *God*!' she lamented, a yawn elongating her face. 'Whoever thought I could be bored by a younger man?'

She pressed her nose against the window pane and looked longingly up the river to the crenellated Houses of Parliament and the smugly squat Big Ben. All around her London was throbbing with life. Jack, whimpering, gave himself a yoghurt facial, splattering as he did so Gillian's last remaining unpawned piece of clothing. 'Controlled crying,' she realized, was the art of *not* shattering into tears when a baby wiped his hands on your cherished Christian Lacroix.

Jack lolled listlessly on the cushions she had shored up around him on the art-deco bed. Two red spots had appeared, high on his cheeks. They'd been there since yesterday. As had the rivulet of mucus emanating from his nostrils. He whined plaintively.

'Look, fluff-grazer, this is not going to work. As I told your Mama, pets I can deal with. When you've had enough, you simply put them out the cat flap.' Gillian offered Jack his milk bottle, but he couldn't suck and breathe at the same time. He vomited then, all down his front and started to cry. She felt a twitch of anxiety. 'I think, kiddo, it's baby-flap time.'

To avoid the accusing vulnerability of his small face, Gillian padded into the black-tiled bathroom. 'The point is, you're sick. And I don't know how to look after you.' Jack howled more insistently. 'You are! You've got a temperature. Your dummy is melting. See?' She held it aloft around the door frame. 'It looks like some kind of Dali creation.'

Jack, still bawling, gave her one of his dubious 'Cut the crap, face-ache' expressions. Gillian wondered, briefly, whether babies could smell fear.

'I'm too old for this, I really am.' Trying to contain the rising panic in her chest, she returned to the bathroom mirror to plump up her hair and stopped short at the sight of her reflection. 'It's hideous, this . . . dwindling. Consider, if you will, child, my sex life.' She uncased her concealer and trowelled a slick beige stroke across the bags beneath both eyes. 'The woman in dominant position, astride, is naturally my preference. But I realized recently it makes my face fall forward. Ten chins. Now suddenly I find myself bleating – rather pathetically I might add, "No. No. I like the *mis*sionary. Missionary is *fine*." And yet lying on my back, my tits fall to the side, despite the silicone.'

Dropping her fluffy, monogrammed hotel robe on to the milky tiles, she dusted blusher between her breasts, before hoiking them indelicately into a cantilevered bra. 'My whole life I've insisted on leaving the lights on for added eroticism. But that, dear Jack, was before cellulite.' She eased herself into a pair of thickly deniered tights to hide her spider veins. 'I saw it! Crinkling. In the ceiling mirror. Now it's – "No, no. I like the lights off. Lights off is good." Yes, if you're Stevie-fucking-Wonder.' She spooned sugar into her cappuccino and watched the foam sag symbolically.

The baby, lethargic once more, looked at Gillian in a grave, official way. It put her instantly on the defensive. 'It was only supposed to be for a few days. That was almost three weeks ago! I've done everything I humanly could.' She slipped on her designer jacket and gazed despondently at the epaulette of vomit on her left shoulder. 'Period cramps I can cope with. But *style* cramping? Well, there's just no pills for that one, sweetie.'

The chandeliered Savoy foyer was thick with earnest Japanese tourists famished for some olde worlde cardboard cut-out culture. The cashier's mouth dropped open when Gillian, claiming she'd lost her credit cards, offered to leave her child as collateral.

'Your small son?' he asked astonished.

'Yes. As a deposit. While I pop to the bank. I'd leave my wedding ring' – Gillian pretended to tug at her jewellery – 'but it's welded, you see. Unlike my husband.' She flashed one of her man-hunting smiles, the sort she usually reserved for sexual safari. 'It *is* rather a large bill. And as we know' – she applied her vocal Vaseline with arch vivacity – 'size does count. I wouldn't want you to think I was fiscally challenged and contemplating absconding.' She became aware that she was absently stroking Jack's foot, and stopped immediately.

'Now, remember,' she lectured the cashier, suddenly stern, 'there are different types of cry. There's the hungry cry, the tired cry, the—' Gillian cut short her regurgitated lecture and set her lips resolutely. 'Have the porter collect my bags.' Jack looked up at Gillian with such trust – just as she handed him over to a complete stranger.

The cashier, claret-red with bewildered blushes and polite to the point of insignificance, was too flustered to reply before Gillian had strutted through the revolving doors, past the grey top-hatted doormen and out on to the Strand. She did not look back. The mystified menial placed the carry cot beside the cash register and called House-Keeping. Unbeknownst to him, nestled inside was a note addressed, 'Return to Sender: Ms Madeline Wolfe, c/o Holloway Prison.'

*

The sense of relief was intoxicating. Gliding sinuously through the pedestrian flow on this smoggy May morning, Gillian mulled over a plethora of possible indulgences. Back to the Concorde lounge to pick up a rich ride to New York? Some brass-rubbing? (Gillian's term for rubbing shoulder-pads with wealthy art dealers at Sotheby's.) Or it was only a leisurely stroll to the real-estate offices of Belgravia. Then the plot would thicken ... preferably into a country estate in Dorset. Oh, how she liked a man with charming manors. These delicious thoughts occupied her all the way down the Strand, past the Reform Club and up St James's to Piccadilly. First, she thought, a glass of icy champagne at Fortnum & Mason's and a perusal of the morning papers.

By the time she got to the Lifestyle section of *The Times*, she was wondering why she wasn't enjoying herself. This was just the beginning of her Hedonistic Hit List, and yet the whole experience was strangely leeched of joy. The kid would be better off with his mother. It was Darwinism. Survival of the fittest ... not that he *was* very fit at the moment. Which was why he needed proper care! Care she couldn't give. After all, it was only supposed to be for a week. It wasn't her fault. She'd tried, she really had. It's just that she wasn't the type. A lifetime of boarding schools and step-parents will have that effect on you ... Gillian body-surfed on a wave of self-pity.

The job offers she'd had to refuse! The dates she'd had to turn down! lamented the winner of the Long Distance Cross Bearing Competition . . . Then why did her stomach feel as if it was being trampolined by sumo wrestlers?

The newspaper headlines dissolved. She kept seeing Jack in that Raj-Prince Mode of his, losing interest in some toy, then stretching out his hand and simply dropping it as though there were four million servants just waiting to pick up after him. Gillian could relate to that. The way he'd see something he wanted and get that steely, Margaret Thatcher 'I've got to have it' look in his eye. A character trait of which to be proud. The way his face lit up when he saw her – as though she were the Sex Goddess of the Universe, even when she was hung over, hadn't shaved her pits or washed her hair. The haystack smell of *his* hair.

Before she knew what she was doing, her Charles Jourdan high heels were in her hand and she was running, sprinting back through Trafalgar Square. A blind, panic-stricken terror tore at her entrails all the way. She barrelled through the revolving doors of the Savoy, heaving for air. She blinked like a neon sign. For Christ's sake. Where was he? And then she saw him, being passed around the clucking staff. They were making the same coo-ing sound as the puréed pigeons which her high-speed dash had left plastered all around Nelson's column. Seeing Jack stretching his tiny arms towards a chambermaid left her gutted.

'What have you done to him?' she jack-hammered, in disc-jockey delivery. 'Can't you see he's sick?' She pushed aside the armada of uniformed flunkies. 'Would someone please call a doctor?' Whispered asides, like rustling insects, surrounded her. 'It's the air-conditioning in that poky little room. If he's caught pneumonia, I'll sue!'

The threat of litigation had staff backing off faster than Bob Geldof from a bath tub. 'Would Madam like to see something in our suite range?' entreated a flummoxed desk clerk.

Something in the range of – Gillian checked her purse – twenty-two pounds fifty would be more appropriate. 'What I'd like to see, you moron, is a paediatrician.'

Pretending to retreat to change Jack in the restroom, she exited instead down the side corridor to the banqueting rooms on the river and out on to the Embankment. She thought moving target. She thought rifle sights. She thought hunted quarry. She thought – you soppy donut.

*

'Some advice for Life,' Gillian said staunchly, as she offered Jack a spoonful of pâté in the luxurious drawing room of a penthouse apartment on Cheyne Walk in Chelsea. 'In a restaurant, never order anything described as a "medley" or an "extravagance of".'

Jack, dosed up on Calpol and smothered in Vicks Vapour Rub, replied happily in his native Lithuanian.

The private doctor her wealthy friend had 'on call' had taken Jack off milk and put him on to water and weak juice. Gillian had amended this prison diet to include smoked salmon, liver pâté and zabaglione. (The Harley Street quack had advised against solids at this young age, but what would *he* know? Jack had a *palate*, didn't he?)

'Never put your face in the sun or have anything to do with a man with a pierced nipple or a gold chain in his chest. Don't believe in love. And, if seriously considering suicide, make sure you look your best. Let us remember, Jack, dear, how we had to consider our options, shall we? They were: one – a spending spree on tranquillizers in the local pharmacists; two – finding a conveniently lonely railway bridge I can easily scale at the sound of an oncoming train, or three – parting men from their money with the art of . . . genital persuasion.'

Jack surveyed her with sombre censoriousness.

'Do you mind? I do *not* need a prudish, sanctimonious stare from a person who sits in his own faeces all day, all right? Now, as I didn't have enough money for a root tint and couldn't trust the London constabulary to dress me in something flattering for the casket, we decided to take up a long-standing offer from an old school chum of mine. So be *nice*.'

Annabelle Crump entered on cue, bearing a silver tray cluttered with Royal Doulton porcelain and *petits fours*. Her mutton-dressed-as-lamb attire was accentuated with a scarf, the knotted ends of which met atop her forehead like two floral propellers. The only thing she was taking off, however, was a BBC broadcaster's voice.

'I say, you're not doing this to exorcise your personal problems with Mummy and Daddy, are you, Gilly?' The exaggerated roundness of her vowels echoed the rotundity of her girdled form. 'Can't bear those gels who get addicted to the degradation.'

Gillian wondered if this was the time to remind Annabelle about the end of school 'Come As The Person You Most Detest Party' when nine people had come as *her*. 'What's spurred my career change, *Bel*,' – Gillian recalled how she hated having her name amputated – 'is a desire never again to frequent the sort of restaurant where the carpet sticks to the soles of my shoes.'

Annabelle's propellers quivered with catty curiosity. 'You're broke?' Her pudgy fingers squeezed around the teapot handle.

'Let's just say that the attention I give to my debt is unremitting.'

'The Lloyd's crash?' Gillian's silence confirmed her guess. Annabelle guffawed with such relish that she spilt the tea. 'And now you've come to me . . . You were such a prig at school, you know. That relentless, niggardly mockery of yours used to drive me insane.'

'Well, you'll be pleased to know that beneath my apostolic demeanour . . .'

'You're a slut, like the rest of us.'

Gillian handed Jack a plastic non-chewable book. He looked like somebody else's husband, disappearing discreetly behind his copy of *The Economist*. 'Does Mark Thatcher say he's an arms trader? No. He says he's in High-Tech Hardware. Does Nick Leeson say he's a thief? No, he says he's in banking. And I am having a brief dabble in philanthropy. *Amorous* philanthropy.' Gillian's teacup gave an irritable rattle as it returned to the saucer. 'Haven't you got anything more robust than tea?'

'Like what?'

'I don't know . . . *Heroin*, perhaps?'

Annabelle's man-handled thighs swished together as she minced to the drinks cabinet. Gillian remembered how she and her school friends had applied thigh-reducing cream to one of Annabelle's legs while she slept. Despite the fact that such a cream would have to contain a flesh-eating virus to have any effect, Annabelle had believed their endless taunts that she'd forever more have one thigh thinner than the other.

The posh 'finishing school' they'd attended had lived up to its name; it had finished them off for life. Their tutelage had primarily consisted of how best to avoid paying tax on inherited wealth – a skill which had made them about as useful as a chocolate teapot. Trained to ensnare 'saccharine daddies' (i.e. sugar daddies, without the sex) Gillian had been prepared *emotionally* for prostitution. At least this was what she told herself as Madam Annabelle set down the glass of whisky within Gillian's reach and opened her client book, gold embossed with the words 'Elite Escorts'.

'What about starting with a French chap? Businessman. Regular.'

Gillian shook her head. 'Wellington was the last Brit to have a satisfactory encounter with the French.'

'Saudi Arabian oil sheik?'

'What about language?'

'They all speak sterling, Gillian.'

'Who else?'

'We got a call from an Australian computer company. A conference. They've ordered five girls. Mean but clean, I'd say.'

'We're not doing anything illegal are we, Annabelle? Jail definitely does not appeal.' Gillian panicked, thinking of Maddy. 'I do *not* wish to spend my time in the company of women who care nothing for Dolce and Gabbanna.'

'You're not breaking the law, *I* am,' snapped the Madam, all of a sudden professional. 'Which is why I take forty per cent of the reasonably large fees I can probably still obtain for you despite your age. *You* only have to worry about wonderbraing those sagging tits of yours into submission.'

Annabelle wrote out Gillian's instructions on scented rose paper calligraphied with the words 'Elite and Discreet'.

'How's the thigh? Still swimming in circles are you, Bel?'

Gillian retrieved the note from between Annabelle's false red fingernails in preparation for her new vocation. Now *there* was job fulfilment – relying on the kindness of passing serial killers.

12. Relying On The Kindness Of Passing Serial Killers

If he brought a video camera to bed or there were any traces of blood on the valance or bodily fluids on the headboard, a career rethink would be in order. This is what Gillian decided as the lift swept her up to the seventh floor of the Swallow Hotel, Victoria. (*Not* a place to take a girl on her first date, she conjectured.)

'You're late,' said the man, opening door 735 in answer to her knock. 'I had my pre-intercourse shower three-quarters of a bloody hour ago.'

A crease of mild curiosity momentarily blemished Gillian's forehead. Her impromptu Prostitution Etiquette Guide had not included what to do if the client was young. Really young. The sort of male who has trainer wheels on his car. The room smelled of aeroplane air and was decorated with musak-banality. What Gillian referred to as a No Star Hotel. Keeping composed, she crossed the threshold, her heels sending up static from the acrylic carpet. Carefully, she placed her carpetbag on the sofa, beneath a colour reproduction of grouse being gunned down. The nervous client shut the door, then turned to make an embarrassed appraisal of his purchase.

'I'm gunna complain . . .'

Gillian tensed. She had detected a slight flicker of disappointment on his face at the door.

'You've been undersold.'

She realized with amusement that he was trying to be suave; Dustin, to her Mrs Robinson. An unsatisfactory film, *The Graduate*. In her version, Mrs R would get to keep her Toy Boy. 'Drink?' His smile revealed a mouth full of steel. Not just bridgework . . . the poor bastard was housing the Golden Gate in there.

As he bent back nail after nail trying to coerse the champagne bottle to give up its cork, rabbiting on about how this computer conference was his first time 'overseas', Gillian appraised him. Late twenties and already the proud owner of a bloated beer-belly, he looked like the sort of guy whose favourite pastime involved adulterating his mates' drinks then shaving off their eyebrows.

'I don't do tongues, armpits or toes. No elbow is to be inserted into any part of my body and it's no, no, no to petroleum jelly.'

'What?' he enquired, petulantly. 'No extras? The fellas told me I could pay for extras.'

Gillian surveyed his terry-towelling robe which gaped uninspiringly. 'Under the circumstances, my idea of sexual inventiveness is not to wear my plastic anti-contamination gloves, savvy?' Gillian removed her coat to reveal her leather basque. Eyes magnetized at suspender-belt level, his lips trailing a labrador drool, the computer engineer unexpectedly lunged. Gillian side-stepped effortlessly, sending him sinking into the duvet with a forlorn phhht.

'I believe you were instructed to make a fiscal remuneration up front.'

The big boy made the wet, gasping noise of a beached walrus. With great reluctance he extracted his wallet from a side drawer. 'So, what brought you to this?' he asked conversationally.

Gillian bristled. She refused to see herself as a fallen woman. She'd just lost her balance momentarily – her *bank* balance. 'And no fellatio,' she added tersely. 'It clogs my sinuses.'

Gillian's L-plated Lothario watched as she arranged her long pale limbs on the Sheridan sheets. He ran his stubby fingers over her skin. 'Let's turn the lights off,' he said, frankly. 'It's just you kinda *feel* younger than you *look*.'

Trying to locate the love muscle of an overweight man in the dark is a little like attempting to land on an aircraft carrier in a hurricane without radar. When Gillian finally tracked down the vital bit of anatomy, it did not respond as enthusiastically as she'd expected.

'Don't take it personally. Been a bit crook in the guts,' apologized the Aussie. 'Been riding the porcelain pony all bloody day.'

'I'm sorry. It's just that I do charge by the hour you know.'

'He's almost there . . . aren't you, Darren . . . I call him Darren.' Gillian mentally added another type to her 'No No' List – men who have pet names for their penises. A male preserve. She had never in her memory been informally introduced to a vagina.

Once aroused, 'Darren' seemed to have just as much trouble reaching any satisfying conclusions about his immediate situation. The gleam of the clock radio glinted on to a Medical Alert pendant glistening in the crease of her client's neck.

Gillian got motion-sickness as she tried, mid-bounce, to decipher the minute writing. 'An S and a Z?' Contagious diseases and bizarre medical complaints flashed through her mind. 'Schizophrenia?' she thought to herself. Oh spiffing. She was about to get a flick-knife through her Fallopians. Exactly how many personalities had she taken to bed with her? she wondered grimly. In the dim green light the silver engraving started to look less like 'schizophrenic' and more like 'psychopathic'. No wonder it was taking such an inordinate amount of time. How could she bonk his brains out, when he obviously didn't have any? Gillian was just contemplating informing him of her dental appointment *in three weeks' time* when, out of the corner of her eye, she saw her handbag move. Then she heard a hiccough. And another.

'What was that?' asked her Oedipal companion.

'What?'

Gillian pre-empted the next tiny explosion with a little gasp of her own which he took to be pleasure. Pleased at his prowess, he re-engaged his attention to his landing gear. Gillian contorted herself into an avant-garde position, more to obscure his view of her handbag than to achieve Kama Sutra credentials. Her computer operator was just about to download, when the snuffles and sniffles emanating from the bag crescendoed into a loud and rasping cry. Gillian simulated an academy-award-winning orgasm as camouflage. Her thrashing movements were so vigorous that her bondage bustier zip got snagged with the boy's mouth braces. Untangling them by braille, she noticed that her punter was up on one elbow, staring in dismayed disbelief across the gloomy room at the squealing handbag inching closer and closer to the edge of the sofa. He snapped on the bedside light.

'It's a baby,' Gillian explained casually, rescuing her bag from the floral precipice and liberating Jack from within.

'Look, what the bloody hell's goin' on, lady?' Her Aussie Love-God was fumbling for his bathrobe. Gillian could see now that it wasn't a Medical Alert pendant at all. It was a silver astrological sign.

'He's got a cold and needs his medicine, that's all.'

There was a flap of terry towelling as he stabbed in vain with his arm at a sleeve. 'Tell me what the hell's going on or I'll call the cops.' Very practical, she recalled, Sagittarians.

'I'm an undercover reporter,' she alibied, 'from *News of the World*.'

'Go fuck yourself.' He was all nerves now and aggro.

'If the alternative is *you*, boy-o, I'll pare my nails, shall I?'

The computer whizz-kid suddenly went green around his after-shaved gills. 'Wait there. Still a bit crook.' He galumphed into the bathroom. When it came to riding the porcelain pony, he obviously still had his spurs on.

The next bit was easy. Gillian pursued him, snatched the key, shut the door and turned the lock. 'Hey!' came a muffled cry from within. She removed the phone from its cradle. The poor bugger was now pounding on the door, letting rip with a catalogue of gutteral expletives. She counted out the money he'd left for her neatly folded on the bedside table. 'What?' she chastised, through the door. 'No tip?'

'Yeah!' he shouted from within, beating his fists with fury. 'Get some liposuction.'

For that, she gutted his wallet. Jack, anchored in her arms, was giving her one of his parsonical expressions. 'We're just borrowing some assets he wasn't aware he was going to lend us, dah-ling. Honestly! You're worse than a *husband*.'

Draping her coat across her shoulder, she hung the 'Do Not Disturb' sign on the door and departed. The maid's trolley was by the lift. On an impulse, Gillian bustled through the open door of room 749. Was her hubby back yet? And would they excuse her? Her baby was fractious because of his cold, poor little poppet, and she had a desperate need to breastfeed . . .

An infant made it so simple – the perfect burglar's tool. All she had to do was locate the maid's trolley on each floor – it was time for the 'turn down' – pretend the room was hers, go into Earth Mother Mode . . . then pocket all the valuables. If only Maddy could see them.

Until now, Gillian had never realized what an aptitude she had for theft. The school of hard knocks has an accelerated curriculum and Gillian had a feeling that there were a lot more lessons where that came from . . .

'I'm stuck with you now, I suppose, you little bastard,' she said to Jack, as they raided another room. But her voice was light and happy.

13. Shoot-out At The Single Mother Corral

Solitary confinement was not something she had bargained on. It would be okay if she were Bette Midler or Whoopi Goldberg: then she could entertain herself. But Maddy felt so dull to start with, how would she be after two weeks of her own company?

Her only guest for the first week was a big, black cockroach. Maddy fed it biscuits and breadcrumbs. It would be pampered beyond belief by the time she got out of here – the insect version of Leona Helmsley.

She switched on her portable radio, but it was all cot deaths, starving children in Somalia, kidnapped babies. Turning down the volume, she filled in a magazine quiz to see whether she was a 'good mother'. She failed. She even failed when she *cheated*.

Shredding *Woman's Journal*, she resolutely set about expressing her milk. Grinding her teeth against the pain as she joggled away with her plastic hand-pump, she remembered the petite, pink, jelly-baby nipples she *used* to have. Now her nipples could stretch to Namibia. You could lasso an elephant with each mauve teat. The way things were going she'd be on HRT by the time she got out of here, yet *still* expressing milk.

During week two, Detective Sergeant Slynne stopped by. 'What kind of mother are you? Dwee was right about you.'

'*Dwee?*'

'Dunno why she gives a toss about you or your kid.'

'You call her *Dwee?*'

'But you're bloody lucky she does – a good woman like that . . . She's your fuckin' good fairy. Notice anything?'

'Um . . . you've taken the bolts out of the side of your head?'

'I've given up smoking, smartass. Thanks to her.'

'She's using you, that's all, to help her find Jack.'

'Yeah. Hopefully before it's too fuckin' late. We're accessing "Lucan".'

'Who?'

'The Missing Persons Bureau's computer,' he boasted. 'The Yard.'

He paused for her to be impressed, but Maddy was too preoccupied by the grey regrowth at his temples. '*Scotland Yard*,' he stressed, piqued. Not just the cigarettes, but the hair dye, and the gold chain were also gone.

'Pointless waiting for a low-life like you to get in touch with your, you know, *remorse*.' The new vernacular didn't suit him. It sat self-consciously – like a man whose wife has dressed him in a shirt far too loud for his personality. 'Stop putting up, um . . . whats-its' – he inserted another three Nicotinells into his cakehole and chewed ferociously – '*barriers*.'

Maddy suffered a sickening intuition. 'Oh shit. You're doing the horizontal tango, aren't you?'

'Eh?'

'You're parallel-parking,' she clarified. 'A team cream. You're having a bloody affair!'

Slynne changed the subject with suspicious celerity. 'How could you leave your baby with a slag like that Cassells? Pissed off without paying her rent in Clapham. Checked into the Savoy Hotel no less. When it dawned on her that she couldn't pay the bloody bill, she *left your baby as collateral*.'

Maddy's stomach pinched sourly. 'What the hell are you talking about?' Slynne rocked on to the balls of his feet. He was enjoying this. 'Where's Jack?!' The terror of it could snap her bones.

'Cassells lost her bottle. Came back. Grabbed him. Then had it on her toes. But what kind of scroat do you think she'll sell him to next time, eh?'

Maddy watched her pet roach scuttle towards the detective, stop abruptly, turn and make for the shadows beneath the toilet. Professional courtesy, she assumed.

'Lemee know when you want to t—' He nearly said 'talk' but changed it at the last moment to 'unburden yourself. The infanticide charge obviously, we're dropping,' he added quickly as he left, 'but given you've a screw loose – why else would you leave your baby with that Cassells slag? – we're maintaining our objection to bail.'

Before Slynne's appearance Gillian, in Maddy's mind, was a tall, elegant, responsible woman friend with received pronunciation and perfect cuticles. Two seconds after Slynne's departure, she'd transmogrified into Rosemary West. By the time the dinner tray was collected, untouched, later that nail-biting night, Gillian was an organ-trafficking satanic worshipper who specialized in the sacrifice of small babies on church altars and the sale of their vital organs to rich Americans.

Where *were* they? What were they *doing*? Maddy was in an eddy of dread. Even if Gillian wasn't a she-devil, was she remembering to put padding on coffee-table corners? Would she get safety gates, safety plugs, fireguards, cupboard locks? Was she stimulating him? What sort of games was she playing? Blind fold games, *by the pool*? She could see Jack now, face down, floating, bloated. Did Gillian know mouth to mouth? Would she remember his immunization shots? He'll get whooping cough. He was probably whooping it up right now. It'd be complicated by diphtheria. He'll contract meningitis. He'll turn blue and die. It'd been two weeks and still no word from her solicitor about her Crown Court hearing. If she lost this bail application she could be left to rot on remand for up to a year. Long, cold fingers of fear clutched at her gizzards. She had to get out of here, pronto. But how? It was about as likely as a UFO piloted by Elvis Presley landing on the Loch Ness Monster.

WARNING TO ALL SCOTTISH MARINE LIFE
Incoming Unidentified Object singing 'Jail House Rock'.

Over the next few days, conditions in Holloway hit the headlines, with the press making innuendoes about human rights abuses: twenty-three hour a day lock ups in six-foot cells already containing the entire population of Belgium; women giving birth in chains; rat infestation . . . Talk shows besieged the new governor with requests to interview a prisoner. As Maddy was one of the few inmates who didn't think an innuendo was an Italian suppository, she was promptly recruited. (She could have cured the vermin problem for them too if they'd asked. Maddy knew from experience that there was only one way of getting rid of rats. Tell them you want a long-term relationship.)

*

The television green room is a charisma-oriented environment. Hovering around the soggy sandwiches on this crisp June morning were the Kylie Minogue Sound-Alike Competition runner-up; the usual, baffled assortment of writers on promotional tours accompanied by twenty-something 'away day' girls exclaiming with vivacious insincerity the importance of 'the Vegetarian Personality' or 'Versailles; the View From Sweden' and the actress Petronella de Winter in a slashed, pink-vinyl dress ingeniously welded back together with a blow torch and bits of bicycle chain – all the better to show off her recent nipple realignment.

Petronella, rising to new platitudes of achievement, was to introduce the live panel discussion on prison reform. 'Keep calm,' the denimed researcher reassured the novice presenter as she was ushered towards the set. Petronella nuked her high-rise hair with one final blast of 505 Stay and Hold.

'I am, like, calm!' Nuke. 'I'm just, like, hys*teri*cal!' Nuke. Nuke.

In the simulated living room on screen, the professionally affable presenters, employing a contrapuntal style popular in America, introduced the audience to the panellists. The hosts' habitual piranha grins, fake tans and brittle, dyed blonde blow-dries made them look like Sindy on HRT and Action Man on acid.

Maddy, who'd been busy inhaling the hospitality tray – oh to eat food which wasn't a decade or two out of date – suddenly gagged on her lemon sponge cake. Through a snowfall of icing sugar, she surveyed two all too familiar faces on the studio monitor. The prematurely balding poet, Humphrey (who, in Maddy's view, had more hair than talent) and the Capital F for Feminist historian, Harriet; Sushi Socialists who dwelt in the stellar realms of London's Celebritocracy, travelling, by limousine, the eternal TV triangle: *Kilroy*, *Channel 4 News* and *Newsnight*. Maddy had met them during her days with Alex, when they'd gone through the motions of befriending her. After his desertion they'd dropped her faster than Woody Allen from the board of a Children's Welfare Trust. Having spent most of their lives at literary cocktail parties in the Groucho Club, it was only natural that the BBC would ask Humphrey and Harriet for their observations on life in Her Majesty's Prisons.

There was no time to register her shock, as her gormless Group 4-supplied jailoress, lips drawn back in a grimace of fascination, eagerly trotted after a sound man down the linoleumed corridor and through a labyrinth of sets to studio 5. Maddy, manacled to her, followed umbilically afterwards. Electric cables snaked across the floor, slimy green and death adder brown. Maddy snagged her toe on one and stumbled forward into the back of a plywood set which gave a palsied shudder. Clipboard-clutching stage hands clung to it with fridge-magnet tenacity.

Maddy heard the show's theme music through numb ears. There was applause. An introduction of the Poet-Laureate-In-

Waiting, the Brown Owl of the Women's Movement and a Tory MP. This was followed by the breathless announcement of a 'Mystery Guest . . .'

'Group 4' removed the handcuffs and clipped them on to hips already heavy with keys, truncheon, torch and other prison utilities. A man in aviator headphones, his lips attached to the mouthpiece like a drip-feed, placed his hand in the small of Maddy's back. 'Have fun!' he insisted, before shoving her like a first-time parachutist into a graceless lurch around the pastel partition.

The audience, sardined in rows, gasped asthmatically as they'd been coached. A camera bore down on Maddy with warp speed. As did the host. He looked identical to one of those life-like male companions with latex appendage you see advertised in women's porn magazines. Except he was talking – telling Maddy how much courage it had taken for her to appear live on national television. The audience gave their Pavlovian response – tiers of clapping seals. Maddy tried not to let it go to her head. There was, after all, a huge neon 'applause' sign strobing above the set, and they had, moments earlier, given a similar show of enthusiasm to a zucchini. It was shaped like Princess Di's profile and would be won later on in the programme.

Maddy was led behind a modular console in the middle of the half moon of pink swivel chairs. She gave a small nod of hello in Harriet's direction. Although Harriet was the kind of woman who believed that isometrically exercising the thirty-two sets of facial muscles it took to smile caused wrinkles, Maddy felt sure she hadn't recognized her. Humphrey, on the other hand, most definitely had. His carefully composed facial features rearranged themselves into the look of someone who'd just been handed a jar of warm sputum.

A Tory MP the shape of a squat research submarine – the sort they send to the ocean floor to take pictures of the *Titanic* and who felt he was just as 'deep' intellectually – launched off. 'It sounds like a special offer in an upmarket travel brochure; bathrooms *en suite*, day trips, gymnasiums galore, theatre on tap . . .'

Petronella clanked her silver slave bracelets up her tanned arms. A twitch in her bleached cranium warned that there was an opportunity for self-promotion approaching. 'When I . . . *we* were making our film in Holloway . . .'

But the opinionated submarine was surfacing for no one. 'To be eligible for this kind of winter break requires a substantial criminal record. Yes. These are just some of the entertainments playing at a Prison Near You.'

'A hotel where the guest is always wrong!' Humphrey depth-charged, his rubbery face babyish in its plumpness. He would not look at her. Maddy couldn't tell if his head was bent so as to avoid her eye, or from the weight of hair gel on his few remaining tufts.

'Entertainment . . . I guess that's, like, where I come in . . .' Petronella tried once more to insinuate her bangle-jangling presence into the conversation. 'There is always a chance of dying on stage, especially when it's shared with a couple of murderers . . .'

While Action Man worked the other end of the studio, Maddy scrawled on to the piece of paper in front of her the message 'How's Alex?' and slid it under Humphrey's nose. The floor manager in the sleeveless anorak who looked as though he had a lot of trouble getting people to remember that his name was Nigel, was making frantic signals for Petronella to remove her clanking bracelets.

Humphrey covered his microphone, tilted his chair and whispered – 'Look, we did all drop you somewhat, after the split up with Alex . . . well, what I'm trying to say is,' he grovelled. 'Um, well, is there anything I can do?'

'Hmmm,' Maddy pondered, covering her own mike. 'I've often wondered about that, Humphrey, and I think the answer is – *lousy poetry*.'

'Unemployment and poverty don't cause crime. *Criminals* commit crime. *Vermin*,' the Tory MP torpedoed in Maddy's direction.

'Hey, mate, go easy.' Maddy leant around Petronella, who was surreptitiously working her silver bracelets over manicured fingers, and placed a placatory hand on the politician's arm. 'The most rebellious thing *I've* ever done is to open the milk carton on the "open other side" side.'

'So, tell us, Madeline' (the desperate host addressed her as though she were a cancer victim; a *deaf* cancer victim, judging by the volume and pace of his speech) 'is It As . . . Luxurious . . . Inside as the . . . Press . . . Have . . . Made . . . Out?'

'Put it this way,' Maddy replied. 'Prison is the only place in the world where you get *promoted* to a job cleaning toilets.'

'You!' When Harriet finally recognized Alex's ex, a look not unlike David Attenborough spotting a rare dung beetle crossed her austere visage. 'I know this remand prisoner!' she gloated. On the Liberal-Left Intellectual Kudos Chart, *knowing* an actual prisoner was on a par with co-authoring a book with a black man. 'The only thing she's guilty of is being a woman!'

A pile of shiny silver quoits lay in Petronella's lap. She painstakingly transferred them to the carpet between herself and Maddy, who wasted no time edging them closer with her foot. Screened by the modular console, she furtively pocketed the lot into her crinoline slacks. 'This young woman would never do anything illegal.'

The chat-show host squeegeed at his brow. A blob of foundation came away on his hanky. Maddy sneaked a sideways glance. Was it fake tan, or merely *rust*?' 'Don't you find it worrying that women are much more likely to be remanded into custody than men for the same crimes?' he asked the Minister for Compassion. 'The fact that women may go into prison as mere shoplifters but leave as drug addicts . . .'

'How! That's what I'd like to know. They didn't smuggle drugs into Alcatraz!'

Petronella turned the smile which was sutured on to her face in Maddy's direction. 'Maybe our remand prisoner can tell us?'

'What? Oh, I don't think you really want to know . . .'

'No. No. We do!' the hostess entreated, enthusiastically.

The entire studio was focused on Maddy. 'Well, okay,' she shrugged. 'Crutching.'

'Crutching?' Petronella enquired, with a farcically solemn expression.

'Yes. You hide things in your fanny and sneak them in that way. One woman I know, her vagina is like Mary Poppins' bag. She could hide a grand *piano* in there.'

A stupefied silence descended on the studio. Both hosts seemed to be in a conversational holding pattern. 'Um . . .' said Sindy. 'Um . . .' added Action Man. Maddy had a feeling that she would *not* be winning the zucchini which looked like Princess Di's profile.

'There is always the chance of, like, dying on stage,' Petronella began talking once more, it was a nervous habit of hers to avoid thinking, 'especially when it's shared with a couple of . . .'

Cued by the anoraked floor manager, Action Man revived his Jack 'o' lantern beam and wrapped up the segment by reciting the day's forthcoming human menu. Next was the transvestite who went shopping with his wife, followed by the mother who stole her daughter's boyfriend, a would-be vampire, two wives who let their husbands date other women; and a straight man who posed for gay magazines. Maddy marvelled at the rubbish television pushed to its public. Chanel sold shit and got ten years. Chat-show hosts got a spread in *Hello!* magazine. Sindy had now coasted to the other wing of their mock living room to introduce the runner-up Kylie Minogue impressionist.

As the pseudo Singing-Budgie warbled into view, the Sleeveless Anorak hissed at the prison panel to remain seated. Maddy's eyes located 'Group 4' in the wings, amid the boa-constrictor cables. She was gazing, awe-struck, mesmerized by the lozenges of coloured lights illuminating the India-rubber breasts of the fledgling pop star. Her head bobbed up and down as she strained for a better view, giving her lacquered, black, centre-parted cranium the look of the beating wings of a beetle.

It was only a hairline crack in her jailer's concentration but, Maddy thought, big enough to slide through. A camera shift offered her a temporary eclipse from view. An opportunity had arisen. It was like a train stopping at an unscheduled station. No time to check the notice board, no idea of destination, it was just now or never. On a dizzying impulse and furtive as a fish, Maddy slipped into the cool, liquid shadows.

By the time Action Man and Sindy had kicked off the next segment of their televised freak show with the kind of soul-searching questions which had plagued Socrates – 'Why do men want to get their leg over other women besides their wives?' – Maddy had crept into a dressing room marked 'Esther Rantzen' and changed into a tweed twin set, complete with curly blonde wig. Looking like an albino merino with a couple of venture capital portfolios up her sleeve, she pocketed as many complimentary honey roast peanut packets and miniature chocolate-bars as she could, and executed a Grand National dash down the corridor. Eyes darting, she made a disorientated reconnaissance. Staunching her terror, she resolved to walk, not run. She would stride purposefully. She would exit straight through reception and take the consequences.

*

The only thing worse than taking the consequences is bumping into one of them. The glass doors of BBC reception hissed open on pneumatic slides. Blinking like a newborn field mouse, Maddy stumbled out into the daylight. She immediately collided with ten or so journalists, hunched into brown leather jackets, a pack of wildebeests, stampeding across the car park towards Alexander Drake. Her heart stopped with a lurch. As did her body. Her legs started to shake. She seemed to be simulating some Elle Macpherson exercise video minus the music.

Alex looked relaxed, dark eyes dancing, hands placed non-chalantly on low-slung hips. A reporter from the *Express* enquired why the voting public should trust the sort of bloke who makes a living out of watching mosquitoes hatch their larvae?

As he paid his taxi driver Alex gave the rich, throaty laugh she remembered so well. His teeth when he smiled, were fluorescent.

A *Daily Mail* journo enquired about his character. A bit of a problem, thought Maddy, in that he didn't seem to have a great deal of it. Who would have thought the light of her life would turn out to be such a bad match?

Alex did the slow smile. He was boyishly tousling his hair when he spotted her. He gave her the sort of look usually reserved for a strangely vacant person you see sauntering into a fast-food restaurant wearing a 'Life Sucks' T-shirt and holding a chainsaw. Maddy contemplated her options. It was a very short contemplation. A complimentary chocolate mashed into his photogenic face was the best she could manage under the circumstances – Death by Toblerone. Flashlights sputtered like popcorn.

By the time 'Group 4' realized she was gone, Maddy was in the back of the taxi Alex had just vacated going through Esther's handbag on her way to White City tube station. From there, she'd go to Hatton Garden to pawn Petronella's bracelets.

Using the heads and shoulders of cameramen and warm-up comedians, 'Group 4' scrambled up a ladder for better visibility, giving national television a perfect view of her support knee-highs. The producer's voice rose to a castrato pitch of panic, 'Where thuhfuck is she?' All across the television studio came the clamorous cry of 'Madeline Wolfe!' – elephant calling to elephant through the jungle.

*

Maddy was too relieved to be frightened. Oh, how she looked forward to getting up at the crack of noon; food which wouldn't introduce new bacteria into her intestinal tract; the feel of a man's body pressed into hers; the smell of her baby – to kiss his sooty eyelashes and tangled, silky hair. She left the dazzle of outdoors and was swallowed up in the warm and noisy gullet of the tube. This was one old rat who was getting off the bloody exercise wheel.

PART TWO

Teething Troubles

'[A boy] models himself on his father, he copies what his father does, he picks up habits from his father . . . The modern father is a full-time parent, not a part-time stranger, and everyone in the family benefits from this.'

Dr Miriam Stoppard's New Baby Care Book

14. Baby, I Want You

Every woman wants to be wanted – but not by the entire Metropolitan Police Force.

The newspaper report was succinct. 'Prime Time' said the headline. 'A Holloway remand prison absconded from BBC television studios in London last night, after an unprovoked assault on well-known naturalist, Alexander Drake. She was taking part in a programme on crime.'

It was not a big story. Maddy was not, after all, exactly Mata frigging Hari. It wasn't as if she had the cops on Chalk Outline Duty or anything. But still, she had to be careful. She thought about getting out of town; a brief holiday at Frostbite Loch or Sewerage Bay; a little lying-low time at one of England's walk-down-this-street-at-night-and-you'll-be-raped seaside resorts . . . but that was not the way to find Jack and Gillian.

Where did people go when they went missing? Maddy had no bloody idea. Perhaps there was one giant condo where Lord Lucan, the crew of the *Marie Celeste*, the missing aircraft of the Bermuda Triangle and Bill Clinton's credibility, were all hiding out together?

During her first week on the run Maddy gave blood regularly. At least you got to lie down somewhere warm, drink hot tea and eat biccies. Five gallons later, Maddy felt it was time for a new plan – only she was too light-headed to make one. She did determine to steer clear of hotels and hostels. Her mother's maiden name, her age, *her cervical cap size*, all were available at the prod of a terminal. So she ended up sleeping rough at the Bullring – a windswept desolate patch of concrete beneath a busy traffic roundabout by Waterloo Station.

Maddy retreated to an empty refrigerator box in this shanty town of cardboard and blankets. It showered sporadically during the night. Rain dripped through her cardboard roof as if it were a Melitta coffee filter. Pavement cracks and corduroy ridges in the cardboard provided impromptu acupuncture. As multi-footed insects feasted on her flesh, Maddy tried to remind herself just who was the dominant species.

Regent's Park seemed a more attractive address, but she only lasted half a night. The trouble was that life was not like Winnie the Pooh. Real animals don't want to befriend you; they want to *eat* you, instantly.

But always, no matter where she was – soup kitchens, churches, the blood bank, St Martin's Day Centre, the Homeless Shelter above the Odeon in Leicester Square – she would check for escape routes, exits, back doors and side alleys. She tried to look enigmatic – not a look which came naturally; Madeline Wolfe was about as inscrutable as a telephone book. Every footstep had her turning, hands rising in surrender.

She had to find Jack. And fast. Her mourning-sickness was getting chronic. In cafés, she'd started reminding men she'd never seen before to wash their hands after going to the toilet. She needed help and she needed it now. Twelve thousand miles from home, there was only one person she could turn to.

Maddy couldn't think of a less appealing rendezvous. A David Koresh Memorial Barbecue held more allure. But what choice did she bloody well have?

In the witching hour of a moonless night, Maddy made her way to Maida Vale.

15. The Sperm Liqueur

....

Maddy lounged on the edge of the bed and observed her ex-lover. He lay naked, half sheathed in a sheet, papers and documents strewn around him. Tortoiseshell specs made a slippery descent along his perfectly sculpted nostrils. His warm, salty smell was so familiar to her. Maddy felt a low spasm of lust. What was the jail sentence, she wondered, for Assault-bonk of a sleeping ex? Resisting the urge to sink her teeth into his flesh, she placed her hand firmly over his mouth and shook him roughly.

Alex's bleary-eyed and vacant look accelerated into a pan-icked stare. His body jolted awake. 'Who are you?' he gulped through her closed fingers.

'You're kidding me? You haven't seen *Fatal Attraction*?' Alex shrank back. 'It's me, you great drongo.'

'Who?'

'*Me.*'

Alex scrutinized her incredulously. His body may have relaxed, but his eyes went tarmac-hard. He pulled the sheet up around him, resurrected his glasses and humphed up on to the pillows. 'Congratulations, Madeline. You have just reached a personal best in psychotic behaviour.'

Maddy couldn't contain a splutter of inappropriate laughter.

'And what the hell are you wearing?'

'What?' Maddy had forgotten she was travelling under an assumed mane. She discarded the merino perm wig and shook free her now neck-length red hair. Alex coyly contorted into his jeans beneath the sheet, catapulted to his feet and, tugging on a T-shirt, strode to the door. 'As I've already had a wife-ectomy, perhaps you'd be kind enough to exercise your man-hating vendetta elsewhere.'

'You and Felicity . . . you're really divorcing?' As he'd told porky-pies about everything else in his life – this was a man who couldn't lie straight in bed – Maddy was disinclined to believe him. But following him into the kitchen, she noted the signs of bachelorhood – the Quentin Tarantino video on the table, the old Grateful Dead albums scattered on the carpet. It was the contents of the fridge which finally convinced her. It was empty, bar a couple of beers, a cracker-barrel cheese left unwrapped and cement-rendering at the edges and a few petrified lumps which could once have been salami.

'If you've never seen a dozen divorce lawyers in a feeding frenzy, don't feel deprived,' Alex snapped, slamming the fridge door in her face. 'Thank you for dooming me to a life of laundry collection from late-night dry cleaners.'

'Pig's arse, Alex. You didn't leave your wife for me, but to spend more time being embraced by the media.'

'Ah, the Chocolate Incident.' He poured himself a large whisky. Maddy waited to be offered a drink. When none was forthcoming, she confiscated the entire bottle and trailed him into the living room. The large bronzed scrotum (otherwise known as a Bafta statuette) lay on the carpet where she'd knocked it during her aerodynamic ascent through his window.

'Yes, thank you for humiliating me in front of the national press,' he stated in a brittle voice. 'I suppose that was just a precursor to the police bursting in and accusing me of harbouring you.'

'Alex, my charge sheet should be on the best-seller list, for *fiction*.'

'Of course! And absconding makes you look completely innocent. Jesus!' He glanced furtively, out the window, before closing it. 'Did anyone see you come in?' He bolted the wooden shutters. 'Your photo will be out on the goddamn lines! Tell me, do you always make friends this fucking easily?'

'Tell me, do you always behave like such a fucking deadshit when a friend's in trouble? Not just a friend, but the *mother of your child* . . .'

'Don't give me that mother of your child crap,' he snarled, creaky-voiced from sleep. 'I begged you not to go ahead with that pregnancy.'

Maddy cradled the whisky bottle. 'No wonder I hate all men.' The fight was draining out of her.

'I failed my first two kids, if you recall,' he justified. 'Parenthood. God, I don't have the qualifications; I just haven't a bloody clue how to make models of space stations using old shoe boxes, at short notice on a school night.'

Maddy kicked off her shoes, flumped on to the sofa and sighed resignedly. 'Look, a lot of sewage has flowed underneath the bridge since then . . .'

'Huh! I'd say *your* river's got too big for its bridges.' He paced in front of her. 'Stealing wallets! Jesus Christ. Let me guess . . . you thought the *change* would do you good. I mean, what the hell did you have to go and . . .?'

'The point is . . .' Maddy dismissed him with a wave of her hand. What was this? she asked herself. International Forgive, Forget and Turn the Other Cheek Day? No, it was just that she was running on empty. 'I had a baby. It was fate . . .'

'Ah, so *that's* what you want . . .' Alex said, with a world-weary groan. 'The moving finger writes and having writ . . . *issues one.*' He folded his arms petulantly. 'The Child Support Agency is a Suicide Act.'

'What?'

'All over the country men are gassing themselves in their cars or stringing themselves up – hounded for payments they can't make. What do you call four divorced fathers with overdue CSA payments? A mobile.'

'Oh, don't be ridiculous. I know you better than that, Alex. You're the type of bloke who thinks a paternity suit is the latest look in leisure wear from Armani.' A hint of a smile flared in his eyes. He quickly extinguished it. 'It's not like you're unique, or anything,' she added. 'Giving up any claim to your child is a trait directly traceable to the Y chromosome.'

'Not according to Felicity. You should see my alimony bills. That bitch has screwed . . .'

'I don't want your money. I don't even want you to hide me.'

'Oh.' That stumped him. 'Well, what do you want?' he asked in a quieter voice, sitting opposite her.

Maddy gulped from the whisky bottle and wiped her mouth with the back of her hand. 'Find Gillian and Jack for me.'

'Where are they?'

'I don't know. Somewhere in Britain.'

'Oh, that narrows the field . . . You called him Jack?'

'He looks just like you.'

They locked eyes for a moment, before Alex got to his feet and stretched langorously. There it was again – the low voltage electric charge in her groin. 'I'll get you some of Flick's old clothes if you like.'

Maddy watched him stand on a chair and reach into a cardboard box on the top shelf of the hall cupboard. His T-shirt rode up, offering a tantalizing glimpse of mohair median strip descending beneath his belt buckle. Maddy felt her crutch moistening insubordinately. This was not going to plan. 'You've lost weight.'

'Is it any wonder? The "Lose Your Wife, Kids and The Love of Your Life Overnight Diet", by Alexander Drake. You could have killed me, you know.' Alex dismounted and sat back down. He crossed his legs; the delicious bulge in his groin disappearing into the conniving denim. 'It's true. Medical opinion now states that you can actually die of a broken heart. Something to do with secretions of stress hormone.' He balled the jeans and shirt he'd scavenged and over-armed them in her direction. 'Nothing Verdi's Violetta or Shakespeare's Ophelia didn't know.'

With a great moan of relief, Maddy groped at her waistband and shucked the heavy skirt. It spilt around her ankles, a pool of tweed. She shook off the jacket with alacrity. Lassoing it over her head, she sent it flying with a whoop of freedom. She was so used to undressing in front of him that it wasn't until she'd also raised her blouse, lariat-style, that Maddy registered this behaviour was no longer appropriate. Alex was letting his eyes travel the length of her prison-issue-underweared body. She caught his gaze. He looked away.

'You ruined my health. If I'm ever tempted to say the words "I want you back", I pray my saliva dries up.' He chugalugged another drink. 'Or that I go mute . . .' There was an animal urgency to his movements. 'Or . . . have a bloody brain haemorrhage . . .'

'*You want me back?*' she said, confounded. When it came to life's experiences, Maddy was a shop-aholic. But this was something she hadn't bargained for.

'I didn't say that,' he replied staunchly. 'Why? Do you want *me* back? Is that why you're here?'

'I didn't say that.' She yanked on Felicity's T-shirt. 'I'll always love *you*, Alex. It's just your life philosophy, pseudo-male Feminism, rotten, ratfink, dirty-dingo lying and dress sense I can't tolerate.'

This time Alex allowed himself an absolving bark of laughter. He threw back his head and guffawed.

'Do do you still love *me*?' she hazarded. Alex stared at her for so long that she felt herself redden under his scrutiny. 'Look, it's not the sort of question you have to swot for.'

He got up out of his chair. He got closer and closer . . . so close he was looking like a Picasso painting. Their noses rubbed together and then their lips did a melting marshmellow impression.

When they drew apart, Maddy was breathing hard. 'Just because I've forgotten what we were fighting about, doesn't mean I've forgiven you.'

'Me neither.'

'What *were* we fighting about?'

'Whatever it was, the fact that we were fighting at all says that this is not a good idea,' he responded, moving away.

Maddy noted the stippled surface of the skin on his neck. *He* might be saying that he didn't want her, but his *body* was saying something else all together.

'Absolutely. I agree.' (At least one or two of her neurones were standing firm. 'The guy's a lying mongrel. Don't do it,' they whimpered into the mental void where her brain used to be.) 'I mean, a soufflé doesn't rise twice, right?'

'Right.'

As Maddy threaded on Felicity's old jeans, Alex pretended not to watch and Maddy pretended not to be aware of Alex watching. He passed her a pair of sandals. Their hands brushed briefly. There was so much electricity between them it could have been privatized.

'It's a shame you hate all men.'

'Oh, I don't know. A month in a women's prison does tend to recalibrate a girl's opinion of the opposite sex, somewhat.'

They sat in heated, awkward silence.

'What are you thinking about?' Maddy probed, finally.

'Me chewing your way out of those clothes you just put on.'

'Me too.'

The next thing either of them knew, their teeth were colliding in mid air with the sort of passion that would require months of periodontal work. It was the kind of sex, Maddy reflected, that you have as a teenager. Sex that wouldn't let you stop thinking about it afterwards in full Technicolored detail. It would be vaginal déjà vu. For weeks. Maddy felt sorry for all the women who would never know what it was like having Alexander Drake take his warm mouth to you.

The sun was tinting the morning sky when they finally

pulled apart. They lay across the sheets, stunned by their sexual symbiosis.

'Playing hard to get, eh?' Maddy panted, adding, 'I don't want you to get the wrong idea. It's just that I'm kinda carnally malnourished at present. I get aroused glancing at that picture of Paul Newman on the salad dressing.'

'Oh, really?' Alex laughed. 'What a shame, 'cause I was thinking it was time we got married. We have, after all, a three-month-old baby,' he bantered. 'People are starting to talk.'

Alex leant up on one elbow. He traced the stretchmarks the baby had branded her with. He bent over her abdomen and tenderly kissed the puckered skin. He suckled the milk beads from her breasts.

'Forget Mother Love. The real reason I have to find Jack,' she explained, 'is my breasts are about to *explode*. The IRA could use me as an incendiary device . . .' Her voice trailed away into a vibrating whisper.

This time he moved over her body slowly – slow as a t'ai chi master going through his paces.

*

'The Sperm Liqueur,' Maddy laughed to herself, wiping a white coruscation from her lips.

Alex's breath was hot in her hair. 'Why am I so bad at relationships?'

This *was* something new: admitting he was wrong. Maddy added it to her mental check list of things she liked about him – his penchant for puns (punnilingus, he called it). The fact that he actually knew all the twenty-five functions of his Swiss Army knife. The curve of his buttocks in black denim. His mischievous streak (he'd once given her oral sex in the Planetarium's Photo Me booth – she still had the Polaroids to prove it). The way his nose crinkled when he laughed. The dedicated scrutiny he gave a wine list, as though he'd written it.

'The truth is, I've never been good enough for you, Maddy.'

'That's true!' She looked at the father of her child. Maybe she'd judged him too harshly. She had been hormonal, for God's sake. And where had going it alone got her? Destination Nowhere.

'Do you know what I've realized? Getting back to the simple things in life . . . that's what's important.'

She yawned, cavernously. 'We'll talk about it tomorrow while we're shopping for His and Her hand towels at Habitat.'

Coiling into his broad back, she replayed their Sex-o-rama on her mental screen. Skin humming with pleasure, the taste of Alex on her tongue, heady on the oxygen of resuscitated hopes, she buried her face in his neck. 'By the way, the only qualification for parenthood is knowing someone who *can* make scale models of NASA space stations using old shoe boxes at short notice on a school night.' And then, muscles like melted butter, body warm as bathwater, she lost consciousness, abseiling into a deep, deep sleep.

16. Fear Of Landing

When Maddy awoke at 2 p.m. to find the bed cold, the flat empty and no note, she didn't panic. After a decade or two of dating blokes and pretending there was no difference between the sexes, she had now decided that men were from a different planet. She couldn't think of one female who waited for the Toilet Fairy to change the roll on the spindle or would prefer to die rather than ask directions (which is why they now always include a token female on the space shuttle). Nor had she ever seen a woman play air guitar in front of a mirror or fiddle with the fridge thermostat *just for fun*. These differences weren't down to nurture, this was *nature*.

The truth was that men were missing the DNA structure which enabled them to find the nail clippers, the TV remote, dry-cleaned shirts, matching socks, Panadol and black bow-ties – the things that were located, *amazingly*, exactly where they'd been for the past ten years.

Men were genetically geared to stand in front of the open refrigerator door and gaze at the interior for hours waiting for something to materialize; to rip holes in the sides of bread packets; blow their noses in the shower and pick them at traffic lights; to insist on driving the car – except at the end of a drunken dinner party when they suddenly announce that *you'd* better drive; to believe that the petrol gauge reading 'Empty' was the signal to drive another 10 K . . . and leave no note declaring undying love after a romantic night of unsurpassed passion. Maddy refused to take it personally.

What she decided to do instead was track him down. It wasn't hard. Rummaging through his desk she found the gold-embossed invitation to a cocktail party to aid the Royal Soil Society at Highgrove House. Alex, more popular than the Heir Apparent, wouldn't have needed it to gain entry. All Maddy had to do was slip into some of the ex-wife's sartorial cast offs, Tipp-Ex out Alex's first name and add the inky curlicues of her own signature. 'Madeline Drake' it now read (she realized, with a jolt, that she liked the way it sounded) and take the train to the Cotswolds.

The harsh apprenticeship of the past month had changed her. It had changed her enough to know that it was stupid to expect men to change too much. She picked up Alex's discarded clothes from the floor and folded them tenderly. It was like her mother always said – better the devil you know . . . than the devil you're not sure about.

Maddy had made her bed and now all she wanted to do was lie in it – *with him*. Was that so terrible? To want to make a go of it with the father of her child? Erica Jong had written *Fear of Flying* about summoning up the courage to cut loose . . . well, Maddy's book would be called *Fear of Landing* – an irrational terror of setting up house and cooking shepherd's pie. Alex had actually said last night that they should get married. Were you joking? she asked the photo on his gym membership card as she untangled the blizzard of bedclothes. But Men never joked about the 'M' word . . . Did they?

Now, for the first time in her life, Maddy admitted that she needed a man. She wanted to be able to talk in the plural – 'we'll do this' and 'we did that'. She wanted to be number one on somebody's speed dial. She wanted to be cherished. She wanted someone to do the harmony line on 'I Got You Babe'. To laugh at her jokes. Damn it. A girl just couldn't kiss her own upper eyelids. This was a woman famished for ordinariness. It was time to make a declaration of Dependence.

Okay, she knew she'd survive without him, but goddamn it: she was sick of surviving. The trouble with being a woman at the end of the twentieth century, she told the toothpaste he'd left enamelled to the bathroom mirror, is having to be so damn strong all the time. Fixing fuses in the middle of the night and fending off muggers and jacking up car tyres in the torrential rain – any more of this equality was going to put her in the bloody loony bin.

Alex would be her human Wonderbra; uplifting, supportive and making her look bigger and better.

Sluicing his shaving stubble from the sink, she buried her face in his dressing gown and inhaled. Alex was the itch around her heart she'd tried for months not to scratch. But God, how she'd missed him. 'Love at second sight', she mused cynically as she scrubbed tea-cup stains from his bedside table. What a labour-saving device for a single mum with a high sex drive! Hell, if it hadn't been for bra fittings at Marks and Spencers, Maddy wouldn't have had any sex life at all for – she made a dismal calculation on her Ajaxed fingertips – *the last nine months*. One thought of Alex naked and her tongue was hanging so far out of her head, his shagpile got a free shampoo.

But no, it was more than that. Much more. And this time she wouldn't let him run out on them.

In a triumph of imagination over intelligence, Maddy, as she dumped crusty plates on the kitchen counter and snapped on the rubber gloves, forgave Alex his faults and foibles. With a shrug of her athletic shoulders, she discarded her mother's favourite warning (besides not putting anything in her mouth which hadn't been peeled) – 'it begins when you sink in his arms . . . and ends with your arms in his sink.'

Maddy swallowed her principles as easily as Alex's sperm liqueur.

With high hopes and a singing heart, she finished her coffee, rinsed the mug and placed it on the sink upside down to drain – unaware that she was about to discover that all Alexander Drake knew about love could be written on the side of it . . .

17. The Middle-Class Hero

The English upper-class have a condescension chromosome. Never does it manifest itself more obviously than at gatherings where they're forced to rub shoulder-pads with the Just-Landed Gentry – the media moguls, lottery winners and Arabic department store owners tolerated because of the obesity of their bank balances. A two-tiered invitation system has been invented to keep the Snobs and the Yobs slightly separated – gold-embossed invitations providing the Aristocracy with entry to the inner sanctum, while plain white invitations relegate the Hellocracy to marquees on the lawn.

But having paid their mandatory 'donation', the plebs and celebs were usually hell-bent on getting their money's worth. As Maddy searched for Alex, she saw them poking their nose-jobs against every windowpane of Prince Charles's neo-classical Highgrove hideaway.

Maddy overheard the Prince explaining his organic sewage system to a small cluster of sycophants who washed his well-meaning words away in an adjectival gush of praise and appreciation. The minute he moved on towards the Herb Garden, it became clear to Maddy that the only thing *these* people knew how to soil was a reputation.

'It's a bowel obsession. That's the trouble. Di, silly cow,

spends £17,000 a year on colonics and Charles has cocktail parties to show off his compost – *that* was last week's menu ... *this* is this week's ...' wittered a woman dressed from feet to facelift in Donna Karan. Her starved body and Big Hair gave her the disproportioned look of a trendy extra-terrestrial.

'Min' you, does explain why Diana's so thick ... Put the enema machine on too high, din they? Sucked her bleedin' brains out.'

Ostentation was banned in the Caring and Sharing Nineties. The men's concession to dressing down was to wear T-shirts with their Versace trousers; neck crystals in lieu of gold ingot.

'Presumin' there was anyfink there to suck out in the first place!' said a man intent on proving the height of his own IQ by sporting a T-shirt which simply read, 'Stacked.'

'The sooner he marries Camilla the better,' predicted a forty-something type recently described in *Hello!* magazine as 'fun-loving'. (This was social-speak for mammoth breasts and alcoholic tendencies.) 'Once he's investitured ...'

'You mean *trans*vestitured,' added another extra-terrestrial. (This one would be described as 'exuberant', which meant that she'd once earned a living doing photographic shoots wearing nothing but a piece of dental floss, otherwise known as a G string.) 'I heard, like, on good authority, like, that he's gay ...'

'You'd be gay too, if you'd been married to a bu*lim*ic. *Ter*rible breath. From throwin' up all the time.' 'Stacked' further proved his Mensa potential by miming the Princess of Wales talking to God on the big, white telephone. 'Ugh. I've no idea how anyone could make love to a bu*lim*ic ...'

'Backwards?' Maddy suggested, impishly.

The men who'd foreclosed on the manors to which they

weren't born, stopped ant-eatering up the hors-d'œuvres to spin round. They might have laughed, except for the coveted gold-embossed invitation she was clutching. The women's outlined-in-lip-pencil lips compressed into a jealous moue before they moved *en masse* into the Sewage Garden.

Maddy, feeling more and more like Stanley in search of Livingstone, thrashed her way through the jungle of famous, photogenic foliage looking for Alex. She stumbled upon assorted wildlife on her journey, the most curious of which were the group of genuine Soil Society types – obvious by their dung-coloured windcheaters which rendered them indistinguishable from the compost – discussing the most effective lightweight climbers: *clematis viticella* versus *aconitum volubile*.

She macheted a path through the throng into Highgrove House. Her A-list invitation pass earned her the privilege of weaving around the endless antique furntiture at shin-whacking level into a library crowded with VIP guests in animated conversation with each other's left breasts – the location of their laminated and invariably hyphenated name tags. Maddy didn't need to read the 'Lord This' and 'Baroness That' to know that she was now amongst the cream of English society – rich, thick and prone to whipping. The 'loo pepper', 'abite the hice' accents said it all. 'Awfullys' and 'frightfullys' exploded around her; consonants crashing down like hail stones.

Maddy ferreted out Alex with her eyes. He was standing by the bookcase, a champagne flute in one hand and a minute square of soggy bread playing host to a piece of fish bait in the other.

'So this is what you meant about getting back to the "*simple things in life*",' Maddy whispered mischievously, goosing him and gobbling his canapé in one bite.

Alex, wheeling around, gave a series of anal-examination grimaces. 'What the hell?' Excusing himself – he was mid-chin-wag with the sort of woman who looked as though she'd have a battleship named after her – he steered Maddy towards a remote corner of the room. 'What the hell are you doing here?' he hissed.

Maddy laughed and pointed to her name tag. 'I'm your wife, obviously.' She ripped Alex's own label from his lapel and Velcroed it onto her right breast. 'Not fair if we don't name the other one. It'll get a complex. What are you *wear*ing?' She tugged light-heartedly at his LL Bean casuals and kicked at his Patagonian climbing boots. 'Where are you off to? *Everest*?'

But Alex had what Maddy called his elevator face on. 'Madeline, this is not funny. I'm here in a work capacity.'

'If you're serious about politics, Alex, let me tell you, the only people who'll follow you in *those* clothes are store detectives.'

'Well, *you'd* know all about that, wouldn't you?' he grated, glancing nervously over his shoulder.

'Just living down to the cultural stereotype, I guess,' she wisecracked.

'You don't seem to be getting this, Madeline. *The long arm of the law is stretching out in your direction* . . .'

'Relax. It'd have to be double-jointed to find me *here* . . . Actually, prison is excellent training for a social event like this. Gaol is just as hierarchical as any stately home.'

'Jesus Christ, Maddy!' He agitatedly jingled the loose change in his pockets. 'Going to work the crowd, are you? Think it's a crowd with a silver lining?'

The female battleship who was now loudly mocking Michael Portillo because his furniture was *bought* rather than in*her*ited, glanced at them suspiciously. Alex burrowed Maddy further into the 'microscopic soil spore' section of the library. 'You must leave – and I mean *now*.'

Maddy leaned up and brushed his mouth with her own. There it was again; the voltage to the groin. 'I'm starting to wish I were back in prison,' she said, lightheartedly. 'Flick-knife-wielding, sex-starved, crack-addicted dyke body builders are more fun than *you* . . . Although you *can* be fun' – she laced her fingers through his belt loops and tugged him towards her – 'when you want to be . . .'

Alex broke free. 'Look, there's something I need to tell you . . . After Felicity left and you severed all romantic ties, I needed to rediscover my sexuality . . . and what I discovered is . . . celibacy.'

Maddy threw back her head and laughed immoderately. 'Oh right, Cliff Richard.'

'I work better, think better and' – he eyed her narrowly – 'there's no fear of scandals in the paper . . . I'm enriching my inner life.' He readjusted his already perfectly tucked-in shirt into his jeans. 'Amazingly easy, actually. Like giving up drinking. What a relief not to have to go to the off-licence so often . . .'

'Really? Gee, carpet-burn, inner-thigh chafing; I could have *sworn* we enjoyed a little carnal nightcap together . . .'

'Lust is celibacy's banana skin. You slip, okay?' Alex sulked.

'But bachelorhood is my natural state, Maddy. Inspector Morse mode – you know, slumped in a favourite armchair listening to a Mozart CD, awash with Chivas Regal . . . collecting model railways and Napoleonic memorabilia . . .'

'Pull the other one, Alex. It's got a fishnet stocking and a suspender on it,' she said impatiently. 'How can you talk like this after last night?'

'Madeline, last night was nothing more than MSB – Maximum Sperm Build-up.'

Maddy felt the bottom fall out of her world. If she'd wanted to be maimed physically as well as emotionally, she'd have gone to Rwanda and made a day of it. 'What about me and Jack?' Her voice sounded as though she were talking with her head underwater.

'You two need me like . . . like, I don't know . . . an Eskimo needs a lawnmower. Our society has moved inexorably to a more matriarchal set-up. The woman is the main controller. The man – a non-essential extra.'

So much for the 'His and Her', this was more of a 'Me and Me' hand-towels situation. Maddy was just Houdini-ing herself to fit the unexpected twist in their conversation when Petronella de Winter attached herself to Alex's arm and planted a big wet kiss on his cheek. 'Hi!' Her vertiginous heels made her nearly as tall as Maddy, who was wearing Felicity's flat 'follow me home and play Scrabble' sandals. Pink-lipsticked and perky, Petronella was so damn cute Disney could make a T-shirt out of her. Her tightly tailored Moschino suit showed off her perfect figure. *Too* perfect. Maddy suspected she was the sort of female you inflate by blowing into her toe. Craning forward, she inspected Petronella's name tag with incredulity.

'Climatic Forecaster?'

'Yeah. I had an employment shift. Three weeks ago.'

A demotion, Maddy deduced, after a certain panel discussion. 'Weather girl' had lately taken over as a career choice from that of actress and trolley-dolly. There wasn't enough weather on television for all the blonde beauties with good profiles, sunny dispositions and 36D bold fronts approaching. Her ample breast size would soon make Petronella the most famous forecaster of them all. She only had to turn sideways to obscure all of East Anglia. Norfolk probably hadn't had any weather indication for weeks. But what the hell was she doing *here*? Maddy felt a distinct cold-front making its way across her emotional isobars.

'It is my belief that smooth inner thighs do not necessarily speak of a rich inner life, Alex,' she said suspiciously.

'Petronella is planning to do a masters degree in environmental studies,' said Alex, shovelling sociable top-soil into the gap in their conversation.

'By presenting TV I was hoping to one day, like, work in you know, Human Rights or Unicef or something . . . but then I found my—'

'Vocation?' supplied Maddy, facetiously.

'Yes! That's it. And you are?' Alex ripped off Maddy's breast labels before the weather girl could read them. Decked out in Felicity's Nicole Farhi and full Estée Lauder war-paint, Petronella hadn't recognized her. Maddy wasn't all *that* surprised. Put it this way. If Petronella had been brunette, her blonde roots would be showing.

'The sucker of the century, apparently. But perhaps I should wear my name tag on my back so that you'll know who you're stabbing?' she asked Alex, who had suddenly discovered a nonexistent stain on his tie.

'And you, like, share our passion for soil conservation?' Petronella probed.

Maddy noted the 'our'. 'Oh, yes. I'm a woman of many convictions.'

Alex shot her a look which read 'a closed mouth gathers no feet'.

'Petronella's joined the Lib Dems. She's helping with my campaign,' he rushed on. 'Speaking of which, Pet, we really must get down to the Celebrity Croquet and meet my new election agent—'

'*Pet?*' Maddy repeated, distrustfully. The trousers of the weather girl's *haute couture* pant suit were so tight, she'd only have to cough to induce orgasm. What Alex had nick-named 'breeches of promise' when Maddy used to wear them for him.

'Lex's campaign aims to dispel the idea that protecting the environment is, like, an expensive luxury.'

This was *not* Maddy's maiden voyage into the Green Seas of jealousy, but this time she had no rudder. '*Lex?*' She sent up her first distress flare.

'Pouring investment into the "greening" of industry, transport and farming, could, you know, save the taxpayer over £3.5 billion in dole payments.' Weather girl *was* her perfect vocation; she obviously knew so much about prevailing wind. Maddy tried to interrupt, but there was more hot air where that came from. 'We plan to, like, shift transport investment from road to rail, you know, abandon nuclear power in favour of wind farms and solar energy, and force industry to, you know, install new technology to, like, clean polluted land and rivers.' Alex was shifting from foot to foot, his expression hooded. 'It's time to stop tinkering around the *edges* and put environmental protection at the, like, *heart* of economic thinking, you know? That's our platform. He's going to make a, like, *brill* Minister for the Environment, aren't you, darling?'

Alex flinched. Maddy's suspicions lurched from Park position into Overdrive. She realized she'd left something out of her list of genetic differences between the sexes: air guitar, fridge thermostat fiddling . . . and the ability to go straight into the underpants of another woman. He probably hadn't even *showered* first. 'Did you know that most murders are committed by people you, *like*, know?' she informed him through gritted teeth.

Petronella strengthened her grasp on Alex's arm. 'Alexander, what's going on?'

'Oh, don't worry,' Maddy assured her. 'Fighting for us is foreplay, isn't it, *darling*?'

'Maddy, that's enough. We're leaving.' He nudged Petronella in the direction of the terrace.

Maddy followed at a furious pace, shin-whacking at every turn. 'Try not to leave any stains on the sheets. I just changed them.'

Petronella froze on the french-doored threshold. She shook free Alex's arm. 'You *slept* with this woman?'

'Oh, yes,' enthused Maddy. 'Apparently he's rediscovering his sexuality . . . and that of as many women as possible.'

HMS Battleship capsized a prawn cocktail down her front.

'For God's sake,' hissed Alex, tugging them outside and behind the topiary. 'Keep it down.'

'Oh, tough titty, Alex. Tell me you're not serious. She's so

159

young. If she were a wine, you wouldn't drink her. Bill Wyman wouldn't even drink her . . . Michael Jackson . . .'

'Look, as you've been, like, insufferably rude,' Petronella pouted, 'I feel I can now speak my mind . . .'

'Why not? *You've got nothing to lose*.'

'What are you insinuating?' prickled Alex. 'That I'm old?'

'You look like Ken's dad, out with his son's girlfriend – Barbie.'

Alex instinctively turned to examine himself in the glass of the drawing-room window.

'Ever since Lex directed me on a shoot at Holloway Prison of all places – we just, you know, "clicked".'

'Face it, Alex. You knew Elvis when he was alive the first time.'

'He rescued me from some kind of *riot*, you know. Alex said that the psychopath who started it was some crazed fan. He was lucky to get out of there alive!'

'How true,' agreed Maddy, eye-slittingly.

'He was, like, *so* brave. We've been in an intimate relationship,' Petronella insisted, 'ever since.'

Maddy hooted. 'Hah! One thing I learnt *inside* is that the best way to a man's heart is through his stomach – by an upwards thrust with a carving knife.'

'In*side*? You don't mean?' Petronella edged backwards. '*You've been in prison?*'

'Ken's *father*? Jesus.' Alex tore himself away from his reflection. 'You make it sound as though I'm about to get a telegram from the Queen.'

'Which is why he had to resort to you, *Pet*. You know . . . any orifice in a storm.'

'Hey, don't I know you?' The weather girl's predictive talents finally asserted themselves.

Alex fired a shut-up-or-die look in her direction. But what Maddy thought was the death-rattle of her relationship turned out to be the thunk! thunk! throb of a helicopter. The aristocracy streamed out of Highgrove House and on to the pleb-laden lawns, pointing ecstatically skywards, as if in anticipation of the New Messiah.

'The McCartneys!' squealed a soap star nearby. Despite her 'Keep It Green. Keep it Natural' T-shirt, any more plastic surgery and she'd just have one big ear at the back of her noggin.

The psychological squall which had threatened to dampen Petronella's spirits blew away. 'It's, like, *terri*bly exciting,' she oozed to Alex. 'Linda has opened a vegetarian food factory which uses ozone-friendly ammonia refrigerators, catalytic converters and, like, natural gas!'

'Gosh,' said Maddy, underwhelmed. 'A Beatle? And I thought Huon Pines were the oldest living thing on the planet.'

Petronella tugged ferociously on Alex's arm, whilst preening her appearance. 'I feel a photographic opportunity coming on,' she gushed, adding the self-conscious justification, 'it'll be good, you know, for the Party.'

'Oh, well, in *that* case, don't bother,' Maddy stated. 'I think it's time Alex considered a career change. A car-park attendant say. Or better – *New Zealand Television*.'

Alex prised himself away from Petronella, who was busy brushing imaginary dandruff from his shoulders. 'What's that supposed to mean?'

Maddy cauterized her feelings and binned her withered dreams once and for all. 'Unless you help me find Jack, I'm going to the press.'

The noise Alex made sounded not unlike a hippopotamus giving birth. '*What?*'

'Can you imagine how many hacks in macks there are drooling for a story like this? Does the word "Planetarium" bring you back into orbit?'

'You'd really do an Antonia De Sancha to me? And that Bienvenida Buck cow? You'd actually put sword to paper?'

Maddy wasn't proud of herself, but she held her fertilizer-enriched ground. 'I'm desperate, Alex. My milk's starting to dry up.'

'Come *on*, Alexander!' Petronella yelled over her shoulder-pad, impervious to their private drama.

Alex lowered his voice to a menacing baritone. 'I'll deny it.'

Petronella, exasperated, satisfied her convolvulus tendencies by latching on to the arm of a passing peer and manoeuvring herself into the welcoming committee. Maddy would have to tell the Compost Conspirators that she had found the hardiest lightweight climber. It wasn't the *clematis viticella* or the *aconitum volubile*. It was the *petronella*: the sort of climber which works its way into the lime mortar and wrecks the foundations.

Once she'd departed, Alex dragooned Maddy behind a piece of dense topiary. 'Come to think of it,' he raged, 'how do I know it's *my* child?'

'Don't be rid*i*culous, Alex. He's *you* in bonsai.'

'Over ten per cent of men in Britain are unwittingly bringing up children that are not their own. Poor buggers.'

'All right then,' Maddy snapped, 'let's have a really public court case with lots of DNA and find out once and for all, eh? Just like Peter Jay and his nanny.'

'You know what I think?' he said darkly. 'I think you got pregnant on purpose.'

'The condom you put on fell off, as I recall,' she seethed.

'And I'm supposed to believe . . . after all the precautions . . . we used a dutch cap every other bloody . . . just one slip up and—'

'It's not a hundred per cent safe you idiot. Spermatozoa can still, you know, swim up the sides—'

'Oh, the Mark Spitz of sperm. Or maybe my spunk had been dieting, is that it?'

'I don't think the Child Support Agency will see it quite that way.'

'The CSA is just a charter to encourage women like you to be single mothers, secure in the knowledge that some poor bastard like me will pay your way. You go to the press and I'll bloody well sue you for entrapment! That's what I'll do.'

'And I'll sue *you* for not telling me you were a married man with two children. If I'd known that I would never have fallen in love with you in the first frigging—'

'And if I'd known you were a preying mantis in disguise . . . that you were going to devour your poor bloody partner after mating—' He broke off. 'There's no winners in this, you know, Maddy,' he said in a subdued voice.

Maddy tore off a flower stem and snapped the stalk in two. 'Yeah, but at least there'll be more than one loser.'

They looked up as the airborne eggbeater descended, drowning out Alex's reply. The propeller spun lazily then stopped. A round of applause went up as the McCartneys' non-leather shoes touched terra firma. The crowd watched as they got into a chauffeured limousine to ferry them the ten yards from helicopter to Highgrove for their appointment with Prince Charles on energy preservation.

Alex and Maddy careered around the hedge to find themselves suddenly smack bang in the middle of the welcoming party. Smiling convulsively, the Inequalitarians, the Just-Landed Gentry and the Compost Conspirators mulched together to greet their popstar patrician paragons.

'Vegetarianism isn't just a, you know, business for her . . . it's like a *mission*,' Petronella, social tendrils spiralling, was telling the Prince of Wales. The McCartneys' chicken-less Kievs and meat-less meat pies made Maddy want to gnaw her own foot off. It made her want to become a cannibal instantly; starting with a certain weather girl.

Prince Charles, looking frail and pale, like a seedling growing in a shoe box, smiled shyly. Despite her Republicanism, Maddy felt quite sympathetic to an heir to the throne who declared his desire to live inside a woman's knickers. This was a man who oozed sincerity from every pore – of which, Maddy noted at this close range, he had many.

'G'day,' said Maddy, extending her hand. Out of the corner of her eye, she could see Alex pulling a face she had previously only associated with the passing of a kidney stone.

'An Awe-stralian?'

'Ah, yes,' said Alex nervously, summoning up a sufficiency of relaxed *bonhomie*. 'You recognized the dulcet tones, eh, Your Highness?'

'I'm awf to Australia shortly,' said the Heir to the Throne. 'Any message?'

'Well, yes,' piped up Maddy, 'you could ring my mum . . .'

Alex gave her a steely stare. 'I think the Prince was referring to a political message for the Prime Minister or the Governor General about environmental issues. The French nuclear testing in the Pacific is, of course, off diplomatic limits.'

'Just tell her,' said Maddy, scrawling the number on a piece of paper, 'that a) I'm not sinking into any arms and b) you can never know *any* devil *that* well.'

18. Kiss And Sell

Later that evening, Maddy and Petronella found themselves marooned next to the hors-d'œuvres on the sidelines of the Celebrity Croquet. Looking like a colony of social sea-birds, the Great and the Good stood nodding at one another on the lawn, uttering the traditional, regional greeting of, 'How's the novel?'

The two women watched Alex thwack a ball through a hoop with insouciant ease. Maddy dipped a biscuit into a mixture of red roe and sour cream. It looked, she thought morbidly, like the stuff women had hoovered out of their thighs during liposuction.

Petronella's sun-lounger creaked defensively as she lowered herself into it. 'We're, like, going to buy a house together,' she announced suddenly.

Maddy's heart skipped a beat. Real estate was nearly always a foundation for marriage. *Where had she heard all this before?*

'We're doing a photo shoot for *Hello!* magazine.'

My God, thought Maddy. It really *was* serious. The bitch! She glumly siphoned up a Pimms. Maddy knew that a woman only called another woman a bitch if she was prettier, wittier, or had won the man of your dreams. Maddy's hand shook, sending tiny tidal waves from one side of the glass to the other.

Ice-cubes collided with lemon slices, capsizing cucumber wedges.

They watched the croquet game in loaded silence. It was cricket, on Valium. Polo for pathetic fat gits. Maddy sucked the flesh from a cucumber slice and frisbeed the rind. She took off her sunglasses and chewed the plastic arm meditatively. She gazed forlornly at the candy-floss clouds scudding across the June sky. 'Look,' she finally announced with quiet fortitude. 'Think of him as toxic waste. In other words – *dump him.*'

'Actually,' her rival goaded, 'we're going to get married – '

'Hey, why give yourself an experience you'll have to pay a lot of money to a therapist to get over? He'll never get married! He's got FOC . . . Fear of Commitment. Chronic!'

' – and, like, have a family.'

Maddy dropped her liposuction-on-rye. 'You aren't getting this are you?' She perched on the end of Petronella's sunlounger. 'Sex for him is like taking a crap. And *you're* his toilet.'

Petronella struggled up out of the lounger and practically pirouetted on her perfectly pedicured pink-painted toes. Her abrupt departure sent Maddy toppling. 'I don't have to sit here and listen to this any—'

'We were in love. I don't think I'll ever be that in love again,' Maddy reluctantly confessed from her improvisatorially prone position. 'Six months and a pregnancy test later, he ditched me.'

Petronella stalked off on to the billiard-table-green lawn; her pert buttocks swinging with metronomic precision.

'IS *THIS* THE MAN WHOSE NAME YOU WANT YOUR BABY TO SEE ON THE CHILD MAINTENANCE

CHEQUES EVERY MONTH!!?' Maddy called out after her, untangling herself from the metal chair legs and scraping roe off her toe.

The eyeballs of the celebrity-croquet players left their sockets and scuttled across the lawn towards Maddy. Alex swiftly followed.

*

As far as Maddy could figure it, psychiatry was a terrible waste of couches. Despite the hampers of emotional dirty linen collected over the decades, Maddy liked to think of herself as fairly shrink-proof. There had to be something amiss in a business where the customer is always wrong. Edwina Phelps had convinced her of this.

As Alex frog-marched her through the Highgrove car park, she deduced that you could tell more about people by what they *drove*. Bentleys said 'smug ponce'. Four-wheeled Land Cruisers said 'pretentious wanker'. Alfas said '*rich* pretentious wanker'. Ferraris, Maseratis and Lamborghinis? Well, they were obviously tax-dodgem cars. But nothing spoke quite so loudly as the red Porsche into which Alex brusquely directed her.

'Well, what do you know. A Meno-porsche. What does the number-plate read?' she mocked. 'Midlife crisis?'

Alex thrust himself behind the wheel in a self-righteous frump of indignation. He remained deep in thought as they ate the exhaust fumes of Petronella's elongated pink sports car down the M40. Maddy wasn't sure what *that* said exactly, – except perhaps 'small clitoris'.

Alex kept up this Marcel Marceau approach until the lazy summer dusk slunk into dark, when he swerved abruptly off the motorway at an obscure exit. He pulled up in the shadow of the Service Area garage. Listening to the engine ticking as it cooled, Maddy watched him cross into the café. It was a cheery little place. The waterlogged buildings wore wigs of green algae. The whole allotment was scattered with the locust husks of burnt out cars and charred bed frames. He returned, slid into the car and handed her a beer. It was warm.

'He who controls the past, controls the future,' Alex said enigmatically, leaning back in the driver's seat. 'George Orwell.' He swivelled to face her, crossing a tanned ankle over one knee. 'So – what do you think the papers are going to say? Cad? Love rat? Philanderer?'

Looking at him by the strobing headlamps of passing cars, Maddy noticed an unexpectedly smug expression had replaced the drowned-corpse countenance.

'Cockroach, more like it.' She took off the bottle cap with her teeth. 'There should be a special test for men like you, where you're lured into a dark kitchen, the lights are snapped on and we see that instinctive dash under the bloody fridge.'

Alex laced his fingers and propped them behind his head. 'What a sad, put-upon little creature you must be, Maddy,' he said sardonically. Maddy couldn't quite decipher his mood. 'All *you* did was ensnare somebody else's husband, trick him into paternity, then blackmail him with exposure threats. Perhaps my friends in the press will be interested in my side of the story?' he continued, shamelessly. 'Innocent family man—'

'Innocent!' Maddy spluttered as the Heineken went up her nose. 'You make Stalin look like, I dunno—'

' – manipulated by a cunning Sexual Career Woman—'

' – John Denver. Career? What a career? You promised me a job but—'

'What you don't realize is the monumental irrelevance of your proposed revelations. The public palate has become jaded with cheap denigration and sensationalism.'

'Oh yeah? Suppose you were a lousy, low-down, loud-mouthed mongrel and suppose you were a *politician* – but, oh, hey, I'm being repetitious . . .'

'Hah, hah, *hah*,' he mocked. 'When it comes to the duplicities of arms to Iraq or the purchase of MPs' favours, okay,' he conceded, smooth as engine lubricant. 'But we Liberal Democrats can weather the odd sexual misdemeanour. Paddy Ashdown's rating went up, remember, when his affair with his secretary came to light. In fact, women all over the country were suddenly desperate to mountaineer his scrotum pole.' In vain, Alex tried to work his hands into the pockets of his fashionable jeans. They were so tight, his testicles had applied for a transfer. Hoping she hadn't noticed, he casually hooked his thumbs through his belt loops and kept talking. 'Even the printing presses have metal fatigue in the Moral Outrage Department.'

With a searching eye, Maddy surveyed her ex in a momentary beam from a truck's headlights. 'You've been doing sit-ups underneath stationary vehicles again, haven't you?'

'The public no longer care if your fly's open . . . as long as your mind is too.' He tousled his mane in the rear-vision mirror. 'I'm standing as a self-made man who—'

' – worships his creator?'

' – who owns up to his past,' Alex corrected imperiously. 'Winning the hearts of everyone through my candour and self-deprecating confessions of how hard it's been as a single father . . .'

Maddy, jerking towards him, hit her head on the sun visor. '*You*? Bringing up a *child*? Alex – try not to panic, but I think you're having some kind of coke and aspirin flashback . . .'

'All we ever hear about is sex discrimination, racial discrimination . . . well, what about the blatant discrimination against *Dads*?'

'With *your* fathering skills,' Maddy predicted with cold amusement, 'his hobbies will include the botched assassinations of female movie stars; an abnormal attachment to ferrets—'

'Ninety per cent of divorces are initiated by women. Yet the poor bloke has only a one in *ten* chance of winning custody of his kids.'

'Oh God, I feel a bumper-bar sticker coming on.'

'Yet when a man is sacked from his family, *he's* the one who has to pay the redundancy! No wonder our sperm count is bloody well dropping!'

The absurdity of Alex's pronouncements jolted a laugh out of her. 'Alex, you couldn't possibly bring up a child on your own. Your fridge is too small. There's nowhere to put all those awful finger paintings.'

'You can now even bloody well fertilize yourselves! A quick squirt with a turkey baster is making us physically redundant,' he swashbuckled. 'Now you're trying to make us emotionally redundant as well.'

'Earth to Alex. Come in . . . It's called Learned Helplessness, you drongo; a special talent perfected by generations of fathers—'

'Fathers now have to categorize themselves as the *genetic* father, the *biological* father, the *legal* father, the *social* father—'

'Tragic.' Maddy said with mock sympathy. 'It's cruelty to dumb animals, really.' She was laughing so hard, she had to unbuckle her seat belt. 'Alex, um, it's a bit late to start playing Bob Cratchit, ya know?'

'Well, I am *not* the feckless father of modern demonology.'

'Get real. Think back. Do you really want to have those little gates all over the house again? To only buy food which harmonizes with animated cooking utensils on day-time TV? I mean puh-*lease*.'

'The point is, Madeline,' he interjected, changing psychological gear, 'at last I've decided to try to be a proper dad.'

With a sinking feeling, Maddy realized that he was serious. Flicking a side lever, Alex scooted the driver's seat backwards and nonchalantly stretched out his legs. Maddy was instantly ambushed by a memory of the time they'd made love in the carwash, during the wax/dry cycle. Now *that* was the true definition of autoeroticism. How the hell had they got *here* from *there*? she pondered, sadly. 'Forget it, Alex. I'll never give Jack up.'

'Depends who finds him first, doesn't it?' There was a thrilling note of triumph in his voice.

Maddy felt a cold hand reach into the pit of her stomach. 'By the time you track him down, we'll have buggered off out of England.'

'That's called child abduction. Under the Hague Convention, to which Britain is a signatory, it's presumed to be in the

172

baby's best interests to stay in the country where he was born.' Alex had suddenly taken on the speech pattern of an android from *Robots From Planet Bastard*. 'Even if you get custody, which I doubt, my access hours will mean that you have to stay in London.'

Maddy couldn't believe that she was the one now in retreat. Alex had turned the tables with the expert ease of a removals company. 'I'll take you to court, you lily-livered piss ant!'

'All being equal the courts come down in favour of the mother . . . but you're an escapee!' He loomed over her, foot flat to the floor on the vocal accelerator. 'An illegal immigrant – facing two charges of theft. And proposing to do that which will lose you the sympathy of every English judge, namely kiss and sell. That will definitely nuke any chance you have of winning custody of Jack. Besides, what kind of mother are you?' With calculated cruelty he set about stripping her down to her emotional chassis. 'You don't even know where your son – *my* son – is.' Maddy reeled from the verbal whiplash of his words. 'My solicitor says if you surrender yourself in order to claim custody against me, you'll be further charged with abandoning a baby under the Offences Against the Person Act, 1861.'

Alex's face was hard, panel-beaten; eyes on high-beam.

'You bastard.' With shot-put aim, she sloshed her beer over his head.

Alex peered at her from beneath his yeasty mask. 'I take it,' he volunteered, 'that we are having a difference of opinion on this?'

Lurching out of the Porsche into air leaden with traffic

fumes, Maddy eyed the ex-love of her life with bitter resentment. She hoped it was the last time she'd ever see him. 'I'll always cherish the initial misconceptions I had about you, Alex, you, you – jerk off.' Maddy felt doddery, concussed: victim of a Hit and Run Romance. 'No. That description's too good for you. Sperm, after all, has a one in a hundred million, trillion, billion, zillion chance of turning into a human bloody being!'

She ran as fast as she could, hurdling the service-area hedge, squeezing through the steel fangs of smashed railings and down through the trees masking the road which would lead her back to London. She stood in the gloaming, hooked her thumb horizontally and waited for a lorry.

What the bloody hell was she doing coming a gutzer, a hemisphere from home, soggy bra-ed and broken-hearted? Not only was she on the run from the cops and Dwina the Czarina of Psychobabble, but now from *Alex*. Eating the dust of car after car, staring at the dark scar of road disappearing into the distance, she drew a bleak conclusion. An Englishman's love is like his central heating; it may keep you warm, but was nothing more than hot air.

With the net closing in around her, Maddy raged against her own absentmindedness. Losing the love of her life was one thing, but losing her *son*? Women didn't *lose* their sons. I mean, what was he? A *sock*?

Biting back tears, she dismally counted up the days since she'd last seen her darling. She panicked at the thought of how the hell Gillian was coping. This was a woman who thought 'crèche' was a French car accident. Maddy had promised it would only be a week. That was *three months ago*. She was probably right now trying to insert Jack into a condom-vending machine for a refund.

She had one question for Gillian, when and *if* she finally found her.

The name of a good psychiatrist.

PART THREE

Weaning

'**Puerperal depressions.** In actual fact there is no such condition, but some women who are liable to mental illness may become emotionally unstable, and pregnancy, delivery, the puerperium and responsibility of the new baby may impose an unreasonable strain upon them, leading to the onset of mental illness. There is nothing specific about pregnancy or delivery which causes a woman to develop a mental illness. Any other stress, strain or emotional disturbance of similar severity may quite easily provoke mental illness in such a person.'

Pregnancy, Gordon Bourne

19. The Blue Eyeshadow Brigade

It took Maddy a moment or two to recognize the woman who answered the door of No 6 Chepingstow Crescent, Milton Keynes. It made her think of those 'before' and 'after' make-over photos in women's magazines. And this person looked like the 'before'.

'What?' Gillian read Maddy's mortified expression and glanced down at her fluorescent stretch leggings and pastel terry towelling scuffs. 'Do I detect slight disapproval pertaining to my attire?'

'Put it this way, Harvey Nichols are flying their flag at half mast.' Even the garden gnomes huddled together on a neighbouring lawn seemed to be gawping at Gillian.

'Where's Jack?' Maddy clamoured, pushing past her.

'Are you implying that I am some kind of fashion victim?'

'Fashion *mortality* would be closer.'

'Well,' said Gillian defensively, following her friend at a trot, 'it's just not practical to wear Chanel whilst making choux pastry with one hand and a patchwork quilt with the other.'

'You're making *choux* pastry?' Gillian seemed to have shed her old identity with chameleon-like nonchalance. This was a woman who'd taken baking lessons from Marie Antoinette. 'Are you nuts?'

'I, my dear, am the Imelda Marcos of choux pastry,' she punned. 'Cuppa?'

Maddy's scepticism dissolved into astonishment as she followed her old friend into her floral-posied, tea-cosy, spotlessly twee kitchen. The decor was vintage Brady Bunch. The laminated counter was lined with minute tupperware containers into which Gillian was spooning small quantities of puréed primary colours Maddy presumed to be vegetables. This woman, who had only ever waxed lyrical about men and money, was now waxing parquet and making her own pot pourri. The food in the pantry was stored in order of expiry dates; the pegs on the clothes-line were colour-coordinated with the washing. On the sink sat a dish of peach-coloured soaps in the shape of shells. A wooden painted pineapple held recipes cut out from women's magazines. An invitation on the noticeboard announced a surprise party for the pet terrapin. There were hospital corners on the newspaper lining of the hamster cage, for Christ's sake.

'Gill, um . . . don't you remember when we used to hunt in packs for men with Mercs?' Maddy wondered if it had been wise to bring this up while *she* was unarmed and Gillian had a loaded spatula in her hand.

'You're thinking of someone else, dah-ling. The only vehicle *I* own is Maclaren buggy.'

On the window sill above the sink sat a china dray pulling a porcelain wagon – the sort of house ornament which indicated the immediate deduction of twenty points from the IQ of the inhabitant. A framed weeney green handprint Maddy assumed to be Jack's was magnetized to the refrigerator door.

'Where is he?' she entreated.

'Beddy-byes.'

Maddy picked up the tiny cocktail frock Gillian was sewing for Jack's cabbage-patch doll. 'What the hell has happened to you? You've become some kind of' – Maddy gulped; the word was like jellied eels in her mouth – '*housewife*.'

'I certainly have not.'

'Well, what would *you* bloody well call it?'

'I'm a domestic engineer, if you please.' She handed Maddy her tea in a mug festooned with euphoric sunbeams and iridescent rainbows. 'A highly skilled operative at the interface between culinary and residential management provision and in-home pedagogy. And now, if you'll just excuse me for a tick, I have to de-mildew the shower curtain before bubby-wubby wakes.' She unselfconsciously slipped on a plastic barbecue apron cutely appliquéd in a double-entendre about love, meat, men and cucumbers.

'Hey! Domestic Engineer!' Maddy called out sneeringly as she trailed Gillian into the living room. 'Better watch out that halo doesn't slip and, you know, choke you to death.'

Her crowing was guillotined by the 'swing-o-matic', a wind-up swing which allows baby to orbit for hours, arcing back and forth across the living room. The airborne seat caught Maddy in the epiglottis. She lurched sideways, only to find herself entangled in some kind of navy canvas pouch suspended from a roof beam, embossed with the name 'Jolly Jumper'. Half harnessed, the velocity of her backwards fall suddenly trampolined her ceiling-wards.

Gillian, impervious to Maddy's impromptu balletic entrance, was half-way up the stairs with a squeegee mop in her hands.

'It's taken me six goddamned weeks to find you, Gill, and yet you don't seem all that bloody pleased to see me.' She gestured to the domestic sceptre in Gillian's hands.

'What? Oh. I'm sorry.' Gillian dragged like an anchor down the stairs. 'It's just this house. It was flats, you know. You could heat a can of baked beans in every room,' she shuddered. 'I've thrown out a couple of Trinidadian families and walled over a few corpses, but there's still so much to do.'

Maddy looked at her old friend mogadonically. 'I'm glad I found out how boring you are *now* and not whilst on a walking tour of the bloody Lake District. But Gillian, really. *Milton Keynes*?'

Milton Keynes was a new town marooned amongst slip roads, spiralling off the expressway into a mish mash of Toys 'R' Us, cash n' carrys and a monarchy of Kings – Burger King, Kebab King, Chicken King. Identical streets full of executive dwellings and brick bungalow 'dream homes' unscrolled mundanely in all directions.

'Do you remember my accountant? The man to whom I used to pay a lot of money to tell me that I didn't have any? It's *his*. I'm decorating it for him. In lieu of rent. Babykins needed a nice place and—'

'Is he okay?' Maddy felt a wave of longing which buckled her knees.

'Okay? My dear, he's not *okay*,' Maddy tensed at Gillian's words, a tearing sensation in her throat. 'He's a *genius*! And so *beautiful*! I'm entering him for the cover competition for *Totler* ... The baby version of *Tatler*, dah-ling,' Gillian explained, eye-rollingly. 'How did you by the way?'

'How did I what?'

'Find me.'

Maddy couldn't help intuiting that Gillian didn't look all that pleased to be found. 'The Missing Persons Helpline. I gave them your photo. They found your ad in some local rag. An Image Palette Consultant? What the hell is that?'

'All I do is advise people what their 'colour' is. You, madam,' her voice took on a fruity, insincere tone, 'are a Cold Spring – and then' – Gillian shrugged – 'they give me fifty quid.'

The meagre remains of Maddy's milk supply tingled as though her nipples were being given Chinese burns. 'I'll have to wake him. I just can't wait any longer.'

'Impossible. He's still got another half an hour,' Gillian over-ruled. But Maddy was already bounding up the stairs.

'Hey!' Gillian protested, behind her.

The pristine nursery was a gelato-bar mix of pistachio and pink. A cot leant up against the farm-animal mural on the back wall. Thick-throated with emotion, Maddy peered over the wooden railings. *And there was Jack.* He was on his tummy, his bottom pyramiding off the mattress, his soft limbs skewed in sleep. She felt a surge of love.

'He always sleeps like that now,' Gillian panted, rapturously.

Jack opened one eye. He looked straight at his mother. But not with the euphoric beam she'd expected. His delicate brows furrowed in a disgruntled 'I'd like to see the manager' kind of way.

Maddy felt awkward and overcome. She picked him up with butterfingers. But Jack didn't want to just see the manager; he wanted to lodge a complaint, which he did, long and loud. Crestfallen, Maddy darted a look towards Gillian.

'Nappy?' she suggested.

Maddy laid him on the change table. 'So *that's* what's upsetting you.' She felt constrained, as though trying to make friends with a stranger in a lift. 'Nappy rash.'

'Ammonia dermatitis,' Gillian corrected, handing Maddy a tube of pink cream.

Maddy was all fingers and thumbs. It was like trying to reverse park with someone watching. 'For God's sake! He's looking at me as though I'm Lorena Bobbitt! Now what?' Demoralized, she held his whimpering form with Ming vase reverence.

'*Feed* him *ob*viously,' Gillian tch-ed.

Maddy fumbled out a breast. But Jack, wearing the prudish expression of a Baptist Minister, kept turning his head away.

'Solids?' suggested Gillian.

Bolstered by pillows in his highchair, Jack kept up his cold shoulder treatment, using his fingers to Jackson Pollock the food on his tray.

'Can you believe how artistic he is!' Gillian enthused. 'In*cred*ible for a four-month-old!'

Jack, having upended his bowl, then proceeded to hurl his food around the room, trashing it in rockstar style. Maddy darted about with a dishcloth.

'Peekaboo!' Gillian peek-a-booed. Jack's eyes lit up, following her around the room. 'And so entertaining! More compelling than Carreras at Covent Garden, despite his F.A.T.H.E.R.'

'Gillian, he's a B.A.B.Y. He doesn't understand English yet.'

'We've been doing flash cards. Feeder preparatory schools are not taking toddlers who score beneath 125 in IQ tests, you know.'

'Gill – um, you keep talking like this and someone's going to have you committed . . . probably *me*.'

Maddy was heating milk in a saucepan on the stove. Gillian ostentatiously switched off the front burner whilst igniting the back. She moved the saucepan to the rear of the stove, handle pointed to the wall and administered an admonishing stare.

Maddy gulped, bewildered, at her tea.

'That's a no no too,' pontificated Gillian, confiscating her cup.

'What?'

'Hot liquids near baba.'

Distracted, Maddy was unaware of the milk boiling over. 'Oh damn!' She searched in vain for some Jiff.

Gillian pursed prim lips and unlocked the cupboard beneath the sink. 'Bleach, detergents, drain cleaners and caustic soda are locked away.' Maddy recalled the times when the only caustic thing about Gillian was her wit. 'Medicines.' In Doris-Day overdrive, Gillian flung open a high cupboard. 'All labelled and up out of reach.'

Now Maddy came to think of it, the *whole room* looked up out of reach. It was as though there had been a King tide, stranding possessions high and dry. 'Gillian, he's not even *crawling* yet.'

'Jackson's the type to get into everything, aren't you, popsy wopsy.'

'Jack*son*?'

'It'll suit him better when he's F.A.M.O.U.S. Don't you think?'

'What I *think* – is that this is the way serial killers get started.'

'Quick!' Gillian tapped a tapered nail on her watch face. 'Must vamoose. It's Tiny Tots time!'

*

Tiny Tots, Tumbler Tots, Aqua Babies, Crescendo, Baby Gym, swimming lessons, followed by music appreciation then taped French tutorials till tea; Jack had a social life Maddy could only dream of. For the first week, she traipsed after Gillian and Jack to one event after another. Still, she was slightly relieved to note that Gillian hadn't changed out of *all* recognition. For these suburban excursions, she dressed Jack in broderie anglaise tops, quilted corduroy trousers and packed a Waterford crystal baby's bottle.

'This is Jackson's *biological* mother,' was Gillian's way of introducing Maddy to the mothers of Milton Keynes – identical, velvet-Alice-banded women in velour tracksuits of every pastel shade; interrupting their PC revisions of *Vertically Challenged Red Riding Hood*. (The 90s Mum treads warily through the semantics of modern nursery rhymes.) 'She's having trouble *bonding*.'

But the only thing preventing Maddy from bonding with Jack was Gillian, the Housewife Hovercraft.

'Haven't you got anything to *do*?' pleaded Maddy, two weeks into her suburban sojourn.

'My social life is comp*let*ely dead, dah-ling,' Gillian announced, cheerily, ritually camcordering another poo deposit for posterity. 'Jackson got hold of my Filofax and *ate* August!'

'But this is the 'burbs! Aren't you supposed to be having steamy mid-afternoon sexual encounters in the neighbour's azaleas?'

'The only thing which shows me any interest these days, dah-ling, is my bank account,' Gillian exhaled, cleaning wax out of Jack's ears and flaking cradle cap off his scalp, 'monkey-ing' she called it – Maddy had never felt closer to Darwinism – 'and that's precious little.'

The few times Gillian did venture out on an Image Palette Consultancy she handed Maddy a list of emergency numbers and pressed upon her what she called her first-aid kit. It was actually more like an entire General Hospital. From dandruff to diarrhoea; from constipation to major convulsions; from warts to whooping cough, all was hypochondriacally catered for.

'That's what I like about you, Gillian,' Maddy marvelled. 'Your low anxiety threshold.'

By mid August, Maddy was chewing the furniture. It wasn't just that she never got to be alone with her baby, but Gillian seemed to have acquired the ability to continue discussing Jack's bowel movements long after Maddy's own interest had waned. She had also become the Cecille B. de Mille of Milton Keynes, videoing every nano-second of the child's life for the archives; then *immediately* viewing the footage.

'Brings back memories doesn't it?' Maddy would repri-mand, facetiously, to no bloody effect whatsoever.

At nights, Jack became a human pancake. Gillian yoyoed up and down till dawn, constantly flipping him on to his back to avoid cot-death.

'As I've told you every night for a month,' Maddy said tersely, colliding with Gillian yet again in the nursery, at sparrow-fart. 'There's no need to get up to him.'

'I always was a bit of a night owl, dah-ling. Jackson keeps

my kind of hours, don't you' – she tweaked his cheek – 'you little party-mammal, you!'

Maddy, repossessing Jack, subsided into the armchair in a pathetic attempt to feed, but her nipples were cracked; the flow glacial. Jack howled with frustration. When Gillian produced her ubiquitous bottle of warm milk, he gave a squawk of sudden joy. Moments later his lips, Mick-Jaggered from sucking, pouted up at Gillian with satisfaction.

She then placed him in his cot on his tummy and patted his bottom rhythmically. 'I notice you put him in disposables today. He prefers terry towelling. It keeps him snug and comfy and much drier.'

Maddy peered at her friend, disbelieving. 'You're talking like a brochure, do ya know that?' she chastised in a piercing whisper.

'Well, then, read my small print.' Gillian boomeranged back an equally judgemental look. 'Better still, *listen*.' She beckoned.

Maddy crouched on the floor beside her. 'What?'

'Can you hear that noise?'

'What noise?'

'That ticking sound? It's my biological clock.'

Maddy shrugged. 'Get a digital.'

Gillian's face caved in. 'I'm getting old, Maddy.'

'God, who isn't? Remember when a "bit of rough" used to mean a night of debauchery with a tattooed rock star? Now it's a leaf of bloody lettuce.'

'My make-up comes with a *trowel*.'

'Gillian, you're only thirty-six.'

'Yes, in *human* years. In Single, Childless Female Years, that's about eighty-six! Soon I'm going to be too old to wear jeans. Maybe I already *am* too old to wear jeans. Maybe people are passing me in the street and whispering, "How path*et*ic . . ."'

'Well, don't think giving birth means you'll be able to wear jeans. Every time I zip up *my* jeans, my neck gets thicker.'

'I'll never have a baby,' she confided. Sadness flowed down her face. 'Loneliness is a growth industry, Madeline. Whilst maintaining an air of optimistic availability, subcutaneously I acknowledge failure. Every single man I know is gay. I'm going to call my memoirs *Dances with Queens*.'

'Memoirs? Hah! Nothing to put in them now you've joined the blue eyeshadow brigade. Hey. Cheer up. Maybe you could be one of those granny test-tube mums?'

'Five-year waiting list,' Gillian said earnestly, massaging Jack's abdomen. 'And, ugh! Dah-ling, I'd be in and out of stirrups more often than *National-fucking-Velvet*.'

'Surrogacy?' Maddy jested.

'You're the only fecund friend I possess.'

'Chinese orphanage?' She refused to take her friend seriously.

'Too expensive. Besides, I don't want just *any* baby.' Her eyes jumped around the room. '*I want Jack*.'

The grin froze to Maddy's face.

'He's the best company I've ever had,' Gillian continued, sincerely. 'And you're talking to the woman who once dated Bryan Ferry.'

Jack seconded her sentiments by emitting a loud burst of wind. Gillian gave a self-satisfied smile. 'I didn't know I could fall in love. And now, suddenly, it's all pouring out of me.'

Maddy's mouth hardened. 'I'm his *mother*. You couldn't possibly love him as much as I do!'

Gillian looked at Maddy evenly. 'When he had a cold I sucked his nose mucus out with my mouth.'

Maddy's eyes popped. 'You don't need a baby, Gillian, you need a *shrink*.'

'Which is why I think you should let me adopt him.'

'Make that a DIY lobotomy.'

'I've put him down for all the top schools. Schools like that look beyond the colt to the stable.'

'So what are you saying? He'll be able to count with his feet?'

'What I'm *saying* is that primary care-givers are as closely scrutinized as pupils in the selection process.'

'He's *my* baby!'

'Yes, but I'm a better mother,' she contended witheringly.

'Why? 'Cause of those hideous baby groups you take him to full of smug parents whose babies sleep through the bloody night?'

'Have you bought fire-resistant nightwear? Have you made your own rusks? Quite large chunks break off the commercially produced one . . .'

'Those groups are legal proof of child abuse.'

'Are you running the cold water tap last in the bath, so he doesn't get scalded by a random hot drip?'

Random drips, yes, she'd met a lot of *them* lately. Maddy, with nothing to lose but her temper, got to her feet. 'So what am *I* exactly? Some kind of *pod*?'

'Are you enhancing co-ordination development? Body and space awareness? Improving his gross motor skills?'

'What the hell's "gross motor skills"? Driving a tacky car?' Maddy plucked Jack out of Gillian's embrace. He responded with a heart-wrenching howl and stretched his plump pink arms back in her direction. 'What bedtime stories have you been reading him? The Wicked Biological Mother?' She frantically rifled through Jack's stuffed toys. They seemed to have reproduced overnight. 'What the hell does he want?' She proffered a teddy which was received with undisguised disdain.

'He wants the bear with the *chewed off* ear, *obv*iously,' Gillian condescendingly translated. 'And *moi*, of course. Come and give Aunty Gilly a kissy wissy, snooky wooky. He's got a lip-lock on him like Sandra Bernhard.' As Gillian's face lowered towards Jack's, he stopped crying immediately. Her mouth curled into a self-congratulatory smile. 'Face it. I'm what he needs, Maddy.'

'What he *needs* is to get to sleep,' Maddy stipulated tartly. Jack's body strained against her as she barrelled down the hall.

Gillian swabbed at her nose with the back of her hand. 'He likes you to blow on his eyes to get him to close them,' she said with sniffy superciliousness. 'He also likes baby massage, deep bath technique,' she called after them. 'Or putting the bouncinette on the washing machine. But only the spin cycle.'

'Go F.U.C.K. yourself,' said Maddy eruditely. Jack was *her* baby. She knew better than anyone how to comfort him.

*

An hour later, Maddy resorted to bribery. 'Exactly what will it take for you to go to sleep? Money? A trip to Disneyland? The promise of one of my organs if you're ever in a plane crash?'

Crouched miserably on the laundry linoleum, watching Gillian's smalls circumnavigating each other, Maddy felt so suave she could hardly stand herself. As if it wasn't bad enough that Holloway's resident trauma critic, Edwina Phelps, Detective Sergeant Chinless Drongo and the entire Metropolitan Police Force were after Jack and her, now she also had to contend with her ex-lover and a maternally correct baby-snatcher.

As far as Gillian and Alex were concerned, this was war . . . If only she didn't have such good taste in enemies.

Maddy contemplated an entry for Jack as the youngest ever plastic-surgery patient. They'd both get Ivana Trump cheekbones and matching Michael Jackson noses. It was either *that* or take up residency on a remote Papuan hilltop. She tried to tell herself that things were always darkest before the dawn, but in Maddy's experience, things were always darkest just before a complete bloody eclipse.

By the time the machine reached spin dry and Jack was dozing soundly, Maddy knew one thing for sure – she would have to go on the run again. But *to where*? She had recently known only one beacon of security in a dark and dangerous world – a twenty-stone beacon with varicose veins and heartburn. But how to find her? She'd just have to play it by foot.

20. Ging Gang Gooly Gooly Gooly Gooly Wash Wash

'What de hell ya been up to!' Maddy would have answered except that she'd emerged completely winded from the vertebrae-crushing embrace of Mamma Joy. 'I bin givin' it a bit of dis' – Mamma Joy bent her elbow in a poor mime of a person drinking a pint of beer – 'an' a bit of dat' – she punched the air boxer-style – 'an' a bit of de udder' – she hydraulicked her massive hips backwards and forwards.

They were sitting in a mildewed flat in a high-rise block on an estate in North London. The aquamarine, fuchsia and red russet walls – suggesting a special deal on discontinued lines of paint – were puckered with water blisters and blobs of mould the colour of guacamole. The television played an old episode of *Father Knows Best*. But the fathers in this area had shot through long ago.

In tracking down Mamma Joy Maddy had expected to be busier than a Bosnian brick layer. But she'd underestimated the old lady's noteriety. Mamma Joy was world famous – in Hackney anyway. She'd beaten her theft charge after a store detective failed to turn up for a court hearing. She had also developed a new line in scams.

'Mamma Joy, says I, Mamma Joy' – her diamond flashed wickedly in her front tooth, as she jounced Jack on her knee –

'dere be a flaw in ya system, gal. Youse gettin' caught far too often.' She winched her left breast, which had wandered too far under her armpit, back into alignment and readjusted the Hermes scarf at her throat. 'De flaw is goin' out of de store.' Her new scam, she explained, was to damage an item of clothing in the changing rooms, then claim her 'refund' from customer services, professing that she had lost her receipt. 'Den I get de minicab to de next store, even better dressed dan de last one!'

With the indefatigable zest of a débutante at her first ball, Mamma Joy showed Maddy a map of England, her shop-lifting future clearly routed from Marylebone Road to Mersey-side. This was a woman with the gift of the grab.

It was good to look into her familiar face, corrugated with laughter lines and to hear the see-saw lilt of her voice, even though Maddy's ears had to strain above the juddering pulse of rap music thundering from a nearby flat by a band she wouldn't have been surprised to discover went by the name of Dead Yak's Smegma.

'Drug dealers. No better neighbours. Dem like a quiet life and dem on de look out twenty four-seven.' Yeah, waiting for an unexpected nark at the door, decoded Maddy.

A young woman who introduced herself in an unruly composite of consonants as 'Chelsea Gore-Plunkett-Fluff', crammed herself into Mamma Joy's flat through a hole in the wall, to heat her baby's bottle. Double-barrelled names, once exclusive property of the upper classes, had been adopted by these Niebelung Estate dwellers with delicious tongue-in-cheekiness. Posh, police-escorted do-gooders visiting the estates for various publicity purposes were now finding themselves out-hyphenated by the proletariat.

Chelsea had pale naked legs, plastic stilettoes, loopy earrings dangling lower than the hem of her micro mini, a complexion pumiced by anxiety and peroxide blonde hair with the roots showing. It seemed mandatory to have roots on the estate. Maddy would have to dye her scalp black.

'The friggin' gas company cut me off again,' the woman complained.

'Won't the council do anything?' asked Maddy.

'They do nowt! When I told 'em I needed a stove for the baby an' that, they told me to buy food that neva needed no cookin'.'

The girl was an expert in one downmanship: 'Round 'ere if you see a bleedin' cat that's still got two ears, it's here on 'oliday,' Chelsea theorized. 'Whyja wanna move 'ere?'

'I think I'll like it.' Maddy squinted through the grimy window into the stagnant summer air, gauzy with smog. 'If only I could *see* it.'

With Mamma Joy off on her 'shopping spree', Maddy was to lie doggo in the flat until things cooled off. This would give the old lady plenty of time to organize fake passports and arrange for her and Jack to be stowed in the hold of a cargo plane of dubious craftsmanship that was not only the pride, but the *entire fleet* of a country Maddy couldn't pronounce. Now *that* was something to look forward to.

It was while escorting Mamma Joy to the mini-cab office later that afternoon (only armour-plated taxis would venture on to this estate) that Maddy got a better idea of her new home. There were five tower blocks, each twelve storeys high, with low-rise battered and burnt-out housing in between. The architectural acne of satellite dishes sprouted from every surface. The whole place had more antennae than Kennedy Space Center. The streets, named with mocking, slit-your-wrist irony – 'Meadow Lane' and 'Buttercup Way' – were deserted except for the odd lone kid on an L-plate motorbike doing wheelies, weepy-eyed dogs with advanced skin conditions and scabs of graffiti written in blood reading 'HIV+'. Britain's inner-city council estates make you believe the world really was built in six days.

'What about the boys in blue?' Maddy asked, nervously, as they neared the Mile End Road.

'De Babylon! Huh!' Contrasting the surrounding neglect and degradation, Mamma Joy gave off a rich, dark glow. Her face split into a mutinous grin. 'Dey come once to see me in de flat. When dey come out, de kids dem take de wheels off de police van!'

As Mamma Joy trundled into the mini-cab office to haggle over the price, Maddy cast a despondent eye upon the sad assortment of crack addicts huddled on the urine-soaked staircases. Kids sniffing solvents dotted the landings: escapees from a Hieronymus Bosch painting.

The car-horn blast of an unmusical bar of 'La Cucaracha' heralded the arrival, in a fug of car fumes, of a young man who introduced himself as Fin. He looked as thick as a plank, only less intelligent. He had zit traces on his mummy's-boy pallor and drove a nicotine-coloured Nissan, the back shelf and dashboard of which were crowded with stuffed mascots. A furry racoon's tail in Arsenal footie colours dangled from the aerial. Maddy had little doubt that Fin was the sort of male who liked movies with 'Pork', 'Death' or 'II' in the title.

'A new mum, eh?' His hairless elbow jutted out of the open window. 'Indefinitely idled then?'

'I'm sorry?' Folding Jack closer Maddy stepped back up on to the kerb.

'Non-waged? Economically marginalized? Voluntarily leisured?' The vocabulary sounded alien wrapped around the wide, slovenly vowels of his East-End twang; an eardrum-shredding accent which sounded like a disease of the throat.

'You mean, am I broke? Yes.' What she wanted to ascertain was whether Fin was 'alternatively schooled' but thought better of calling moronic a man who was capable of road-rage.

Fin slewed open the car door in Maddy's path and ponced to his feet. He was wearing baggy khaki shorts and reflective sunnies. Maddy marvelled at how Britain had ever managed to colonize the globe on such pale and piddly little legs. 'Ten per cent a week,' he said, expansively. 'Them's me terms. Otherwise, it's guts for garters time.'

Fin, Maddy finally deduced, was a Loan Shark. With a disdainful huff, she shoved past him into the office.

'Ya sure you'll be awlright, gal?' The hammocks of Mamma Joy's aubergine-coloured arm flesh swung in the breeze as she bear-hugged Maddy.

'Do you know how long I've been waiting to have some time alone with my baby?' Maddy spluttered from a face concertinaed between Mamma Joy's 38D Bombes Alaskas. 'Four months. It's going to be *heaven*.'

'So dat's why you're grinnin' like a wave on de slop bucket!'

Maddy watched Mamma Joy's cab lurch off at speed. It bounced into a stationary vehicle, taking the wing mirror and half the paint from the passenger-side door. The mini-cab's bumper bar sticker read 'God is my Pilot'.

*

'GING GANG GOOLY GOOLY GOOLY GOOLY WASH WASH, GING GANG GOO . . .' Maddy checked her watch. Six a.m.! God, she'd thought it was going to be *much* later. 'GING GANG GOO . . .'

She placed her insomniacal offspring into his baby walker, which Jack immediately took as a cue to play hockey, scoring a goal with his head. Oh well, Maddy thought, sweeping up the ceramic shrapnel from a fallen vase, at least it wasn't a priceless one. 'Living with you,' she told him, 'is like co-habiting with an entire demolition squad, do you know that? Hey, come on now. Don't cry. Mummy didn't mean to go crook at you . . .' She yanked him into her arms. 'GING GANG GOOLY GOOLY GOOLY GOOLY . . .' She checked her watch again. It was five past six. 'Damn,' she said aloud, 'I thought it was *much* later.'

At breakfast-time, Jack refused his rice cereal. 'Look, pretend it's the slime-coated underbelly of a dead slug, okay?' She knew by now that babies would only eat food which had been dropped on the floor, stamped on, licked all over by a dog, then kicked into the corner and covered in fluff.

'Oh, it's so good for mummy wummy to see bubby-wabby. No one loves you as much as I do. Think of all the wonderful things we'll be able to do together! Like . . .' Maddy checked her watch. 'What time is it again?'

*

For his midday meal, Maddy secured him into a high chair. Jack proceeded to throw everything over the side. It was like dining with Henry VIII. Bugger those books on balanced meals, cursed Maddy. A balanced meal was whatever stayed on the spoon *en route* to Jack's mouth. 'I'M SINGING IN THE RAIN, JUST SINGING IN THE RAIN . . .' The only way she could get him to sit still long enough to sneak something surreptitiously into his moosh was to perform a tap-dancing, umbrella-twirling Busby Berkely spectacular. 'WHAT A GLO-RIOUS FEELING I'M HAPPY AG—' Which was fine, until she noticed the entire gang of resident drug-dealers peering through the hole in the wall. But whenever she stopped, he'd start crying again. 'I'M SINGING IN THE . . .' Shit a brick. This child was more demanding than Frank Rich.

By the end of lunch, there was so much congealed egg in the kitchen, she'd need a blow torch to remove it. The only gourmet treat which *did* interest him was salvaged from a nostril. He offered the grey globule up to Maddy like a party hors-d'œuvre.

The afternoon's activities involved trying to locate the missing goldfish. Maddy saw Jack licking his fingers and hoped to hell he hadn't developed a taste for sushi. Then there was the moment when he discovered that poo could be a decorative option. By mid-afternoon, Mamma Joy's flat was fast resembling the Maze Prison.

The lady on daytime TV was lamenting the fact that the

time with one's baby went so quickly. *Quickly?* Really fucking slowly, was more the observation Maddy was looking for.

*

'ROCK A BYE BABY ON THE TREE TOP, WHEN THE WIND . . .' By one o'clock in the morning Maddy was begging Jack to go to sleep. She'd drive him around the block . . . only she didn't have a car. She'd read him a story only she couldn't find her reading glasses. 'BLOWS . . . THE CRADLE WILL . . . You are *not* Margaret Thatcher, okay?' she told him at 2 a.m.. 'You do *not* need to sit up to do your red boxes . . . ROCK, WHEN THE BOUGH . . . If I have to keep pacing much longer, it's goodbye Julie Andrews, *hello* Myra Hindley, got me?' she told him an hour later. 'Hey, playing "hunt the dummy" at 4 a.m. is not my idea of a good time, okay?'

In the graveyard shift she took him into Mamma Joy's bed which he promptly colonized, playing soccer with her kidneys and leaving Maddy clinging to the side of the mattress for dear life. It was then she found her glasses – *on top of her head*. Glancing over at Jack, she saw, with amazement, that he had finally conked out. 'Thank you, Jesus,' she whispered. 'But hang on . . .' she conjectured, '*is* he sleeping? I can't hear him breathing. Holy Hell! He's stopped bloody breathing! Oh God! Oh God! It's cot death. Jack? Jack? JACK! It's okay. Don't cry . . .'

'GING GANG GOOLY GOOLY GOOLY GOOLY WASH WASH, GING GANG GOO . . . GING GANG GOO . . .'

See Mother Run! Hear Mother Talking to Herself! See

Mother get down the bottle of tranquillizers! See Mother unable to get the child-proof lid off the jar.

*

Some women are born mothers, some achieve motherhood and others have motherhood thrust upon them. Two weeks of living alone with Jack in Mamma Joy's flat and Maddy would have to put herself into the 'thrust' category.

Oh, she still worried and fretted and got toey. The pram merely had to bounce over a bit of clotted shag-pile for her to think he'd be a paraplegic. He only had to gag on his milk for her to think 'blocked wind-pipe' i.e. brain damage. A cough conjured up iron-lungs for life. Two micturations per hour and she practically had him wired up to a kidney dialysis machine.

As there were so many 'no go' areas on the estate, and the areas you *could* go into were chock-a-block with cops no doubt carrying her mug shot, Maddy was forced to become a full-time prison warder, patrolling the perimeter of her kitchen, constantly on the look out for beetles, needles, loose screws. Another week of this and the latter were mainly to be located between her ears. In desperation she constructed a makeshift play-pen . . . only to end up sitting *in* the play-pen, with *Jack* sitting *out* of it.

The fact that Jack was teething didn't help. His whinginess made him cling-film clingy. He was super-glued into her arms at all times. Like an amputee, Maddy learned to do everything with one hand – from changing a lightbulb to changing a tampon. And then there was the spittle. Maddy felt she could white-water raft on the amount of drool oozing out of her kid's mouth. It also meant that he bit her nipple. Now *there* was a bonding experience.

But the brain-boggling blahdeblahdom of it all was the worst. Maddy was so bored she could see her plants engaging in photosynthesis. She started developing a yeast infection for a change of pace. The real highlight of the day, apart from a breast self-examination, was pumicing her callous. She only sandpapered a little at a time to make it last longer.

Desperate for company, the gas-meter reader became the most scintillating person Maddy had ever laid eyeballs on. When he left, she pretended to order carpets, skylights, kitchen gizmos, just to get people over for estimates.

Maddy soon found herself contemplating a roof-top protest – to protest about conditions not being as good as in prison. She hadn't known that society sentenced mothers to such bloody drudgery – with no goddamn parole in sight.

Bone-marrow-melting exhaustion exacerbated things of course. Chelsea lent her a book entitled *Solve Your Child's Sleep Problem*, but she was too tired to read it.

Maddy prided herself on her memory. She could remember what sexual position she'd locked into during Charles and Di's televised marriage; what diet she'd been on when John Lennon was assassinated; every lickable dimple on Alex's toasted-almond-tasting body . . . and yet the morning of the Autumnal equinox she walked to the corner store in her bra.

When realization struck, she dodged and darted up the stairs, bent double, scanning the horizon like a commando for sniper fire. Sticking out like a dog's balls was probably *not* what Mamma Joy had meant by keeping a low profile.

She tried to stay inside and just watch the black and white

television. But the endless husbands coming home to cooked meals to chew over the day's ups and downs made her suicidal. Maddy knew with *her* luck, she'd just get her head in the oven . . . and the gas would be cut off. She'd attempt an OD on pills . . . only to end up in a persistent vegetative state. And let's face it, *she was in that already*.

To make matters even worse, sandwiched between these day-time TV hubbies one afternoon, was the succulent mouth of Alexander Drake, making noises about his love of children. Maddy's heart did a fast fandago.

'Isn't it true,' the female presenter probed, 'that your wife is divorcing you on the grounds of adultery?'

Alex unzipped a self-deprecating smile of devastating sincerity. 'Like all men, Miranda, I need a wife perfect enough to understand why I'm not.'

The interviewer dragged her eyes away from his crotch and, going into bat with her eyelashes, praised Alex for being so nice.

'Nice!' Maddy shrieked at the set. 'Oh yes, he's nice at first, then he will virtually become another person – that person is usually Attila the Hun!' Crash-diving the channel changer, Maddy wondered how she had ever loved such a bottom-feeder? She vowed never to lower her standards again – well, not unless she was really, really horny.

Stock-piling coins, Maddy commandeered the only unvandalized public phone booth on the estate. An hour later she'd tracked down the compulsively sociable Mamma Joy at a cousin's chiropodist's son-in-law's hairdresser's step-daughter's masseuse's in Birmingham. 'Any word on those passports?'

'We won't know nutting for at least a mont; maybe six weeks . . . maybe more—'

'Six weeks? Okay. *I'll hold.*'

'You awright, gal?'

'Oh yes, fine, except that he won't stop crying, he hates me and I'm a hopeless mother.'

'Dere's only one ting to remember, gal,' came Mamma Joy's reassuring tones. 'If you shake de baby too hard, him will get brain damage.'

Maddy laughed. She snuffled back her tears. She cradled Jack to her.

'I know I said to make like de snake's willy and lie low, but you need to get outa dee flat. You *really* do. Dat flat of mine can get to stinkin' like a dead mon*goose*. You hear?'

The payphone cut off. Maddy opened up her wallet. It was a moth graveyard in there. 'Some day, son, all this will be yours,' she informed Jack sarcastically.

Money or no money, there were not a lot of recreational facilities open to Maddy on the estate. She could watch the council ratcatcher. She could watch the rats evading the council ratcatcher. Alternatively, she could watch the loan sharks in a feeding frenzy on the shoals of poverty-stricken single parents.

When Maddy leaned into Fin's Nissan and asked for some cash to tide her over until Mamma Joy's reappearance, he languidly dipped into his Tesco's shopping bag and produced a bundle of fifty pound notes. He smugly peeled off eight.

'Don't forget.' Maddy had to strain to hear him above the tape deck thudding at full throttle. 'I know where you live.'

'Oh, well, hey! Then come on over – *the dog's in heat.*'

'Want any gear?' As there didn't appear to be any bullet

holes in her upper body, Maddy presumed he hadn't heard her. 'How 'bout some blow?' he shouted.

Jack beamed at Fin euphorically, ravenous for experience. Maddy remembered back to the days when she too, had got high on life . . . but lately she'd built up quite a tolerance. Oh, where was Gillian when she needed her? Throughout Maddy's life, men had come (the nights they didn't have Brewers Droop) and gone. It was her female mates who'd remained true blue. Split up with a man and people cluck and sympathize; they read you Dorothy Parker poems and buy you exotic cocktails with umbrellas in them. They rush over with *Tank Girl* video rentals. Break up with a best friend and nobody could give a fig. Bugger it. How the hell had she eneded up with such a pair of warm personal enemies?

As she snatched the money from Fin's grimy fingers, Maddy had an awful feeling about the dice dangling from his rear vision mirror. They were loaded.

21. Eggs Benedict

Gillian, a graduate of the Prudence Prendergast Finishing School, was at a loss to know the correct etiquette in finding a live sperm donor. She'd thought about insemination, but the anonymity of it worried her. What if he had bad teeth? Ingrowing toenails? A tendency to heavy-metal music? The question was: how did one go about enticing a man with whom one wanted to have babies? Perfume ads were full of promises of romantic attraction. Obsession said, 'I'm a fun-loving babe.' Allure said, 'You'll have to buy me an expensive dinner first.' What Gillian needed was a perfume which said, 'Fabulously Shagable Sex Goddess Who Wants You To Father Her Children. And I'm *Ovulating Now*.'

With her eggs counting down to their monthly blast off, she enlisted the help of a computer dating service. Her perfect match, it appeared, was Benedict, a six foot one, thirty-two-year-old Open University lecturer, with hazel eyes who liked travel. He was, Gillian decided, a N.B.F.M.K. (Not Bad For Milton Keynes). But she lost her appetite even before they sat down for dinner.

'What makes Chinese women so wonderful,' said Ben, authoratitively, sucking an olive from it's tiny skewer, 'is the small vagina. It just goes "Pop!"'

What would he make of *her*? Gillian wondered, grimly. *Channel Tunnel*? 'Yes, quite satisfactory,' she retorted snidely, 'if you've got a minute penis. Personally,' she said, pushing up on to her high heels, 'I prefer a man who touches the sides. Like nature, I abhor a vacuum.'

He wasn't a N.B.F.M.K. after all, but an A.A.A. (Absolutely Awful Anywhere).

And so her biological clock ticked on.

22. The Earth Mother Mafia

The little girl in the red jumpsuit was interrogating her minder about why exactly the cow felt compelled to jump over the moon. The freckled three-year-old was meticulously wedging Smarties up her nostrils while explaining to a plastic Power Ranger that she '*had* to do it for the aardvarks'. And the four-year-old wearing a tea cosy as a balaclava was demanding to know if there was a God

'Who cares?' butted in Maddy, winking at the woman the child had been berating. 'Mummy and I are too busy worrying whether or not we can get a babysitter at five minutes' notice, aren't we?'

The young woman in stretch leggings and T-shirt eyed Maddy coolly. '*You're* a mum aren't you? *We're* the nannies. The *Mothers*' – she said the word as though it was carcinogenic – 'are over there.'

'Oh, right.' Maddy reshouldered her nappy bag, hoisted Jack up on to one hip and crossed the old church to join the parents in the pews beneath the ornate organ pipes. The mothers, despite hastily applied lipstick and liberal coatings of Estée Lauder's Beauty Flash Balm, couldn't disguise their exhaustion. The nannies – gregarious, well groomed and Adidas-clad – looked more like personal trainers.

'Are you a Tiny Tots Mum or a Crescendo Mum?' beamed a woman in her early thirties, in a cheesecloth smock through which you could strain tofu.

'Um . . .'

'It's just that I haven't seen you at this group before. I'm the mother of Smarties-Up-Nose. And this' – she indicated the woman on her left – 'is the mother of Squashed-Banana-In-Hair.'

'Um . . . I'm Madeline and this is Jack.'

'Laeticia!' Smarties-Up-Nose embraced Cheesecloth Smock.

'Ophelia!' Banana-In-Hair bounced up to *his* mum.

'Your *kids* call you by your *first* names? Jeepers, you're very informal around here,' Maddy joked. 'I mean, it's not as though you've known each other all that very long.'

The mothers gave Maddy a distrustful look.

Laeticia indicated the nannies on the other side of the room with a slight inclination of her diamanté slide-combed cranium. 'You're one of *us*?' she asked, suspiciously.

'A mum? Oh, yeah . . . from the estate.' 'Estate' made the confusion of tower blocks and dilapidated tenements sound so grand. Hitler's bombs had left London randomly pot-holed. Housing estates had mushroomed, fed on the fertilizer of post-war socialist idealism, and now sat hugger-mugger with the interior-designed homes of the fiercely fashionable. Laeticia's entire demeanour softened into a throb of insincerity. 'Oh . . . Sebastian . . . *do* meet our latest recruit . . .' She was over-enunciating all of a sudden, like a children's TV presenter. 'This is Madeline. From the *estate*. Sebastian is our resident New Man.'

Maddy was yet to be convinced that such a species existed. In her books, having poor musculature and reeking of patchouli oil did not a Male Feminist make. 'Sebastian's writing a book about his fathering experiences . . .'

'I'm in it!' bragged Ophelia.

'So am *I* . . .' amended Laeticia, proprietorially.

Sebastian, a sleeping newborn cocooned up against his chest, looked up languorously from his lined notebook. He examined Maddy over his fashionable John Lennon specs. 'Hi.' The lone man in the midst of a group of lonely women, Sebastian didn't have to make much effort to be riveting. By the look of his crisp jeans and spotless jumper, no doubt hand-knitted by Peruvian lesbians, Maddy suspected him of being a Gentleman Father: the type who held forth at every opportunity about the joys of fatherhood . . . but farmed his kids out at the drop of a small turd.

'So, what do you think, Sebastian?' beamed Ophelia, holding up a Peter Pan costume she'd been working on.

'Seb! Seb!' Sebastian's toddler waddled up to him. 'Poopies.'

Sebastian's eyes darted around helplessly. Ophelia and Laeticia both sprang into action.

'I *was* tempted to work on a Disney characterization . . .' simpered Laeticia, beating Ophelia to the honour of bum-wiping Sebastian's two year old, 'but then I chided myself for not being more *original*.' Ophelia's smile deflated with the speed of a ruptured party balloon. '*I've* been stitching away at a little ladybird ensemble,' Laeticia added with mock modesty.

'And what about you?' Sebastian asked Maddy, sucking on

his Mont Blanc fountain pen. 'Are you helping to extend your child creatively?'

'Well . . . he's got an ear-wax deposit you could sculpt. Will that do?'

Maddy sensed all three of the Creative Play Evangelists place a cross next to Maddy's name in the mental box marked 'Good Mother?'

'I found that flash cards helped kick-start creativity,' Ophelia advised. 'Tarquin started talking at six months!'

'Winsome couldn't wait to talk!' Laeticia gushed. 'Didn't bother to crawl either. Just up and off!'

'I didn't mean to imply that Tarquin's not physically advanced as well! We *are* in my family. My grandma is ninety-two.'

'Really?' one-upped Laeticia. 'My Granny's one hundred.'

'Which is why I got back into my pre-pregnancy clothes so quickly!' Ophelia gestured to her labia-hugging Versace strides, causing Laeticia, in her billowing cheesecloth, to cram herself into a tight, ill-fitting smile.

Gene snobs, thought Maddy. With a couple of competitive mothers like this, *both* kids were bound to grow up to be sadistic traffic wardens with thick ankles and boils on their bums.

'Practically potty-trained by five months . . .'

'Gobbledee-gooking by four . . .'

'Well,' Maddy said facetiously. 'Jack came out of the womb playing concert piano, mastered CD ROM with built-in modem in the hospital and is currently learning Sanskrit.'

Make that two crosses, she forecast.

'I only wish Portia didn't sleep so much so that I could play with her more,' confided Sebastian, patting his baby papoose. The Earth Mother Mafia melted in his direction.

Maddy, who hadn't slept for six weeks, eyed him narrowly. It was a little like Twiggy complaining to Liz Taylor that she just *can't* keep the weight on, no matter *what* she eats. 'Doesn't getting up four or five times a night kinda get to you?'

'Winsome's a *fab*ulous sleeper,' Laeticia boasted. 'It's all in the parenting, you know.'

'I'm *desp*erate for another child,' Ophelia confided, looking into Sebastian's eyes. 'I had a Caesarian the first time. I feel, I don't know . . . cheated. As though I haven't found the Fertility Goddess within me . . .'

Maddy gawped at her. '*That's* like Terry Waite saying he felt cheated by being released before the electrode torture to his testicles.'

Sebastian flinched as if she'd personally flayed him.

'Though vaginally I'm beautifully intact. You had a rather . . . traumatic delivery, didn't you Laeticia . . .'

A hateful look flared into Laeticia's eyes. 'Yes, but giving birth naturally . . . it did so make me feel like a *Real Woman*.'

Ophelia smiled with asperity. 'So did eating my placenta – freeze-dried.'

'*Dried?*' upstated Laeticia. 'I ate mine *raw*.'

While the babies and toddlers romped unattended on the church floor, this Breast-is-Best Brigade – all divorced, separated or married to workaholic left-wing barristers – pretended that they weren't flirting with the Earth Father whilst lecturing Maddy on ways to become a Better Mother.

'You're not giving him fluoride?! Oh, well, don't worry. He does have another set of teeth to come and it *might* not affect them,' volunteered a woman whose baby was delivered to the strains of Mozart by a Leboyeur-trained spiritualist in a heated swimming pool beneath a full moon.

'If he's not sleeping, he must be insecure. Perhaps you don't spend enough time with him?' prompted a woman who spent *her* spare time knitting organic mung beans.

'Perhaps you're spending too *much* time with him?' advised the Leboyeur Lobbyist. 'What a child needs is independence.'

'You let him watch *television*? Tobias is only allowed one animated short – the Eastern European ones are best – per week. Otherwise he'd never fit in his gestalt therapy and Suzuki lessons,' pontificated the sort of woman who volunteered for medical research in order to save rats and monkeys the discomfort of being used to advance the health of human beings.

Sebastian, too, was not short of advice on how to be a Good Mother. 'Best to begin sex instruction, including oral, at about four or five.' (Such instruction on the estates, Maddy brooded, would guarantee you four or five years inside, *minimum*.) 'My children will know the erotic details of their conceptions, and they'll be closer to me because of it.' The Earth Mother Mafia sighed audibly, feminine nails sucked to his masculine magnet. 'I lie my children on the floor and draw outlines of them on paper, then encourage them to stick cut out penises and vaginas on the outlines, and chat about them.'

'And what does your wife think about this?' Maddy asked, flabbergasted.

Sebastian was swift to point out that he preferred the word

'companion'. 'It's a gender-inclusive, non-heterosexist substitute for the word 'Spouse', he explained.

What it *meant*, Maddy decoded, was that he screwed around.

Beaming at each other like Christian Scientists, the Maternally Correct went on to recommend cottonwool balls over nappy-wipes, professionally fitted shoes over hand-me-downs, home-made food over the canned variety. Maddy mused that far more irritating than a baby who won't sleep, eat or behave, is some Ayatollah of Baby Care advising you on *why* your baby won't sleep, eat or behave.

'The only parental tip *I* have is how to find his missing Lego. Turn off the lights and saunter round in bare feet. One crushed instep later and, ouch! You've found it!' Maddy volunteered, determined to be sociable. 'Oh, and to blame everything which happens on teething. Including giving up breastfeeding.'

'Oh, you mustn't give up! Breastfed babies have a higher intelligence,' effervesced Sebastian, his orbs riveted on Ophelia's stupendous mammaries.

'Oh, what the fuck would *you* know about it? First off, you have no tits and second off, when you're not coming to mothers groups in a pathetic attempt to come on to mothers, your baby is no doubt tended by tribes of domestics from the Developing World who live on *my* estate.'

Maddy caught herself. She hadn't come to fight with the Islington New Labourites. She'd come to make friends. To have a conversation which didn't involve drool or stool. To actually see people synchronizing their lips with their brains. It was just a shame that here the trains of thought were so self deluded. All passengers for Self Delusion, we are now approaching your station . . .

'I'm sorry ... it's just ... I dunno,' Maddy acquiesced. 'Every time I get a handle on this mothering bizzo, the training manual seems to get revised. Still, I guess there's only one thing you *really* need to remember as a mum ...' She smiled warmly, trying to make amends. 'If you shake him too hard he'll get brain damage!'

The stunned mullet expressions on the faces encircling her suggested to Maddy that Mamma Joy's quip had not gone over quite as she'd intended. 'It's a joke ... Honestly,' she jibed. 'I only hit my kid in self-defence.'

The Stepford Mums shrank away from her.

'Oh, you must never hit your baby,' chided Ophelia.

'Tell me,' asked Laeticia, stuffing her daughter's limbs into the half-finished ladybird costume, 'have you thought about therapy?' God, thought Maddy, give a kid Calpol and they'd arrest you for membership of a Columbian drug cartel.

'*Do* give me your address ...' pressed the man who liked to give his kids pin-on penises. '*What* was your surname again?'

'Sebastian has contacts with social services,' Laeticia patronized, uncapping his fountain pen and handing it to him. 'People who can *help*.'

Authorities on the sniff. That was just what she needed. 'Hey, Laeticia,' Maddy stalled, as she extracted Jack from the clutches of Smarties-Up-Nose and Mashed-Banana-In-Hair. 'Did you know that ladybirds have a dark side? Oh yeah. Promiscuous Cannibals. Actually, the females often feed and bonk at the same time. Not to mention rampant VD.' It was something Alex had told her.

Bolting out into the rose garden of the church grounds,

Maddy was pulled up short by the sight of a young mother, weeping. At last, empathized Maddy, a soulmate.

'It's my four-year-old son,' she sobbingly replied to Maddy's kind enquiry.

'I know . . . I know . . .' Maddy sympathized, ready to offer tissues, whisky, bulk order Mars Bars.

'*He's not taking to his French!*'

Maddy ran, sprinted almost back to the estate. She refused to believe that she was the only mum who didn't cope. Okay, they may look like the Perfect Mothers pictures on Life Insurance Brochures, but to Maddy's mind they were either lying . . . or taking a *lot* of drugs.

23. Egg-flip

....

Gillian admitted that there were always going to be things about which one could do nothing – husbands being unfaithful, the supermarket Express check-out queue moving more slowly than the other lanes, freak asteroids . . . but an underutilized womb wasn't one of them.

'That "ideal man" you so kindly sorted out for me.' Gillian poked the polystyrene chest of the Milton Keynes computer dating agency expert. 'He's *worn out*. What else do you have in stock?'

The assistant, whose desk bore the plastic name-plate 'Marina', busied her fingers over the chattering computer keys.

'Ah . . .' She looked up, wreathed in smiles. 'Now, this fella's a catch. Just come free again. The best on our books.'

'A little like saying Rafsanjani is a nice Muslim' – Gillian snatched the print-out – 'he's *still* a fundamentalist, dah-ling.'

'Ap*par*ently' – Marina leant conspiratorially close – 'he's got a beef bayonet which could double as a draught excluder.'

Gillian was not disappointed. At first. It wasn't until halfway through their amorous encounter that he informed her about his operation. Sorry, *her* operation, at a gender re-alignment clinic.

'What?' Gillian gasped, as the hideous reality dawned. 'You're shooting *eggs* into me?'

So far so good. Next month, Gillian vowed to be more discriminating. Before going out with a man in October she promised always to ask herself one very important question: *does he have his own penis?*

24. Mad Cow's Disease

If motherhood were advertized in a job column, it would read:

'Hours – constant. Time off – nil. All food and entertainment supplied by you. No over-time. No sick pay. No holiday pay. No weekend leave. No pension. Must be good at athletics, home repairs, making mince interesting and finding the pair to the other glove. Fringe benefits, none.'

Now *there's* a career move, Maddy lectured herself. Would *you* take this job? *I don't think so.*

By October Maddy's self-esteem was on a par with Kafka's cockroach. The repetition, the banality; her life had become bad wallpaper. Maddy couldn't believe she had done this to herself, of her own volition.

Sod it. How can you be responsible for anyone else, she lashed at herself, when you can't even find an unused nursing pad?

Oblivious to his mother's angst, six-and-a-half-month-old Jack continued practising his pre-crawl rock, as though he had an invisible Sony Walkman strapped to his head. Maddy watched him doing chin-ups on the cot side. It'd be steroids and jockstraps next. No one had told her that babies resemble the most selfish, demanding lover you ever had. Always hungry, but won't eat what you cook. Always tired, yet won't sleep. Chucking things all over the house, yet never picking up after himself. Throwing tantrums, yet never saying he was sorry. And possessive! Jack was jealous of other people coming anywhere near her. He hated her being on the phone ... wouldn't even let her go to the loo on her own. All day long, he just sat around in his vest, waiting to be amused.

But amusing him was hard. No matter where Maddy ventured on the estate, the feeling that she was being watched intensified. Her skin crawled and the hairs on the back of her neck looked as if they'd been spiked with gel. She felt sure it was the police. But the only life form she bumped into on a regular basis was Fin. On Maddy's list of People You'd Least Like to Be Stuck in A Lift With, the loan shark was number 5 ... After Dwina, Peregrine, Slynne and Newt Gingrich.

'Ya know, it's single mums like you what provide me regular income. Hand over their child benefit book every two weeks and I'll keep off their back for a while.' He had her pinned up against a poster: 'A safer, happier place to live,' promoting the success of the local Neighbourhood Watch scheme. 'Uverwise ... just cause you're female, don't fink you can get away wiv not payin' me back. I'm not opposed to a bit of slappin'. Usually get anuva girl to do it for me. If that don't work ... well, negative client care outcome is not unheard of, right?'

'Sorry?'

'A terminal episode.' Fin crushed his can of Foster's up against his forehead then jet-propelled the flattened end product at a passing pedestrian, proving her suspicion that this was a bloke who'd been given his brain for nothing. Just a spinal column would have done.

Barricaded back in the crumbling flat of Edifice Wrecks –

on the whole she'd decided against high-rise living. There were just too many things to jump off. Maddy sat epoxy-resined to the radio (She'd despaired of television. It was too full of families who made the *Waltons* look depressed) . . . until the day she found herself imploding at the sound of Alex's creamy confidences to Sue Lawley on *Desert Island Discs*.

'The truth is, Sue . . . do you mind if I call you Sue?' Even on radio, his sex appeal was deadly. It really should be registered at Police Headquarters as a lethal weapon. 'I didn't cut the marital mustard. Hell, I wasn't even in the *jar* . . . But I love my kids.' *He loved his kids?* 'Children need their fathers.'

'Pig's arse! Jack needs you as much as the bloody Emperor needs a wardrobe for his new bloody clothes!' Maddy fumed. She was buggered if she knew why all the men in her life had been such duds. She would never date again – well, not without a Dudometer surgically attached. That way she may finally fall for a bloke who didn't belong to the Fig Jam fraternity – Fuck I'm Good, Just Ask Me.

She furiously swivelled the dial, only to get an earbashing from a Tory politician, flapping his gums about the sponging existence of single mothers. 'Mad cows,' he called them. She looked around her dismal little flat and thought of her imminent pulverization, courtesy of Fin.

'Yes, this is why I became a single mum,' she sobbed, face like a wet week, to the wilted aspidistra. 'I just couldn't resist the bloody *glamour* of it all.'

25. Eggs Over Easy

On the whole, certain conversational openings are not as prudent as others. 'You've put on a little weight, haven't you?' is, for example, not a particularly endearing question. Nor is, 'May I have the name of your plastic surgeon?' But these were positively winning compared to the dialogue Gillian found herself having with the men she met through the Lonely Hearts columns of England's leading newspapers.

A confession from one latent Lothario that he bought his sex toys from a surgical supply shop brought the conversation to a flaccid conclusion.

Gillian's next male selection fared no better after he had suggested she come up and see his press cuttings: a rare collection of every story ever published about homicidal American postal workers.

Her third potential partner did at least manage to exchange a few pleasantries about favourite holiday destinations before commenting that Gillian was the first partner he'd had who was biodegradable.

By the end of October, Gillian had a feeling she would give up on finding a sperm donor through the personal ads; she figured it was foolish to bonk outside her species.

This view was confirmed when her fourth and final feasible Romeo, having confided his preference for eel insertion, asked Gillian what *she* really liked in bed.

'Breakfast,' Gillian found herself replying, rather dismally.

26. Missing Persons Bureau

By November, Maddy was seriously considering going to the Missing Persons Bureau.

'And who's missing?' they would ask.

'The person I was B.C. . . . Before Childbirth.'

It was a strange combination – never a nanosecond alone, yet constantly lonely. When pushing a pram you might as well be swaddled in the Invisible Man's bandages. Society had handed Maddy her eviction notice. She was a runner-up in the Human Race.

Forget her 'chequered past'. What Maddy desperately wanted was a chequered *present*. She found herself yearning for someone with whom she could be intimate. Someone to tell her that her bum didn't look fat in ski pants and to remind her she was due for a pap smear. Bloody hell. It was just as well she didn't have enough money to go out to restaurants. The lovey-dovey couples would be a torture too great to bear. They should be in a segregated section: she would rather breathe in cigarette smoke than poison herself with images of smoochie goochie, kissy wissy.

Even if Maddy *did* have a god-damned social life, which she didn't, she had turned into one of those women who are always seated down-table at dinner parties. And who could blame the hosts? She was now a mother: more worried about teething rash than Tehran; breast engorgement than Belfast. The Government may be involved in yet another scandal, yet what did Maddy lie awake at night worrying about? Whether the light in the fridge was going off properly when she closed the door.

She floated in the bath, surrounded by wind-up turtles, rubber whales and Postman Pat sponges, turning the hot and cold taps on and off with her toes, for what felt like three days at a time, dreaming of when she'd be able to eat her way down through the cereal packet and *not* break a crown on a grinning plastic Disney character.

Her first sign of impending insanity was finding herself playing with the playdough . . . *with the baby nowhere in sight.*

She thought about taking anti-depressants to shut out her feelings of inadequacy and bereavement, but they'd cross over into the breast milk. And eight-month-old Jack, scooting around on his bottom in a circular direction, was *already* resembling a malfunctioning sputnik. Besides, motherhood was a slower and quieter means of self-destruction. Quieter than, say, a suicide bombing of Pet and Lex's apartment and less messy than a small handgun.

Maddy loved her son desperately, but felt duped by the Motherhood Myth – the way you feel duped after a facial when the beautician has talked you into £100 worth of Swiss rehydration cream and pore-pampering gel you can't afford.

And yet the women's magazines she picked up at the laundromat were full of slick articles on how to increase your baby's wordpower whilst simultaneously fellating your lover, filleting fish, and stir-frying a Thai extravaganza; pausing only to swallow. The articles were outnumbered by the books. 'Fair, Firm and Fun! Bring Out the Perfect Mum in *You*.' 'Mothering, not Smother,' invisibly subtitled, 'Babies, the Bushel You'll Forever More Be Hiding Your Light Under.'

Maddy's problem was that these publications had led her to believe that parenthood would be like getting a goldfish. Now she knew such books could lie. Something she should have realized after reading Sheila Kitzinger's infamous claim that giving birth is the ultimate orgasm. *Hel-lo?*

The second sign that she was loose in her top storey was that if someone offered her a night of earth-shattering orgasms or a full night's sleep, she'd take the zeds. It was tragic, but true.

The only thing on offer, however, was Fin. His interest rates for what he called 'petty cash clients' had suddenly, on a whim, gone up to 140 per cent. He suggested that Maddy work off her payment by acting as a drug courier or by lending a hand, literally, in his brother's massage parlour.

'So tell me, how long have you known about your third chromosome?' Maddy felt that this was a fairly good retort, seeing as she was in the middle of a nervous bloody breakdown.

Fin's formica table-top complexion, greyish white, flecked with freckles, turned puce. 'Enjoy bein' involuntarily undomiciled, do ya?'

'I'm sorry?'

'Let's call it' – he placed his foot on Maddy's doorstep like a conquistador – 'underhoused.'

'Come again?' Maddy drew Mamma Joy's voluminous dressing gown more tightly around her.

'Pay me or I'll torch ya fuckin' flat.'

That kind of brute vocabulary even Maddy could understand.

Like all mothers, Maddy wanted Jack to warm his hands before the fire of life (only she didn't have the pound coin for the meter) but torching Mamma Joy's flat she felt was going just a tad too far.

Maddy was busy incorporating every obscene term for the male reproductive organs into their cosy little chat when Fin thrust a newspaper clipping under her nostrils. Maddy found herself looking at her own mugshot, under the headline – 'Unlawfully At Large'. It was part of a colour-supplement article on the number of escapees currently roaming British streets.

From then on, whenever Maddy ventured on to the estate, she felt as though she was wearing pork chop jeans in a dog pound. She took to not looking back, in case something was gaining on her. In the supermarket, as the groceries belched down the conveyor belt, the cashier surveyed her with mild curiosity – a scientist examining a microbe. She bought a balaclava. Now there was a fashion statement. Especially indoors. But at least people couldn't read between the worry-lines on her face.

Oh, it was bad enough England being an island . . . but it was now entirely surrounded by hot water. Without passports, she would never get back to Australia with Jack no matter how much she longed to be shipwrecked on the shore of that uninhibited island.

'Oh, beam me back to the mother ship,' begged Maddy. 'Mission on earth aborted.'

27. Scrambled Eggs

With the months ticking by, Gillian's quest for an Artificial Inseminator became more urgent. During November's ovulation period, she went freelance. Her first choice was a footballer from the English team . . . but he proved a little uncooperative. This particular species of male has to go to Ibiza to mate.

This convinced her to settle for brains over brawn. But she lost interest in the newspaper proprietor when his foreplay included tethering her to the chair with an Old Etonian tie. 'But, my dear,' Gillian pointed out to him, scathingly, 'I've read *Who's Who*. You went to *Leek Boys High*.' She left then and there. After all, pretentious snobberies are hereditary.

Despite reaching the qualifying rounds for the doubles at Wimbledon, the local tennis talent was also disappointing. His post-coital comment of 'That was brilliant! No kidding. I was that desparate I could have shagged a dead dog!' definitely merited a morning-after pill.

In a fit of desperation and déjà vu, Gillian even sneaked into the boudoir of an ex-lover. At first she thought the Mono-Fibre Hair Extension King had been eating toast in bed; that would explain the little crumbs stuck to his backside. Except they wouldn't brush off. Gillian snapped on the light and peeled back the bedclothes to find – boils. His entire bottom was pebble-creted in craters. Now *there* was an effective contraceptive.

The Popular Novelist seemed a good biological match. But he insisted on neck-to-knee condoms and femidoms big enough to pitch for a garden party. She should have guessed about his anal retention when he arrived carrying a disposable medicated cover to put over her toilet seat.

There was the Aussie sea captain of some press baron's cruise ship. Now *he* was delicious. The sort of guy you could write home about – if your parents were into whisky chasers, flavoured French ticklers and doing it standing up backwards. But Maddy and the Computer Nerd had warned her off Australian men. According to Maddy, when it came to sex they had few criteria beyond a hole and a heartbeat.

The Tory backbencher. For a while she thought him her best bet. He had drive, determination, a Mensa club qualification and the cutest buns she'd seen all season . . . but he withdrew just before ejaculation to pleasure himself. 'Women,' he panted, 'just don't do this bit right.'

And then she got her period. Now the end of November, it was fair to say that on the breeding front, all systems were phut.

There may be one in every crowd, pondered Gillian morosely, but he never finds me. Who would have thought it would be so hard locating a sperm happy to get egg all over its face?

Gillian felt a change of plan coming on. She couldn't exactly say she was looking forward to it – well, maybe the way a turkey looks forward to Christmas.

28. Stop The World! I Want To Get Back On!

By December, Maddy never wanted to see a moist towellette again. There should be compounds, she thought, where first babies are stored: the kids we all made our mistakes on. Mind you, Philip Larkin's poor oldies were never given the chance to reply to that famous stanza of his. She reckoned if they *had*, it'd be to say that *Philip* had fucked *them* up something bad. Yes he meant to. And he did.

As if reading Maddy's thoughts, Jack, who at 8½ months was already pulling himself up on the furniture, gave her one of those 'hey, I gave you the best *year* of my life' looks.

Maddy was trying to forget the fact that it was her birthday. Looking in the kitchen, all she could find was the torso of a Ninja turtle and a piece of fruit about to pay homage to Lister. How can I mother, Maddy moaned inwardly, when I want to be mothered myself? Lightly poached eggs, Vegemite soldiers and a few renditions of 'Why Was I Born So Beautiful' would have done nicely.

Maddy wheeled Jack out into the raw rain and inhaled what was left of the air. It had been drizzling for weeks now. Londoners would soon be evolving webbed feet. The tower blocks loomed in the dark like massive gravestones; their epitaphs reading 'unemployed, pissed off and totally friggin' 'miserable'. There was a tourniqueted atmosphere, as if the buildings themselves were about to choke from the coils of anguish.

Moving out of the poisonous yellow light of the stairwell into the sort of pea-souper incomplete without Sherlock Holmes, two rough hands tentacled toward her throat. Fingers smelling of dog and McDonald's hamburger clamped over her mouth.

'Hey, Fin, you know I'm really not your type,' she said, biting one of his fingers and breaking free. 'For starters, I have a *pulse*.'

'Ja have anyfink to say to me?'

Maddy paused as if in thought. 'Um . . . *who moved the rock*?' If only Darwinism could be rewritten as Survival of the Wittiest.

'I was finkin' more along the lines of, "Fanks, Fin old son. Here's your dosh."'

'Look, it's been lovely, it really has,' Maddy clasped the pram handle, 'but I have to hyperventilate now.'

'How's that fat, black cow whose flat you're in? Still resortin' to non-traditional shoppin'? Reckon the cops would be interested in her "differently acquired" possessions, don't chew? Not to mention her lodger. Still keepin' you a nice cosy little spot in Holloway at the taxpayer's expense, in't they? I want that money by this time tomorra . . . uverwise . . .' He cast his cold reptilian eyes in Jack's direction.

'What the hell do you mean?' Maddy lurched back into the oasis of toxic light in the stairwell.

Fin took hold of Jack's stuffed Winnie the Pooh and decapitated it with his teeth. Evidently *not* the parental type. Maddy's heart contracted.

A police helicopter swooped into view, its searchlight raking the street. A calisthenics workout erupted in her ribcage. Prickles of fear tap-danced up and down her spine. Displaying all the athleticism of a tree-sloth, Fin sauntered casually into the nearest cul-de-sac of his miserable kingdom.

Maddy tried to tell herself that they weren't looking for *her*. 'You're obviously paranoid. *Just ask any one of the psychotic multitudes who are after you.*'

On jellied limbs, she quivered towards the supermarket. On the corner two men offered her some smack in exchange for sex. It had got so bad of late that even prostitutes were refusing to come on to the estate. The press euphemistically referred to this inner-city war zone as having 'special policing needs'.

In the market she bought fresh vegetables for Jack, adding it to a tab she couldn't pay. Children weren't a necessity, they were a bloody luxury item. What if Jack got sick? How would she cope? Maddy knew that on these estates, kids died at twice the rate of their middle-class counterparts. Their diets were worse, they were shorter, they weighed less. No wonder Jack was grinding his *tooth*. The poor kid was tense. Lately he got hysterical whenever she went near him. Maddy presumed he'd thought the Gonk slippers she'd borrowed from Mamma Joy were going to savage him. But maybe he too was having a nervous breakdown?

The truth was that Gillian and Alex were spot on. She was not worth a pinch of pelican shit. At first Maddy tried to ignore her guilt feelings. And yet, the sonar echo was there in all her thoughts. It resonated from the murky depths like a wreck: *she was a bad mother*. Maddy felt she made *Medea* look like good mother material. Jack didn't need a Child Disability Allowance; he needed a *Mother* Disability Allowance. He'd be one of those kids who won the right to divorce his parent. It was a dead cert. The god-damned humiliation of it was too much to bear. Why didn't she just get it over and done with now? Dwina was right. There were lots of wed un-mothers out there desperate for a little one. There was a birth dearth, wasn't there? She lay awake at nights drafting the ad: 'Adoption. One nine-month-old. One prev. owner. A Steal. Take tyke out for a test perambulation.'

Eyes peeled for the King of the Kleenex Climax, Maddy darted back out into the rain. She was ploughing across the street when Alex's Adonic face loomed at her out of the gloom from the side of a double-decker bus. She skittered to a halt, spot-welded to the road. Her face levelled with his Cheshire cat grin – the tip of his tongue a pink colossus of temptation as he advertised his new BBC series. At this porous proximity, she felt an unexpected pang; the pang, she admitted wretchedly, of unrequited love. Oh well, it *was* the safest form of sex. She'd have to ring Lex and Pet and tell them how happy she was for them say, at 3 o'clock in the bloody morning.

She was still soldered to the spot when the prowl-car skimmed around the corner. It fish-tailed to avoid her; the metre-wide speed bump laid in the tarmac to deter joy riders acted as a Thorpe Park amusement attraction, sending the cop-crammed Panda rocketing ozone-wards. Maddy took the traditional option of the wanted felon and did a runner. Dodging potholes, she grand-prixed the pram down a sidestreet, realizing, with a sickening chill, it was a dead-end. An underground car park afforded an exit, but Fin was already scuttling into it – a spider into his hole. Bloody hell. Some people get all the breaks – County Mounties behind and the Pooh Decapitator in front. It was like being asked to choose between lethal injection and the electric chair.

Terror-stricken, she wheeled around to see eight huge, shiny black shoes speeding towards her. Maddy experienced the pressure of pure terror. It felt not unlike trying to open a car door underwater – seconds away from sinking without trace.

'Where's the fire?' demanded one wheezing constable, braceleting her wrists with his hands.

'I think we should have a little chat,' coaxed another. This, thought Maddy, was police talk for 'You're nicked, dillbrain.'

'Um, is this the little chat where you warn me of my legal rights? Or where I warn you that my old man's the police Commissioner?' Maddy bluffed, half-heartedly.

'I'm turning out your pockets.' Pine-fresh breath Listerined its way into Maddy's face, as a second gumshoe rummaged through her soggy collection of snotty hankies, gnawed carrot stubs and corroded dummies.

The third cop cocked his bald head and considered her. He wore the kind of glasses which magnified his eyes. 'What's yer name?'

Maddy faced him, feet leaden, face ashen. Always tell the truth, even if you have to lie to do so; it was something living with Alex had taught her.

He scratched his St Paul's Cathedral dome. 'We'll have to take you down the nick.'

God almighty, now *there* was some oppressively familiar dialogue. 'Petronella,' she replied, effortlessly. 'Petronella de Winter.'

'I'll have to do a PNC check. Delta Tango Receiving 493. Name check. Over.' The first cop stroked his pelt of facial fur with one hand, while cradling his walkie-talkie with the other. 'Hackney Estate. Paradise Way. Stop and search,' he staccatoed. 'De Winter ... Petronella ... Foxtrot ... White ... Over.'

This was it then. The epicentre of terror. When Jack did file for parental divorce, *this* would be the first incident he'd cite in the proceedings. She clung to him, a Himalayan range of goose pimples up and down both legs, while fate secreted the lead weights into its boxing glove for another bloody round.

The radio sputtered. 'No trace.'

'Garn on then. Piss off.' The eight shiny black shoes, looking like a fleet of miniature limousines, went into reverse. 'Go on. Fuck off before I change my mind.'

Shit a brick, Maddy thought profoundly.

After tongue-kissing Mamma June's doormat, Maddy put the butt of a birthday candle in a rissole which would have been better employed as a tennis ball, and surveyed the wreckage of her life. The psychotic psychiatrist with an inter-fere-iority complex, the *Defective* Sergeant, the Great White Loan Shark, Alex the Earth Father, Gillian and her biological time bomb with the dicky fuse and the four policemen she'd lied to who, right this minute, were back at the Clue Factory contemplating her wanted poster. The list of people after her was getting longer than the Trump-Maples pre-nuptial agreement. No wonder she had the spiritual buoyancy of the bloody *Titanic*.

Maddy flicked around the TV but the only movies available were *The Three Faces of Eve*, *Sophie's Choice* and *Rosemary's*

Baby. 'Happy Bloody Birthday,' she said to herself, shuddering at the inauthentic taste of processed meat. Jack, who was cruising his way around the furniture, turned to her and said his first word.

It was 'Dad'.

It was then that Maddy decided motherhood did not have to be a game of solitaire. It was time to let the whole family play.

29. Girls' Night In

'Shock! Horror! Incomprehensible amazement!' Sonia, a 'warm spring' with a corrugated permanent which had gone from brown to grey to brown again, flopped into one of Gillian's velvet armchairs. 'Old what's-his-name openly displayed an interest in how to turn on the dishwasher today.' Ignoring the wineglass Gillian offered, she seized the bottle, chug-a-lugging. 'It's only taken him ten frigging years of marriage.'

Marion, a 'cold summer', appeared at the bottom of the stairs. 'Asleep. *Fin*ally,' she said, plugging in her baby intercom.

'How's *your* husband?' Gillian enquired, tilting a wineglass in Marion's direction. 'Does *he* help with the "domestics"?'

She too humphed into an armchair. 'Love, he *does* the domestics. Got another note yesterday. "Dear Marion, Gone off with Personal Trainer. Have tuned carburettor; topped up dishwasher salt; new video in machine."'

'No!' Gayle, a young 'warm autumn', appeared, readjusting her maternity bra. She too connected her baby alarm. The living room wall was now bristling with plastic illuminated boxes. 'What did you do?'

'Checked out what video he'd rented. *Four Weddings and a Funeral.*'

'Aren't you upset?' Gillian probed, with ill-disguised intrigue.

'Yeah. I've bloody well seen it.' Marion stuffed a wodge of cheese into her lipsticked jaws. 'It was the au-pair last time. She'll kick him out soon. If she values her ozone layer, that is. Potent digestive tract. The after-effects of a rich meal have often forced me to wear *scuba gear* to bed.'

'When I married' – Gayle, with scientific precision, was sorting through the peanut bowl with a long, lacquered talon, extracting all the cashews – 'I wanted a big happy family: six kids. Well, two years later, it's one and a half' – she slapped her pregnant belly – 'and flagging.'

'You think it's hideous *now*!' shrieked Sonia, the mother of a ten-, an eight- and a four-year-old, and therefore the group's matriarch. 'Wait till they take up the descant recorder!'

A small whimper came over one of the intercoms. All three mothers sagged begrudgingly into their chairs and exchanged unenthusiastic looks.

'It's not mine!' announced Gayle, authoritatively.

Marion swigged at her wine. 'Well, it's definitely not mine.'

'Mine neither.' Sonia was equally certain.

'I wish my toe-rag of a husband *would* go and have affairs.' Gayle placed a pillow behind the small of her back. 'Believe me, girls, marriage is the chief cause of single Motherhood.'

'I suppose your hubby never helps you around the house, either,' urged Gillian, topping up the glasses.

Sonia hooted. 'Husbands always get colds on Saturdays, have you noticed?' She snapped a toothpick between her manicured claws. 'Old what's-his-name has a metabolism which ensures that he simply *must* spend the weekend in bed with the papers.'

'If scrotum-breath *does* take the children,' added Marion, 'he develops some sort of nasal congestion, preventing the detection of dirty nappies. And selective hearing. "Oh, sorry love,"' she mimicked, '"was the baby crying?"'

'Not to mention selective amnesia.' Gayle put her hand over her wineglass, pointing, by way of explanation, to her protruding belly. 'He's forgotten how jealous he got of the last one. "Who's Mummy's lovely baby boy?" I said to my newborn, and my husband answered, all sulkily, "*I* am actually."'

Another staticcy whimper came over one of the baby alarms.

'It's *yours*,' asserted Sonia, pointing a painted toe-nail in Marion's direction.

'It's not *mine*. It's *hers*.' Marion tipped her hennaed head towards Gayle.'

'It's a cat,' counter-claimed Gayle.

'The books do warn that after the birth, men may feel usurped,' prompted Gillian. 'The books say that men like this—'

'Should be castrated immediately.' Marion bit into a party frankfurter deftly illustrating her point.

Gayle shifted uncomfortably, rubbing her distended abdomen. 'Fart-face was desperate for another one. Came over all masterful. Even when I still had stitches.'

'I thought children were a contraceptive?' proposed Gillian. 'I thought that every time you went to make love the baby cried or the toddler toddled in.'

'Vaseline,' said Gayle. 'On the doorknobs.'

'Oh, I tried that, love,' said Marion. 'Too painful.'

One of the intercoms hiccoughed into life, silencing the women's cyclone of cackles and guffaws. They strained tensely, before slumping collectively into subsiding cushions.

'Let's give it a few minutes,' yawned Gayle, inspecting a cuticle.

'Five,' added Marion, lazily wrapping her crimson mouth around a canapé so as to avoid lippy reapplication.

'I'm sorry,' Sonia spoke into the nearest monitor, 'but the mother you are trying to reach is temporarily disconnected. Please try again.'

The other mothers, mid-bite, swallowed and spluttered and brayed, then recovered and cast a rapacious glance over the remaining crudités.

'The last time that Life Support System to a testicle came over all "masterful" he slipped a disc,' Marion confided, chewing meditatively. 'Whenever he comes near me I know it'll be casualty in half an hour.'

'You lucky tart,' screeched Sonia. 'The only rash thing about my husband is his eczema. Last week I wore my Janet Reger lingerie with latex rubber trapdoors, dripped honey into my navel and sugar-coated both nipples. Old what's-his-name kept reading his *Telegraph*. "Sorry, what were you saying?"' she mimicked her husband's voice. '"Something about me not noticing you any more?"'

'I don't call it "being noticed" when he pounces on you, with the words – "We've just got time to do it, *I've got the bath running*,"' complained Marion.

'Or arrives with two cups of coffee, for *afterwards* . . .' added Gayle.

The women laughed with guilty gratification. Having recovered, Sonia then turned her attention to Gillian. 'And what about *you*?' she sticky beaked.

'Well, that's an interesting question . . .' Gillian, opening another bottle of ice-cold Californian Chardonnay, sloshed it liberally into her guests' glasses. 'I'm your unmarried friend who desperately wants what you all hate.'

'Call yourself a *friend*?' Sonia scoffed, agreeably acerbic. 'You never tell me *any*thing any of our *other* women friends have told you in Complete Confidence.'

'You want to have babies?' Gayle asked, amazed. 'I always picked you for the total career woman, what with the colour charts and . . .'

'Actually, it's the reason I've gathered you all here tonight.' Gillian discharged the most engaging smile in her social armoury. It was time to call a spade a penis. 'I am thirty-seven years old. I am losing skin elasticity, I have a greying mons and bum-droop. Add to that the fact that there are currently three times as many single women as unmarried men in England and you will no doubt deduce, as have I, that my chances of having a child the conventional way are rather slim. Anorexic, actually. Even if I *find* a partner, oestrogen-mimicking pollutants have produced a sharp drop in sperm counts.'

'Oestro-what?' quibbled Gayle.

'I could waste *months* with such a man only to find that we need fertility treatment which we won't be able to get because the NHS upper age limit is thirty-five. A donor is a possibility, but let's face it, dah-lings, the filter which applies to sperm donors is not terribly fine. Besides which, it *can* get complicated. The sperm-donor's parents suing for grandparental visitation rights, blah-de-blah. Can you imagine it? Which is why' – Gillian took a deep breath and zig-zagged the shortest distance between two half-full glasses – '*I thought you could lend me your husbands.*'

All three of Gillian's guests centred her in their uncomprehending, goggle-eyed gaze.

Sonia bit down hard. A trajectory of mayonnaise torpedoed out of the end of her canapé. 'Lend you,' she gasped, '*Ray?*'

'My *Andrew?*' gawped Marion.

'You want to have Justin's *baby?*' winced Gayle, gulping gratefully at the Chardonnay she'd refused earlier.

Husbands who'd only been referred to as 'that bastard', 'toe-rag', 'scrotum-breath' and 'old what's-his-name' all evening suddenly acquired names, good qualities – *haloes* even.

'Well, yes. That's why, out of my many clients, I selected you three. I mean, from listening to you all, I got the impression we weren't dealing with tiny friendship fissures in otherwise perfect partnerships, but Monumental Matrimonial Rifts. I can pay, of course.'

'Which one did you have in mind?' asked Marion, in an awed whisper.

'All three,' said Gillian, evenly. 'It increases my odds, does it not?'

The younger women looked to Sonia for a cue on how to respond. It seemed that Huffs of Moral Indignation were called for.

'It's prep*ost*erous!' Sonia huffed. 'How could you ask such a thing?'

'What kind of a *mon*ster do you think Justin *is?*' huffed Gayle, crabbing away from her.

'Marriage for me and Andrew is a life-long commitment,' huffed Marion, on behalf of her genitally incontinent hubby.

HMS Relationships, with the buoyancy of Robert Maxwell only moments before, had been salvaged with astounding alacrity. Into the icy silence whimpered another crackly bleat over one of the baby monitors.

'It's *mine!*' shrieked the pregnant Gayle, hefalumping to her feet.

'It's *mine!*' declaimed Marion, springing up the steps two at a time.

'It's *mine!*' announced Sonia, high-tailing after her.

Gillian flumped on to the ottoman. Well, *that* went over well, she thought to herself. Like Marlon Brando over a bloody pole vault. Through her blur of dejection, she became dimly aware of the doorbell.

The dishevelled shape huddled on the steps in the wintry damp, thrust a swaddled bundle into Gillian's arms and shambled over the threshold uninvited. 'Do you think it's too late for that termination?' it said.

'Madeline!' Gillian, spluttering in surprise, found herself choking. 'Must be a pubic hair,' she rasped, flippantly.

'What were you doing?' Maddy joshed, half-way down the hall. 'Yoga?'

'Ha bloody ha,' said Gillian, closing the door against the cold. 'A left over from last night.'

'Oh, a typical Milton Keynes dinner party.'

'I'm trying to get pregnant, if you must know.'

Now it was Maddy's turn to choke. Jack, who'd been asleep, woke with a jolt. He lay still, all eyes.

243

'Dah-ling, I have spent the last four months, ever since you . . .' – Gillian skewered Maddy on a look of utter betrayal – 'abandoned me, in the quest for an AI.'

'AI?' Maddy lay Jack down and shed her coat.

'Artificial Inseminator.'

'What?' asked Maddy, siphoning up the remaining eats. 'How? You just walk up to some guy and say "Hi, would you father my child?" Tell me every detail. Don't leave any genital unturned.'

'Well, agencies at first. Then those personal ads.' Gillian unravelled Jack and marvelled cluckingly at the changes in him. 'I've had every oddball known to womankind. I could have had a direct line to Doctor Ruth.'

'Anyway, you know you never get pregnant when you're *trying* to,' Maddy said between mouthfuls. 'What you should do is plan a month's scuba holiday, paid in advance. Buy a teeny weenie Yves Saint Laurent bikini. Get the job you've always coveted as a lab technician in an X-ray department. Train for a space shuttle mission. Honestly' – Maddy choreographed her long limbs on the ottoman – 'you'll be pregnant, pronto.'

Gillian clinched Jack to her breast, cooing and raspberry blowing and chortling ecstatically.

'But enough about *you*,' sulked Maddy. 'What about *me*?'

'Sorry, dah-ling.' Gillian placed Jack on her knee and jiggled him contentedly. 'How *are* you?'

'Fine. Me and this rock are just about to bludge the bus fare to the Thames.'

'Why? What's happened?' Using one hand, Gillian expertly poured Maddy a tumbler of wine.

'I'm running away from home,' Maddy said, quietly. 'You were right, Gillian. I – I can't cope.'

'Of course you can, my dear. It just takes getting used to. That time I had with Jack . . . well, motherhood, I don't know exactly, but it makes you a much more rounded person.'

'Yeah. In a square world . . . Will you mind him while I go and see Alex?'

'My God, dah-ling. The desperation of a mother to converse with someone whose nose isn't running is truly tragic.'

'I'm going to give him the baby, Gill.'

Gillian raised a topiarized eyebrow. 'You're *what*?'

'The point is, Alex is rich, well-connected, stable. Jack'll grow up to be happy and well-adjusted—'

'He'll grow up to write *Daddy Dearest*.'

'He'll have a much better life with his father '

'Maddy,' Gillian said urgently, 'I know I was insanely possessive. But I'm over it now. I'll have my *own* baby. We'll bring them up together . . .'

'How? On what? How long before the owner kicks you out of this place? I'll have to sell myself at King's Cross to psychotic kerb crawlers – except that nobody will want me 'cause of stretch marks. We'll have to eat dung-beetle shish-kebabs and canned dog food. We'll live in a discarded cardboard box under a railway bridge and he'll grow stunted and pneumonic and hate me.'

'Maddy how can you just *give away your baby*? What are you going to tell him? That you're at that "awkward age"? That it's just a "phase you're going through"?'

'I've made up my mind, Gillian. We have to stop being selfish. It's the best thing. For Jack. I mean, put yourself in *his* booties. Where would *you* rather be?' By convincing Gillian, Maddy hoped to convince herself.

The two women looked at each other in glum silence, then at Jack who was happily gumming to death a cardboard drink coaster.

Gillian's body started to vibrate with pent-up laughter; the sort of laughter that usually went with a padded room and a straitjacket.

'What?' asked Maddy, mournfully.

'Nothing. I was just thinking – it's the female dilemma. All the women I know who are endowed with progeny are sitting in friends' kitchens sobbing that if they *didn't* have children they'd be fulfilled as a female. And all the women *without* offspring are sitting in kitchens sobbing that if only they *did* have children they'd be fulfilled as a female.'

'Yeah, the other woman's grass is not greener – it's just bloody astroturf.'

They smiled faintly at each other, pained at the piquancy of their reunion.

'I've missed you, old thing,' Gillian confessed.

'Yeah, me too.'

A moment imbued with a dangerous amount of hug-potential was salvaged by the sound of clattering high heels on the uncarpeted stairs. A flurry of scarves and coats, carry-cots and nappy bags, cascaded into the living room. The haughty brigade unplugged baby alarms with disapproving thwacks, and backed, sleeping toddlers draped on over-coated shoulders, into the hall and out the door.

'Pervert!' came Sonia's parting, mock-righteous hiss.

Gillian held Jack aloft. 'Re*sult*,' she crowed, 'dah-lings.'

30. The Nick Of Time

Life is full of mortifying moments. Peeing in a train toilet, when the door is suddenly opened by a man and you're *hovering*. Scales which speak your weight. Asking a friend when the baby's due – and she replies that she's not pregnant. Eating bananas in front of blokes. Discovering, during the over the head-thigh-extension exercises in your mixed aerobics class, that there's a hole in the crutch of your leotard. All these things were blush-inducing, but nothing compared to the embarrassment level of having to admit to an enemy that you're wrong.

She had called Alex at the BBC. His new secretary, off-balanced by the genuineness of Maddy's urgency, had revealed his whereabouts at a private clinic. Maddy was surprised at the residue of sympathy which welled up inside her at the thought of his hospitalization. Her steps became more and more agitated as she strode up Harley Street. She was shown into a plush private room, with the creamy pink decor of a pastry shop. There, propped up on a bed in a white hospital gown, his face obscured by *The Times*, was the father of her child.

'Don't make me eat my own words, okay?' she said, bluntly, having barged in on him. 'I mean, think of the calorie count.'

'What the—? Oh *no*.' The editorial page wafted on to his lap. 'This can*not* be happening.'

'What happened to your *hair*?' A conspicuous fault line of yellow follicles zigzagged across his cranium.

'Oh, yes.' His hand flew instinctively to his head. 'Bit of a disaster. A failed attempt to lighten the hair colour so that the grey bits would blend in. Pet's idea. A' – he searched for the right word – 'rehabilitation procedure is required, called, I believe, "reverse streaking".'

Maddy tried to suppress her amusement, but it burst from its seams in a gravelly chortle. 'Sounds like a naked dash backwards across a footy field.'

'It's all right for *you*,' Alex sulked, overcome by a gust of absolving self-pity. 'You're yet to be mugged by time. In fact, now that you're a mother, you have time on your hands. I'm so jealous of you not having to go out to work. It's very ageing, you know . . .'

Maddy thought of her hours of vegetable mashing and pram pushing, and sighed deeply. People were always asking new mums when they were going back to work. *Back*? As far as Maddy could see, motherhood seemed to involve standing still while *work* came to *her*.

'So, what "words" were you about to ingest, Madeline? Perhaps you could make it an eat-and-run scenario.'

Maddy looked at Alex, lying there, his supple limbs brown against the sheets. She felt an urgent desire flicker through her body. It didn't seem surprising that she had loved him. There was no doubt that Alex had sex appeal – the trouble was, that he gave generously. She took a tortured breath.

'I've come to tell you . . .' It was the hardest sentence she'd ever had to utter. 'I've come to tell you that you can have Jack.'

Her sudden ability to hear the man in the next room trimming his nostril hairs, suggested to Maddy that she had come up against what's known as an awkward silence.

'Well?' she urged, touching his arm. The place where their skin brushed seemed to burn briefly.

'I – I can't.'

'Is it the . . . surgery?' she asked delicately. She could never go anywhere near him without every molecule of her blood heating and her heart racing. Another minute and you'd have to *soak* them apart.

'Yes, yes. That's it.'

'What's wrong?' she whispered, itching with residual affection.

'It's serious, Maddy. Life threatening. I don't want to go into it. Must be stoic.' He smiled bravely.

A nurse clattered through the swing door with a pre-op trolley. 'Drake, Alexander.' She recited from a clipboard in a metallic voice. 'Facial and abdominal liposuction, minimal hair replacement and blepharoplasty. Doctor Brennan, yes?'

Alex gave a sheepish nod of his streaked head. Maddy fixed him with a venomous stare.

'Oh,' she said, with pseudo sincerity, '*very* serious. Life-bloody-threatening.'

'All right. All right. The point is, Madeline . . .' Alex paused, as the nurse hauled up his hospital gown and lathered his abdomen. 'I don't want him.'

'*What?*'

'You've sucked out enough of my life blood. The Down Under Dracula, that's what Petronella calls you. And now you're out for another haemoglobin cocktail.'

'But, but you said you'd be the best parent. That you could give him the best start in life.'

'I just wanted to punish you. Good God!' he exclaimed, as the nurse bent over his stomach with a razor blade. 'Is that en*tire*ly necessary?'

'What the *hell* for?'

'Rejecting me.'

'That was nearly a year ago.'

'Oh, I didn't realize there was a statute of limitations on revenge.'

'Alexander, you may be fifty years older than your son, but you are just as mature. *Facial liposuction?*'

'Jowls, neck and eyelids. Purely professional motivation. The emphasis on youth in face-to-face contact with the public cannot be underestimated.'

'A case of mutton dressed as ram.'

'He's doing it for *me*.' The voice was so treacly sweet it wouldn't have been out of place on a crumpet. Maddy turned to see Petronella prancing through the swing door. '*Aren't* you, darling?' She hastily dashed the victorious glint from her eyes before gazing devotedly upon Alex. 'To look lovely on our wedding day.'

*

The colour chart on the wall of Gillian's living room was divided into four quadrants, named after each season.

'Now, let's examine your true colouring,' Gillian

announced with the remote but friendly tones of a tour guide. After removing the woman's insipid make-up (she was a full day-planner sort, Gillian felt, with not one single redeeming vice), Gillian seated her before a harshly lit mirror and stared hard into her face. There was nothing more cruel you could do to a woman. But killing a customer's confidence (Youthanasia, she called it) was a vital part of a colour-chartist's technique.

Making a lot of 'hmmm' and 'ah-huh' noises which Gillian hoped sounded wise and authentic, she then draped her client in a white muslin cloth and proceeded to hold various coloured panels up against her sallow complexion.

'Warm winter,' she finally pronounced, a cuisinart chop to her authoritative consonants. Gillian unstoppered her 'beauty flash balm' and began a rapid restoration of the woman's face. 'Watch the difference.' Women were generally so relieved to look human again that they'd believe it was the Image Palette Consultation which had redeemed them, and not Gillian's lavish application of half a kilo of Kohl.

'I need clothes which don't show the dirt,' the woman volunteered, with exaggerated affability. 'What with my baby and all.'

'Oh, you have a baby?' asked Gillian, swathing her victim in acres of turquoise. Standing back, she gasped, hand over mouth, as though discovering the eighth wonder of the world. 'That colour *speaks* to me.'

'Oh, yes. He's nearly one. And you?' the client asked, in a faintly interrogative tone.

'No terracottas,' Gillian ad-libbed, 'rusts or maroons. Never, ever. I'm godmother to a baby. He's upstairs, asleep.'

She held a cornea-sizzling swatch of aquamarine material up to her client's face and nodded euphorically.

'Crawling?'

'Mostly in reverse. And *pas*tels are *poi*son.'

'Where is he? I'd love to see him. Do you mind?' she insisted.

Gillian glowed proudly. 'Dah-ling, does Zsa Zsa Gabor turn down a wedding proposal? I'd like nothing more . . . than a sale,' she added under her breath.

There was an affected ease about the woman's smile. 'My baby does this rather amusing little bottom shuffle . . .'

'Sounds like he's dealing from the bottom of the deck!' Gillian said conversationally. She went to fetch Jack from the nursery, completely unaware that life was about to do just that.

*

'May I hold him?' asked Cool Summer, her voice the consistency of tepid mayonnaise.

'Of course,' Gillian complied, the fifty pounds for the course of Palette Consultations already spent in her mind.

The baby tugged happily on the pussy bow which frothed so frivolously at the woman's neck.

*

'For Christ's sake, Alex,' Maddy entreated, aghast. '*A weather girl?*'

'What's, like, wrong with that?' Petronella demanded, bristling.

'Oh, nothing. It's just, you'd be better off marrying a god-

252

damned shopping trolley. I mean, at least it has a mind of its bloody own.'

'We're rushing things' – Petronella planted a proprietorial kiss on Alex's perspiring forehead – 'because of the baby.'

She might as well have pushed Maddy out of an aeroplane with a cast-iron parachute. 'I'm sorry?'

'We're, you know, *expecting*.' She patted her concave stomach.

'Nurse,' Maddy said, feigning calm, 'when they're doing Mr Drake's hair transplant, get them to sew the hairplugs in the shape of the word "Bastard", will you? . . . What about Jack?' she pleaded.

Alex looked at Petronella, then gave a helpless flap of his arms. Maddy turned to the weather girl. 'It's strange, isn't it, this recycling urge which hits men in midlife. He dumped his wife for me. Dumped me for you. I give it one year before you're checking his hairbrush for strands which are not *his* . . . Pretending you like to take his coats to the dry cleaners, so that you can go through his pockets . . . Reading between the lines of every Amex statement, and the figures you'll be looking for will add up to "dinner for two".'

'I happen to believe marriage to be sacred,' huffed Alex, his lips protruding from a duvet of shaving foam. 'My affair with you was a complete aberration. A mutual aberration society. A' – he groped for the right words – 'sexual swan song.'

'Yeah, and Jack's our cygneture tune,' Maddy out-punned him.

The nurse checked her watch, braced open the door and manoeuvred the bed towards the hall.

Maddy held on to the end of the bed. 'Why the hell are you going through with this, Alex?'

'To keep myself young,' he said, with all the ebullience of a limpet. Maddy realized then that Alex *would* make a good politician after all; he possessed an infinite faculty for self-deception.

Petronella gave the bed an irritable tug aisle-wards.

'Alex, it's a midlife crisis. Women shoplift and get hot flushes.' Maddy yanked back on the bed rails, her shoes skid-marking the linoleum. 'A man's symptoms are remarriage with a bimbo, a Porsche purchase . . .'

'Bimbo!' Petronella's face clouded, appropriately for a weather girl, with fury. 'Could someone, like, call security?'

'That's how Porsches are advertised,' Maddy persevered. 'Used to drive through midlife crisis. As new . . . And plastic surgery.'

Alex suddenly appeared wracked, dwindled. The look in his eye was not unlike that on the face of a fish on a slab of ice in the Harrods food hall. Maddy's anger muted into an abstract feeling of pity. She felt a sentimental fondness for Alex; similar to her feelings for the picture postcard England she'd come all this way to find no longer existed.

The mobile bed was approaching a sign which read, in Maddy's heightened state, hilariously: 'Medical Staff Only. This door is alarmed.' And so, thought Maddy, am I. Grabbing at him, she could feel his backbone through the starched tunic. 'Alex,' she implored, 'don't do it!'

'Security!' The cry was echoed down the hall.

'Alex, I need you,' she begged from a mouth which was little more than an unsutured wound. 'Please help me.'

Petronella shoved the nurse out of the way and propelled Alex towards his vile but somehow inevitable fate.

'The only thing I ask is that you get him circumcised,' Alex said, his voice plaintive with defeat. 'After all, *I* was.'

'Yeah,' acquiesced Maddy, darkly, 'and they threw away the wrong part.' It struck her, grievously, that Alex was empty inside. She had been sucked towards him, really, like an astronaut in the gravitational pull of a black hole.

An arm-flailing commotion erupted by the lifts. Maddy didn't recognize the encroaching figure at first because it was running down the corridor. The only thing Gillian ever ran down were reputations.

'It's Jack!' she puffed, hurling her asthmatic form across Alex's bed. The rapidity of her descent sent the bed on wheels scuttling into a medication trolley which capsized a spectacular confetti of coloured pills all over Petronella. Maddy's belly churned and shrivelled as she gazed upon Gillian's ashen visage. 'She took Jack.'

Maddy gasped, loss filling her lungs. '*What?*' She shook Gillian by her bony shoulders. '*Who?*'

'Edwina Phelps.'

PART FOUR

Bonding

'Watch your baby; let him gaze into your eyes so that the outside world does not distract either of you. Never leave him in strange situations.'

The Baby Pack, Penelope Leach

31. Handbags At Dawn

Gillian, in an uncharacteristically Papal gesture, flung herself horizontal and kissed the pavement of a side alley in Soho. 'Somebody mug me! I can't tell you how div-ine it is to be out of the suburbs.'

'Gillian, for God's sake,' Maddy hissed, taut as a wire. At the loss of Jack, her maternal instincts had come tidal-waving back.

'Maddy told me you love dat place.' While Gillian and Maddy played 'Spot the Cop', Mamma Joy was threading a wire coat-hanger down the inside window of the passenger side of Rupert Peregrine's decrepit XJ6.

'A Milton Keynes shop assistant asked me if I was moving in permanently. "Can you get mangoes all year round?" I enquired. "Mangoes?" she queried. "Pre*cise*ly," I replied.'

The light in Peregrine's second-floor office was extinguished just as Mamma Joy eased the lock upwards.

'Gillian! Get in.'

Maddy and Gillian shrunk down into the rancid darkness of a back seat filthy with fag ends and waited for the sound of the key in the lock. The news on the sour-grapevine was that one of the Holloway 'lifers' was pregnant. Rupert Peregrine was the prime sleazy suspect.

The car lurched as Maddy's solicitor squeezed his waistline of Ordnance Survey dimensions behind the wheel. Mimicking the move she'd seen on endless TV cop dramas, Maddy held what she hoped felt like a gun (but was really one of Jack's Tommee Tippee trainer cups) up against the base of Peregrine's dandruffy skull. Gillian leaned over and extracted the keys from the ignition.

'Dwina has taken Jack.' Maddy's throat was so constricted with grief that her voice came out in grave, low tones she didn't recognize.

'Well, well, well,' Peregrine said, snidely contemptuous. 'Isn't Life bedevilled with perplexing little conundrums.'

Maddy thrust the baby's beaker harder into the blubbery folds of his neck. 'If you don't help me, I'll testify against you. Oh, yes. It was a pleasure working *under* him, your Honour. Very *laid-back* attitude.'

'*Really*? I would have thought absconding from Ye Olde Women's Prison could perhaps put a small indentation in one's credibility . . . but what would *I* know, a humble lawyer.' Peregrine shrugged, not a dent in his scabrous charisma.

'Listen, you swivel-eyed, impotent inebriate—'

'I see that your grasp of the Mother Tongue has not improved. There is no such thing as an impotent man,' he replied, scathingly, 'only *blemished women*.'

This called for female reinforcements. Maddy gave the nod and Mamma Joy thundered out of the shadows and origamied herself in beside the truculent solicitor. With scornful nonchalance, Peregrine made a sluggish move to open his door.

'Oooh, I tink you is in too much of a hurry.' Mamma Joy's chin rolls quivered with mirth.

'Especially when she's got a loaded cat in her pocket,' Maddy added triumphantly.

The fleshy acreage of Peregrine's face fell. 'You've got Butter Truffles?' he asked in a clammy voice.

Mamma Joy produced the over-fed fur ball and held it just out of Peregrine's reach. The cat whined harrowingly. Butter Truffle's owner twitched, perspired, fidgeted. 'Well?' she asked, stretching the feline's neck to a wringable length.

'I didn't want to do it,' he bleated.

'Do what?' demanded Maddy.

'It's genetic. A primitive instinct for survival . . .'

Mamma Joy tightened her lock on the cat's larynx.

'But various psychological nooses seemed to be drawing closer . . . and a career change appeared suddenly desirable.' He spluttered, catching his carbolic breath. 'Somewhere humid which involved cocktails with pastel parasols in them . . . Ms Phelps is helping me finance my . . . early retirement. All I had to do was draw up some fake adoption papers.'

A cry of anguish unrolled down Maddy's face like a window blind. 'Who for?' Her voice grated in her dry throat. It hurt her to spit out the words. 'When? Where?'

'Her niece picked them up this evening. New Zealand lass. On the traditional trek to Europe. The transaction, I believe, is to take place tomorrow. A vested interest, masquerading as magnanimity.'

'You're the one whose English hasn't improved,' Maddy yowled.

'Talk proper so's I can understand what youse sayin'.' The cat's Pernod coloured eyes bulged balefully as Mamma Joy tightened her grip.

'Ten thousand pounds, I believe, was the payment.'

The women gasped, as a trio.

'Nice couple, though. He's in advertising.'

Maddy fought back a debilitating fit of crying.

'What we goin' to do wid you now?' Mamma Joy tweaked his flabby cheek. 'Maybe I should just rape you?'

'No!' Peregrine mewled with febrile anxiety.

'You *say* no,' Gillian teased disdainfully, 'but do you really *mean* no?'

'Please don't labour under the misconception that this little contretemps of ours will not remain strictly *entre nous*,' he Uriah Heeped. 'Butter Truffles and I were going to satiate our hacienda hankering in a week or two, but we could depart earlier. Today perhaps. Hey, why be a slave to self-control?'

Maddy wailed. Why indeed? Her fist had come down on Peregrine's head before she realized it was raised.

*

Their rushed plan had to be simple. It was hatched over hot chocolate huddled together in Mamma Joy's fetid living room. Gillian fought recruitment. As far as she was concerned, breaking and entering was a much more terrifying, nail-nibbling experience for the break and enterer, than the person being broken in *to*. The person being broken in *to* only had to worry that you might forget to take the family heirlooms they hate and have over-insured. The breaker-*in*, on the other hand, had to worry about being skewered on gate railings, barbecued on electric fences, gnawed by Rottweilers and caught on closed-circuit security cameras *whilst having a bad hair day*. (A 'Lockerbie', she called it. A Hair Disaster.)

Then there was the trauma of finding a ladder in your stocking, once you've got in on over your face.

Gillian was saved the ordeal by the arrival of Sputnik. As Mamma Joy ushered her into the flat, Maddy was surprised to detect a meek look in her eyes; defeat in her rounded shoulders. Removed from the prison environment, she was like a bat in daylight – dazed and disorientated. Her predatory expression had collapsed into one of troubling humility. Her once purple hair had grown long and lank. The slave bracelet around her scrawny ankle made her look like a plucked chicken.

'What the hell is *she* doing here?' Maddy shrilled. As the hours ticked by, she'd become more wound up than a Taiwanese watch.

'She goin' to set de fire for us.' Mamma Joy had a burning desire to smoke Dwina out of her house by the means of a spot of arson at her office. Maddy, using forged social service documents (Mamma Joy's recipe for Cat Creole had proved an excellent Peregrine motivator) would then steal back her baby from the dim New Zealander.

'Why?' Maddy asked suspiciously. 'Friggin' hell! You're not still trying to take up residency in my undies, are you?'

'Wassat? I wanted ya to get it down, that's all . . .'

'*Go* down is the expression I think you're looking for.'

'On paper. Me life story,' Sputnik said, declining her stereotype. 'I can't write, see.'

'Wait. You wanted me to write your *memoirs*?'

'That Tonya Harding cow, Amy Fisher and Joey Bottafuoco, those Menendez Bruvers – the ones what murdered their parents. All them geezers got movie deals an' that. Who said, crime don't pay, eh? That's why I planted the Malteser. To have somefink over ya.'

Prisoners used to dream of escape, thought Maddy. Now they dreamed of feature films and book rights – *How to Kill Friends and Influence Morons.* 'You mean, you didn't want to have sex with me?'

'Shit, no. Wiv a skinny-arsed bitch like you?'

'But why do you want to help me now?' interrogated Maddy, with more hostility than she felt.

Sputnik picked at the hole in the sole of her tennis shoe.

'You could end up back inside.' Maddy watched her nibble at the skin on the side of her nails. They were fairly well gnawed already and she drew blood quickly. Her glazed eyes darted to and fro.

'Everybody knows me Inside,' she appealed softly. 'I'm a Somebody in there. Out 'ere, well, it does me 'ed in.'

There was a sad silence, while this wretched information was absorbed. A life of children's homes and detention centres and 'giving up' was all she could succeed in.

'Sweet Lord, gal!' Mamma Joy slapped her herculean thighs. 'Let her do it.'

Sputnik, taking Maddy's silence as a yes, was suddenly possessed with the radiance and energy of a girl in a tampon ad. Like a warrior going into battle, the first thing she did was shave her head.

As she watched Sputnik assembling her incendiary calling card, Maddy willed herself to stay calm. She had to bluff her way into Edwina Phelps's house, be convincing as a Scarf Draper and rescue Jack. She must *not* take to Dwina's furnishings with a chainsaw. Nor should she wait and strafe her with a machine gun. She might just put some Nair Hair Remover in her enemy's shampoo if there was time, but that was *all*.

*

'What the hell's happened to your tooth?' Maddy asked when they rendezvoused with Mamma Joy a few hours later in the estate's car park. The sparkle was missing from her smile.

'Dat nutin', gal. I soon get anudder one when tings pick up.' A majestic sweep of her arms revealed the proceeds of the diamond sale – a hot yellow VW Beetle holed up behind a graffitied lamp-post. The car was so dilapidated, no one would insure it – they'd just give you a survival kit. The stickers covering the chassis read 'My other husband's a stud muffin', 'We're staying together for the sake of the cats' and 'Smile, its the second best thing you can do with your lips'.

It seemed to Maddy that the stickers were the only thing holding the rust-bucket together.

'De get-away car,' Mamma Joy grinned.

'Did you *have* to purchase a vehicle with red flames licking their way up the bonnet?' asked Gillian, mortified. She was not having a good day. The grot and grime of Mamma Joy's flat ('That's not *dust*,' she had said, running a finger along a shelf, 'that's *topsoil*!') was bad enough, but she was now expected to get into a car whose bumper stickers she didn't agree with. 'What is left of my reputation will be ruined, you understand.'

'Your reputation is like your virginity, gal; just sometin' extra to carry around. It's de first time me have intermittent wipers!' Mamma Joy trilled. 'Hmmm, *yes*! I is comin' up in de world.'

With Mamma Joy driving and Gillian navigating (using the

map-reading technique made famous by millions of finishing-school females before her – 'It's one fingernail's length further towards the red dot and then veer left') they deposited Sputnik, beaming like a demented cherub, outside Dwina's office. Maddy disembarked near the Highgate address Peregrine had given them.

The freezing air punched into her like a fist; it was colder than a polar-bear's bum. Maddy couldn't believe the Gothic twist to the plot – plot being the operative word. The best position for Dwina-surveillance was from the shrubbery of Highgate cemetery. Maddy, dodging frozen blobs of dog shit, crouched amid the skewed tombstones – it was like being inside the dank mouth of someone dentally challenged – and strained to see through the ten-denier fog until her eyes ached. Branches scrabbled at the air above her. A feeble dawn tinged leaden clouds. In the livid light, London stretched out below, bleak and desolate. Something touched her in the dark. Her heart pogoed into her mouth. Before she could scream, the shape purred. Maddy looked down at a half-starved cat, performing a minuet around her trembling legs.

At cock-crow, as planned, Maddy, willing her teeth to stop castanetting, detected a smudge of light in Dwina's house. An eternity of minutes later, the front door of the gaunt terrace wheezed open. A spoke of light fell on the path. Dwina, still stabbing her arms into her coat, scuffled out from the dimly lit hall and hurled herself behind the wheel of her maroon Montego.

At first it wouldn't start. In an agony of dread, she waited and watched as Dwina tried to fire the ignition. The emphysemic engine strained. Maddy held her breath. Finally the yolk-yellow headlights reflected in the wet bitumen, wavered in the rain and she was gone.

Layered in coats and cardigans, Maddy the Michelin woman levered herself down from her eerie perch and, clutching her fake papers, rolled across the deserted road and punched the bell. She was so psyched up that when the door eventually opened to reveal a young woman with an eyelash curler clamped to one eye-socket and a mascara wand hovering near the other, the ordinariness, the indifference made her gasp. 'Yiss?'

Maddy extended her papers. 'Social Services.'

It was easier than Maddy had ever imagined. Jack was sitting on the living-room couch in front of a Disney video, flinging food in his renowned imitation of a lidless blender. He squealed with joy, put out his arms and, much to her astonishment, stepped towards her, legs wide apart like a gunslinger.

Maddy's heart beat gave a ragged thud. 'He walked!' In a daze of joy, she lavished him with loud kisses, even on his creamy, dreamy eyelids.

The niece picked black globules off the tips of her lashes. 'So what?' she shrugged, eyeing Maddy narrowly. 'You'd bitter hang round till my Aunty gits back. I'm jist babysitting.'

Maddy looked at her tangle-toed darling, his plump pink mouth gurgling, his eyes glittering with glee, and tried hard to swallow her elation. 'No time. It's all official.' She made a dart for the door.

'Hey, what's goan on?'

The niece's question was answered by the chilling voice of Edwina Phelps. Maddy hadn't heard the key clicking in the lock, but rounding into the hall, there was her enemy blocking the exit in a paisley dress disconcertingly similar to her living-room curtains.

'Hello, Madeline,' Dwina said with greeting-card courtesy. 'How are you? In all the chaos I forgot my office keys.'

'Oh, thank you, Fate Fairy.' Maddy cursed inwardly. This was the same Fate Fairy who'd given her a mother who knew the difference between marjoram and marijuana. The same Fate Fairy who'd sent Maddy into Harrods to buy a packet of prunes.

'A patient,' Dwina explained to her niece, in a voice of unfathomable composure. 'I'm her psychotherapist.'

'With the emphasis on psycho.' Maddy cleaved Jack tightly to her. 'Think "social worker" by day . . . Norman Bates by night.'

'You're projecting again, Maddy! Now give me the baby.'

'No! You stole him and now you're going to sell him to the highest bidder!'

The niece poked absentmindedly at a pimple.

'These women. They'll say *any*thing.' Dwina's voice was even, conversational, as though discussing a bus timetable. 'As if I could ever do such a thing. I *adore* children.'

'Yeah, I bet that's what it says on your charge sheet.'

'Now, come on, lovey. Give me the baby.' She made a move towards Maddy.

'Why?' Maddy shoved her backwards with one hand, into an armchair. 'Why the hell are you doing this to me?'

'Good! Vent! Vent! Let go!'

'What have Jack and I ever done to you?'

'She thinks *all* babies are hers,' Dwina explained with quiet lucidity. She was breathtakingly plausible. 'The trouble is, she hasn't found her inner child.'

'No, but you've obviously found your *inner arsehole* . . . If she's not lying,' Maddy implored the girl, 'why doesn't she call the cops?'

The niece, holding her eyelash curler like a handgun, turned on her relation. 'You *did* say you'd take me to a restaurant which revolves, Aunt Dwee, for my twinny-first,' she said, sincere with petulance. 'And all you gave me was that bloody salad dryer. I hate salad!'

'Sweetie,' Dwina said, placing her hands just so on her panty-hosed knees. 'Why don't you take my car to work? You're always pestering me about it. I won't be needing it today,' came her clotted cream consonants, 'except to take you to a' – she raised her index finger ceilingwards and twirled it – '*certain restaurant* for dinner.'

The New Zealand niece's plain impudent face lit up. 'Brill.' In a wave of her mascara wand, she was gone.

With bolt of lightning speed, Dwina's five foot three inch body flew across the room as though propelled by a poltergeist. Grasping Jack under her left arm, Maddy lashed out with her right. She felt like King Kong, swatting planes with one paw, whilst maintaining her precarious perch atop the Empire State Building with the other. Dwina yanked Jack's arm. He yelped. Maddy got a retaliatory hold on Dwina's hair. Dwina tugged harder on Jack. He screamed in pain.

'Stop!' Maddy begged. 'You'll break his arm!'

'Let him go then!' Dwina spat, looking at her murderously.

Maddy, her nose bleeding, scratch marks down her face, her heart drilling against her ribs, did the only thing she could. She let go of her darling.

'Make one move and I'll hurt him.' A rictus smile spread over Edwina's face. 'Women like you shouldn't have babies,' she said with cold-blooded complacency. 'You should be forced to wear contraceptive patches. With an IQ test required before removal. Woman like you should be spayed.'

Maddy stood still, mesmerized with horror. She tried not to hyperventilate. She told herself this wasn't happening. She told herself that Life was probably just a strange experiment being carried out on a lesser planet.

'Meanwhile, it's a simple equation. Too many single mothers parasitically oppressing the welfare system, and married, intellectually elite couples, who can afford babies – unable to conceive.' She gave Maddy a shrivelling look. 'We simply take from the poor . . . and give to the rich.'

Jack was whimpering: his angelic face streaked with dirty tears. Maddy's arms ached for him. 'And *you* get to make a heap of dough on the way.'

'Citizen's arrest.' Dwina snatched the key from the utility cupboard and gestured for Maddy to climb inside. 'I'll hand you over to Detective Sergeant Slynne, just as soon as I've handed over my other little delivery.'

Maddy's blood curdled. 'No!'

Dwina pinched Jack, hard enough to make him gasp. 'Well?'

Maddy's desperate wail was drowned out by the baby's sonic apocalypse. Numb with terror, Maddy was just inserting herself into the cupboard's musty maw when Mamma Joy and Sputnik moved into the living room in tandem.

'It's Cagney and fucking Lacey,' announced Sputnik, cheerfully.

In Maddy's fight with Dwina, exhaustion, poor nutrition and breastfeeding had taken their toll. All Mamma Joy had to do however, was launch herself at the social worker – a whale in flummery – and simply sit on her. Oh, thank you, Fate Fairy. All is forgiven, pledged Maddy, sweeping Jack into her arms and pressing him to her heart.

'I'm finkin' of gettin' anuver tattoo – a phoenix risin' from the ashes,' announced Sputnik, tethering the arms of the psychotherapist with a dressing-gown cord. Dwina twitched and fidgeted; a wasp in a jar.

'Lord have mercy! Gal, on *your* arms it's goin' to look more like a budgie over a Bunsen burner. Come on, now, move your arse.'

Ensconced in the back of the yellow VW, Maddy marvelled at Jack afresh. She inhaled his small cinnamon sigh and held him close. As Mamma Joy gunned the motor, Maddy's euphoric smile frosted. Coming down the street towards them was a blue Vauxhall Astra with an aerial mid roof: the unmistabale mark of an "unmarked" poice-car' – Detective Sergeant Slynne behind the wheel.

'Okay, okay. Let's not panic,' stipulated Sputnik.

'Christ!' Maddy panicked. Well, why not stick with what she was good at? 'Ram him!'

'Lord have mercy! An' mess wid me nice white wall tyres?'

Sputnik lunged sideways and hijacked the wheel. The Beetle lurched to the right, buffeting the copper's car off the road and smack bang into a red post-box. A cheeky grin split Sputnik's face. Slynne arabesqued in slow motion out of his vehicle, his springy ruff of hair squashed back on his skull like an Indian headdress. Mamma Joy waved him away with regal indifference and flattened her elephantine foot to the flimsy floor. Slynne tried pursuit. With one headlight smashed, he swerved through the grey drizzle, a cyclops shaft of light leaping in front of him.

As the getaway car rounded the corner under protest, Sputnik, trumpeting that she wasn't ''alf fond of you daft bitches' and reminding them to crutch some dope on visiting day, jettisoned herself from the passenger seat and rolled into the policeman's path. The last Maddy ever heard of her was a jubilant whoop as Slynne's car was forced into a rubber-burning, metal-crunching tailspin.

Beyond Sputnik, Maddy glimpsed a gleaming Saab pulling up sedately in front of Dwina's terrace. She knew, with a sickening stomach, that it held Jack's adoptive parents. Her baby boy flung his podgy little arms around his mother's neck, as passionate as Rhett Butler. His fingers rigamortized on to hers. Maddy couldn't prise them free. Her heart soared in her body. She smiled a smile big enough to admit a banana, sideways.

32. If You Can't Stand The Heat
... Get Take Away

The rendezvous address Gillian had given Mamma Joy turned out to be a private clinic in a formal, tree-lined crescent in St John's Wood. 'Never spit up in de air – it'll fall on your nose,' was Mamma Joy's parting advice as she grappled Maddy and Jack into an asthma-inducing embrace. Maddy loved her friend, but was not sad to see her getting out of the car and undulating down the road towards the nearest department store. Mamma Joy's driving motto was along the lines of 'So many pedestrians . . . so little time.'

Gillian appeared on the street moments later, staggering beneath the weight of two suitcases, three pot plants, six cardboard boxes and a fish tank.

'Think Thelma. Think Louise,' Maddy snapped, helping to shoe-horn Gillian's possessions into the flame-hooded beetle. 'We are on the *run*, you know. What the hell is this place?'

'Well, in the basement, a steady stream of men masturbate, helped along by soft porn videos – or for the real wankers, certain passages of Melvyn Bragg. And upstairs, women have their eggs extracted under anaesthetic.'

'What is it with you English people who can't speak English?' Maddy crow-barred Jack off her hip and gently deposited him on the driver's seat.

'A classified advertisement in the personal column of a quality newspaper. Well, the *Telegraph*. "Egg donor wanted." There's a national shortage apparently. The ad was placed by a sort of "egg broker". At £4,000 per omelette, it was an offer I just couldn't refuse.'

Maddy rocked back on her heels. '*You sold your eggs?*'

'Having babies in test-tubes – much less agonizing, dahling.'

'Why?'

Gillian's colour drained; her emotions held in check. 'You are looking, my dear Madeline, at an anomaly. Brought up to live luxuriously ever after, yet the only stately pile I've inherited is my father's tendency to haemorrhoids. Brought up to marry someone rich, yet not blessed with any particular pulchritude. With the onslaught of the epidermal sabotage you euphemistically refer to as "character lines", my only means of obtaining a sugar daddy is with a dowry. Post Lloyd's-crash, my chances of becoming a wife are, well, remote is the kindest conclusion. As for becoming a mother? Ah . . .' she sighed, her trademark bravado rekindling, 'so many men, and *so many reasons not to bonk any of them.*' Gillian rallied a smile. 'So, I thought to myself, why put all your eggs in one basket? Or, one bastard, if I were prone to the lowest form of wit. This way I get to have *thou*sands of little *me's* running around. Isn't that *fab*-u-lous?'

Maddy gawped at the idea. *One* Gillian had nearly upset the balance of the universe. She did, after all, think the world revolved around her.

'This way I get to make babies *and* money.' She handed

Maddy a thick wad of the same. 'Down payment now, dah-ling. More when I complete the three-month programme.'

'You did this for *me*?' Maddy blushed. She'd been on a regular diet of her own words of late.

'Not entirely,' Gillian bluffed. 'There is the odd incentive for remaining unfettered in the familial sense; a house free of televised sports for one. Now . . .' Lifting Jack, Gillian slid in behind the wheel and traced a crimson nail over a road map. 'I presume it was a member of the male species who devised a navigational system where one inch equals 100 kilometres.'

Gillian, thought Maddy with deep admiration, was the type who would have danced on the eve of the Battle of Waterloo.

*

'Where are we going?' Maddy demanded, as Gillian turned on to the M3. 'This is the motorway. She who hesitates is not just lost, but, you know, *ten miles from the next exit*.' Maddy's nerves were more than frayed. They were starting to resemble the hairstyle of a Rastafarian.

'Trust me, dah-ling,' Gillian advised, cocking an elbow out the window. For some reason Maddy did not find this thought a great comfort.

As they beetled south, Maddy kept a constant vigil for the police – scanning ahead for road blocks, searching the thundery skies for incoming choppers. Gillian was more worried about whether or not she could drive without spilling water from the terrapin's fish bowl clenched between her legs. Nor would she drive fast, in case the pot plants fell over in the back of the car.

'Gillian, it's a *getaway car*. We're *supposed* to go fast, for Christ's sake.'

'I nurtured that rhododendron from a seedling,' Gillian protested. 'It's indis*pen*sible, dah-ling.'

Maddy made a half-hearted poke through the junk stuffed to roof level. 'Oh *right*, like the glass snow-storm of Kuwait and the paper *"Piglet and Tigger Too"* party hats?'

As Maddy worried about how the hell she was going to get out of the country without a passport, Gillian admitted that she was also agonizing – had she turned off the heating? 'Did I disconnect the milkman, and the meter reader?' she mewled aloud.

'Gillian, repeat after me, *"My velour track-suit days are over."* Just concentrate on the road, okay?'

Gillian's driving technique chiefly involved a continual readjustment of the rear-vision mirror to lip level. When Maddy made the panic-stricken suggestion that stationary make-up application might be preferable to the Pointillist look, Gillian refused to pull over. 'We're only stopping for essential purposes.'

'Oh, you mean a tanning bed and the use of a curling wand? What about *food*?' Maddy asked, as the bitumen arteries leading back to the heart of London became fewer and fewer. 'That's an essential service – even to a pretzel like you.'

'We might be recognized.'

'What do you bloody well suggest we *do* then? Catch wild game and eat it?'

'Well, yes, dah-ling. Why not?'

'Oh, and what are we going to trap it in? Your *jeans' zipper*?

Let's just stop for a coffee?' Maddy pleaded, one hour down the motorway.

'Too dangerous,' Gillian insisted. 'There could be police.'

'What are they going to charge you with? Driving under the influence of caffeine?'

'I packed tea,' Gillian said, defensively, gesturing over her shoulder. '*Some*where.'

'Of course! English penicillin.'

'Well, perhaps we could stop and make a fire.'

'How?'

'You're Aust*ralian*. You're supposed to know how to do these things. Outback ingenuity and all that. Rubbing together two sticks, I presume.'

'Fine,' said Maddy, curtly. 'As long as one of them's a match . . . Where the hell are we going, Gill?' Maddy nagged, two hours later.

'Must you always bring up such contentious subjects while we're travelling at speed on a motorway? You'll know soon enough, dah-ling,' she stated, mystifyingly.

Maddy had a sinking feeling. Flying blind with Gillian Cassells inspired the same confidence as, say, an episiotomy performed by Helen Keller.

33. A Few Nappies Short Of The Full Load

I t took Gillian three circumnavigations of the misty car park and ten hair-raising attempts before she manoeuvred their flame-flecked neon yellow car into a disabled parking place.

'Why can't they have parking spots for *abled* drivers?' she asked, killing the ignition. 'That's what I'd like to know.'

Maddy peered out of the passenger window at a scant nebula of lights – bobbing lights. Her suspicion that she could discern boats at anchor was confirmed by the percussion of aluminium masts clanking in the wind. 'Gillian, where the hell are we?'

'Poole,' she answered, mysteriously.

'Um . . .' Gulls bickered tetchily overhead. Maddy knew just how they felt. '*Why?*'

'Because you are going on a little trip,' Gillian stated. 'It's a beautiful boat. A 44 metre Benetti. Belongs to a press baron. A mogul. The skipper's sailing it to the Caribbean. Tonight. And you and Jack are going with him.' Gillian strode off down the pier.

Maddy's eyebrows nearly shot off her forehead. They looked as though they were having a party without the rest of her face. 'Ah, Gill, I don't know if you're aware of this . . .'

Maddy, zipping Jack into his snow suit, stalked after her. 'But the Atlantic is famous for having no land mass at which to disembark when you get sea-sick.'

'It's the only way to elude Customs. Pretend the baby was born at sea or somesuch. Then you can apply for a passport in the Grenadines. Or simply buy one from a corrupt politician in Antigua.

'Gill,' Maddy panted, catching her up. 'Remember when you said you might be too old for jeans? Well, guess what? You *are*. In fact, I think it's senility, the way you're bloody well talking.'

'From there, Skip tells me you can hitch a ride with a "boatie", I believe was the vulgar vernacular – homewards.'

'Skip?'

'He was one of my AIs. A favourite, actually. My Swiss Army Man. Handy for everything, dah-ling. Can mend fuses, change car tyres, open bottles with his teeth and, oh! what nifty additional extras.'

Maddy openly gawped at her friend. 'You're putting me in the hands of a one-night-stand? Oh, that's comforting.'

'He showed me a lot of things actually.'

'Like what? His *gun collection*?'

'That Australian men aren't as abhorrent as you maintain.' Gillian had reached the side of a long, dark boat, riding high in the inky water. It was sleek and shark-like beside the other vessels. 'I was going through a stage where I had my heart set on having a little girl,' Gillian stepped lithely on to the ladder. 'I read an article about deep-sea divers being more likely to father baby girls than boys.'

'I bet he was a dud lay,' Maddy disparaged. 'Aussie blokes think Kama Sutra is some kind of Indian take-away.'

'Hyperbaric chambers, you know those tanks which are used to reduce pressure after diving—?'

'I know what they are!' Maddy irritably handed Jack up to Gillian on deck.

' – significantly reduce testosterone levels. Studies of Australian abalone divers and navy frogmen in Sweden showed fewer male offspring than average.'

'What was his idea of foreplay? Did he ejaculate into a mate's sandwich just for fun?' Maddy jeered. In the hair-brained preposterousness stakes, Gillian's plan was first-past-the-post. 'Lace a groom's drink with laxatives? Did you need sub-titles to decode the grunts he uses for language?'

'That's me all right,' drawled a laconic voice from above. 'Completely inarticulate. Communicate via the vibrations of my testicles.'

Maddy was eye level with a pair of muscly, leathery legs. She looked upwards into the weatherbeaten face of a 40-ish man, wearing a peaked yachting cap without irony. A hand of similar sun-tanned texture thrust downwards to haul her aboard.

'This is *him*?' asked Maddy.

'Hey . . . if I'd known I was going to live this long, I'd have moisturized now and then,' he replied, impiously. He offered Maddy a card. Her eyes strained to read the embossed lettering through the gloom. 'Skip,' it said, simply. 'Expert.'

'What in?' Maddy asked, trying to camouflage her embarrassment. 'Eavesdropping?'

'Parallel parking for one,' he replied, laughingly.

'*I* wasn't driving,' Maddy said, flustered. '*She* was . . . Anyway, what's it to you?'

'Come on down,' he invited, leading the way into the galley where he flopped into a leather banquette, indicating for the women to follow suit.

'I've cleared Customs. We leave in the hour. The guys, Bristoe – he's the galley-hag, the ginger-beer – engineer, and the two deckies – the lowest form of marine life, aren't all that chuffed about it. Women are bad luck on board. Sexual roulette, you see. We only spend three months in dry dock, the rest of the year, cruising. Bloke gets barnacles on his balls, savvy? Believe me, the second bang you hear when we hit port is the door closing. Sleep with one of the crew and the others get toey. But as I'm the window watcher' – the two women looked at him perplexed – 'the boat aimer.' They still didn't comprehend. 'The *skipper*,' he finally deciphered, 'tough shit. So here's the rules. No nooky. We hit the fart-sack by ten. And no red emperors in the head. Tampons,' he generously decoded, 'in the toilet.'

'What's in it for you?' asked Maddy, suspiciously, thinking of his barnacled balls. 'Some kind of sexual keel-haul?'

The skipper winked. 'A bottle of whisky at the other end,' he said breezily.

'I don't even know why we're having this discussion. Like I said, you've lost the plot, Gillian. Senile dementia's set in. There's no frigging way I'm going to sea, got it?'

'Dah-ling, *I* may have a grey pube, but *you're* stupid and *I* can pluck.'

'I have a baby! You can't take a baby to sea. It may have escaped your notice, Gillian, but sailors and babies, you know, they don't have a lot in common.'

Jack was holding his bottle skyward, like a triumphant

trombonist, improvising a silent rift. He dropped the bottle, belched magnificently, then plunged unceremoniously into sleep.

The captain grinned. 'Hey, my type of guy,' he said.

Maddy tried another conversational tack. 'But I don't want to leave England. I love England.'

The Skipper's forehead creased incredulously. 'Come again?'

'I do! The beautiful buildings, the leafy squares, Dickens and Doctor Johnson. The quirky little umbrella shops and ornate little theatres and – '

'England's the reason God invented the Greenhouse Effect,' Skip philosophized. 'This sucker's gunna sink.'

'To be tired of London,' Maddy parroted, undaunted, 'is to be tired of—'

' – Traffic jams, dog shit, water-logged leggings, the Hammersmith flyover, and haughty, child-hating, class ridden-ness,' Gillian surmised. 'Thanks to the Luftwaffe, the London you colonials talk about, the architectural genius of Wren and Nash, has been trans-bloody-mogrified into an arid waste of tower blocks full of people who end up in documentaries about chain-smoking.' She shuddered.

'Okay,' Maddy conceded, 'but Hitler didn't do anything to the people. Your dry wit. Your self-deprecating sense of humour.'

'Crikey, the English have so little *joie de vivre*,' intellectualized their cavalier host, 'they ain't even got their own word for it.'

'Who asked you?' hollered Maddy. 'I didn't know your testicles vibrated in French also. Jeez.'

'I can't see that there's a choice.' The Captain knotted his nut-brown hands behind his head and leaned back on his digital pillow. 'A bunch of perfidious Poms or a—'

' – Rod-walloper like you,' added Maddy sourly. *Perfidious?* Cripes. These were the best-read testicles she'd ever encountered.

'Well, make up your mind.' Skip pushed up on to his undone docksidered feet. 'We're throwing the strings off now-ish.'

Maddy got up also. She made for the deck. At the top of the stairs, as the cold hit, Jack's little body went rigid. He let out a wail with the audial appeal of a guitar solo by Sid Vicious.

'You see? Can you imagine *that* for three whole weeks?' Maddy justified, tossing the comment back down the stairs.

Skip shrugged. 'You'd cry too if you only came up to beer-gut level on adults; had to look up people's nostrils all day; couldn't speak the local lingo and were financially dependent on a moronic mother who doesn't know when she's being given the break of a bloody lifetime.' His eyes were ice blue; clear but not cold. 'From what I hear, it's your only way out.'

Gillian reached up and tugged on the cuff of Maddy's jeans. 'I have one thought for you,' she said, succinctly. '*Jack and Edwina Phelps in matching mother-and-son outfits.*'

Miraculously, Maddy's head cleared in an instant. It was only three weeks, after all. From the Caribbean she could hitch another ride, south, to the Galapagos Islands, Tuamotu, Tahiti, then on home via Samoa, Fiji, New Guinea. Maybe it would be good to give her enemies some latitude. The truth was that a birth, a broken heart, and a nervous breakdown or ten had left her too drained to go against the tide. She retraced her steps into the galley. 'What about you?' Maddy seized Gillian's arm. 'You're coming too?'

Gillian cringed, breaking free. 'In, out, in, out, all night.'

'Who?' Maddy asked.

'The *sea*. In, out, in, out, that's all it does, dah-ling. When I met Skip, we went for a walk up to the cliff – do you remember, sweetie? We finally reached the wretched summit. And there was nothing there. Just *down*. And again with the in, out, in, out. Ugh.'

'But, Gill, Australia, it's such a—' On the whole Maddy thought it best to avoid clichés with a ten-inch pole, but this was an emergency. ' – well, such a young country. You could start all over again.'

'No need, dah-ling. I have recently ascertained the secret of staying young.'

'What? Sperm facials?'

'Lie about your age.'

Leaving Jack toe-sucking on a berth (according to Gillian, since he was Maddy's progeny, a predisposition to putting his foot in his mouth was only to be expected) the two women returned to Gillian's overflowing car.

'Now, don't forget to keep up the flash cards,' fretted Gillian, trotting after Maddy. 'And don't de-gunk his ears with Q-tips; you can perforate the drum and—'

'Stop! As far as motherhood's concerned, I've amputated the old Guilt Gland, okay?' In a daze, Maddy selected essentials – bottles, nappies, rattles, rusks, enough powdered milk to sink a battleship – an image she briskly discarded.

'Oh. Well, just don't amputate it too quickly. You've got a hazardous journey coming up.' Gillian fussed, the confidence sapping from her voice. 'Wean yourself slowly. Only one neurosis at a time, dah-ling. Promise?'

They were facing each other, beside the Baretti. An uncomfortable self-consciousness stole over the old friends.

'Hey, um, I didn't mean it. What I said about the jeans.'

'I didn't mean what I said about you being stupid. Or a hopeless mother.'

'Yeah, I mean, Mowgli survived, right?'

'Exactly, dah-ling. Azaria is probably out there somewhere right now, being brought up by dingoes.'

It was more of a collision than a kiss.

'Are you sure?' asked Maddy, staunchly, one foot on the rung.

'Dah-ling' – Gillian slapped her abdomen – 'I have a battery-farm to run.' Though waving exuberantly, Gillian hurriedly shoved on a pair of designer sunglasses; not exactly requisite clobber for an English midwinter at ten below.

Maddy ascended. She did not look back. Slipping below decks, she gave a very good impression of a duck's back.

*

In the unlikely event of a conscientious Customs officer boarding to check the bonded stores, the Captain stowed Maddy and Jack in the engine room until they cleared port. It smelled of salt, fish heads and diesel fuel which throbbed through the engines like blood in a temple. Soothed by the motorized pulse, Jack suckled contentedly. Maddy curled around him like a mother cat. They dozed, Cleopatraed in milk, until the Skipper appeared with the all-clear.

On the bridge, they sat in silence, watching the lights of

Maddy's beloved England fade. Skip pulled off a hunk of bread, slathered it in butter and strawberry jam, dipped the crust in piping hot tea and handed it to Maddy. She realized with a twinge that she hadn't eaten in twenty-four hours and hoed in with relish. Improvising a little party, Skip poured a nip of whisky into the purple plastic top of Jack's bottle.

'Ah,' he exclaimed, post swig. 'Like angels pissing on yer tonsils. Go on,' he urged, offering her the plastic vessel. 'You could get work in the Caribbean,' he suggested. 'Or hitch a ride south. I've got a mate heading down through Micronesia.'

'Maybe I'll work a little first.' She caught her breath as she briefly espied Alex's roguish, impudent expression echoed in Jack's sweet face.

'A career and family juggler, eh?'

Maddy looked again and it was gone. 'Yeah. Do tend to drop a lot of hubbies, though.'

Skip shrugged. 'Baby kangaroos live in single-parent homes and they're pretty okay. Unless you miss the bastard, that is.'

'Miss him?' snapped Maddy, defensively. 'I'm as nostalgic about Alex as I am about the stitches in my perineum. I fell in love with a man with a high IQ,' she found herself confessing, 'but no brains – you know?'

Skip fiddled with instruments and logged charts before handing her another nip of whisky. 'Gillian didn't tell me much and I'm not stickin' me nose in, but it's taken a lot of guts what you've been through.'

Maddy felt liquidized by exhaustion. With Jack nestled in her arms she sank back, the leather upholstery sighing. 'Not really.'

'Don't reckon I could have done it. Mind you, I was gunna get me ear pierced, but I squibbed it.'

'Why?

'The pain! Haven't been to the dentist for twenty years.'

'Er. Remind me not to tongue kiss *you* then.'

'Well, if you *do*, check my upper left molar, would ya?'

Maddy laughed warmly. Jack, his four hair strands combed horizontally over his head in a fashion favoured by gerontophile newsreaders, was giving her a funny look; the look her father used to give her if she was wearing too much lipstick. But Jack had no competition. The only grand passion in Maddy's mind was between her and her small son. She touched his angelic little face, amazed. She kissed his warm head, over and over. Jack babbled back at her. She didn't know what he was saying, but he was talking in exclamation marks, punctuated with peals of silver laughter. Maddy felt a tremendous joy squeeze into her bone marrow. She knew then that this was the greatest love affair she'd ever have. For life. Unconditional . . . Although, on second thoughts, there *were* a few conditions: no more nursery rhymes dipped in disinfectant, crèche courses, nor was poo ever again to be considered a decorative option.

The sails of passing boats sucked in their cheeks to the wind. Water lapped at the bow like a cat. Take Two on the convict scenario, thought Maddy. Just like her ancestors two hundred years before, she too was making an inglorious, aquatic exit from the Motherland. England had lured her; a geographic love letter, unscrolling from Jane Austen to Vita Sackville-West; from John Donne to Alexander Drake. And Jack was its precious postscript. That was the Motherland which mattered to her now. The trouble was, she'd believed the sanctified, disinfected myth of the Perfect Mother. She'd climbed – no, pole-vaulted on to that pedestal. But like anything on a pedestal, real life flows on past, leaving you lonely, exposed, and covered in bird shit.

England was groaning beneath weighty statues of mouldy old Admirals and long forgotten prime ministers. What Maddy wanted to see were statues to 'The Unknown Soldier – a Mother of Five'. She wanted an inscription which read 'A Toddler *and* a Day Job'.

On and on bishops and cabinet ministers droned about Traditional Family Values. But Maddy couldn't actually remember ever experiencing them. Not on the poverty-stricken estates. Not with the Stepford Mums in the Mother and Baby Groups. Not amongst the boarding-school-bred, nanny-dependent middle classes. The truth was that the 'traditional family' was nothing more than a psychological theme park which politicians and Baby Book gurus visited occasionally, but in which nobody actually lived. Bloody hell, mused Maddy, uneasily, that sounded almost wise. Wisdom. Huh! She slurped at her whisky. Wisdom was the bikini Fate gave you, post-birth, when you had stretch marks, cellulite and acres of thunder thighs.

Above the horizon sat a lop-sided moon. The sun was going down over the land. A shaft of hazy vanilla light intercepted the gloomy clouds and bathed the deck. The spray from their boat glinted with rainbow fragments of light.

Just for a moment she glimpsed, there in the luminous foam, the possibility of happiness. She kissed Jack's eyelids, half shuttered as he fought off sleep. At least she was now wise enough to know that as far as Happily Ever After went – well, it was best to take it on a day-to-day basis.

Epilogue

34. The First Year Check-up

GILLIAN donated dozens of eggs to happy couples, then fell pregnant with quads, naturally – to her gynaecologist. The birth isn't covered by private insurance, but it is by the national media. She sold the exclusive rights to a baked-bean company making her incredibly rich and resulting in five proposals of marriage.

The run up to the General Election was marked by the sheer number of photographic spreads in glossy magazines celebrating ALEXANDER DRAKE'S happy marriage to Petronella de Winter. Personally he had come to the conclusion that he *could* be happily married . . . all that was stopping him was his wife. Alex's anxieties were exacerbated when his hair transplant, which had started to grow back in, seemed to be sprouting in the shape of the word 'bastard'.

DWINA PHELPS was arrested for a string of child abductions and sentenced to six years in Holloway where she is now preyed on by a vindictive psychologist of her *own*. Her appeal is pending, but she has little faith in a system of twelve people too moronic to get out of jury duty.

DETECTIVE SERGEANT SLYNNE retired from the force to join a psycho-dynamic Buddhist rebirthing centre in

Brighton. Having left his wife for Edwina Phelps, only to be rejected, his mind is wandering (a shame, as it really is too small to be allowed out on its own) towards the Men's Movement. He was last glimpsed clutching other hairy middle-aged men in a forest in Connecticut.

PETRONELLA DE WINTER was finding that it could take *years* to become an overnight sensation. She staves off the boredom by going through Alex's suit pockets and reading between the lines of his Amex statements for signs of infidelity. The press has begun to test the temperature of their relationship ... with a rectal thermometer. Her only solace is her weekly riding lessons with one Captain James Hewitt.

MAMMA JOY finally hung up her balaclava when she was head-hunted by a large PR company. Her strategic planning potential (escaping from a prison van) and bold competitive initiative (avoiding recapture) and shop-lifting scams (creative accounting) made her excellent entrepreneurial material for New Labour's stake-holder society.

SPUTNIK's autobiography, *Inside Me Inside*, got favourable reviews from the pro-prison reform lobby led by Feminist Harriet Fielding. She sold the film rights to Michael Winner. And in this case, you *could* judge a book by its film.

RUPERT PEREGRINE washed up as an 'entertainment's officer' at the floating Club Med Resort moored by the French at Mururoa Atoll. Soon after, Butter Truffles was eaten by an iguana.

HUMPHREY. Well, they said he'd never make it; and he didn't. Humphrey lost his position as Poet-Laureate-In-Waiting when a drunken spoof he wrote on the Royal Family, entitled 'I, Corgi', was published in *Private Eye*.

Madeline's mother, MRS NARELLE WOLFE, received a prank call from someone claiming to be the Prince of Wales. She used her rape whistle.

JACK WOLFE enjoyed his first birthday on March 25th, sitting on Bondi Beach, strewn with drunken Pommy backpackers, eating sand. Despite his quirky gene pool, Jack was now running (a kind of bow-legged, professional jockey look) and talking (the Virginia Woolf stream-of-consciousness, what's-on-his-lung-is-on-his-tongue, goo-goo-gar stage). It was also beginning to dawn on him that he would soon be able to out-run his mother by about eighty CPSs (collisions per second) and was probably capable of putting the guinea pig into the blender and turning it on *all by himself*.

MADELINE WOLFE had begun to tell her little boy an unbelievable story. 'Once upon a time, Mummy had a brain, career opportunities and no stretch marks. Then she met your daddy, went to the other side of the world on a great adventure . . . and ended up a few nappies short of the full load.' She hadn't decided whether or not the story had a happy ending. Her friends, however, maintained that they had never seen her so content. Maddy concluded that, yes, it could be happiness . . . but then again it could be a chemical imbalance.

ENGLAND'S OFFICIAL MOTHER OF THE YEAR washed and dressed her children, deposited them at play group, cleaned her house impeccably, then jumped to her death off Archway 'Suicide Bridge'. Her suicide note read, 'Billions and trillions of lemmings can't be wrong.'

KIDDIE COMMISSARS Penelope Leach, Miriam Stoppard, Sheila Kitzinger, et al. are still writing sanctimonious, guilt-inducing books about perfect mothers, who, unlike Santa Claus and the tooth fairy, cannot possibly exist.